by Gail Parent

HARPER & ROW, PUBLISHERS

New York, Evanston, San Francisco, London

FIRST EDITION

Library of Congress Cataloging in Publication Data

Parent, Gail.
   David Meyer is a mother.

   I. Title
[PZ4.P2314Dav PS3566.A64]   813'.5'4   74–15885
ISBN 0–06–013274–4

76 77 78 79 10 9 8 7 6 5 4 3 2 1

FOR KEVIN

Prologue

When I was twenty, you figure about thirteen years ago, I got a job as a lifeguard for the summer in a hotel in the mountains. Since I was going with this girl Felice Friedman (we were both at B.U. at the time) and since I had this great sex thing going with her (Felice was the first girl I made it with in a bed), I suggested that she get work at the same hotel. She landed a job as a counselor and we were both excited about spending the whole summer together. In those days, if you made it with someone in a bed instead of a car, you got pretty damned excited about spending the summer with them. You knew that you were going to have sex without a steering wheel in your side.

I got to the hotel about a week before Felice, since the pool opened before the camp did. We had it all planned. The day she arrived, she was going to meet me down at the pool at four o'clock, which was when I knocked off work.

She showed up at the pool on the appointed day at the appointed time. She came running down to me. I saw her from my high chair, which was facing the pool so no one would drown.

I took one look at Felice in this white bathing suit and there was no way that I was going to spend the whole summer with her. She had a pretty good figure, but right at the bottom of

1

this white suit I could see a whole mess of dark pubic hair sticking out. It turned me off and it drove me crazy.

I asked her to go home, back to New Rochelle. She cried and asked why. I couldn't tell her. What could I say? "I'm turned off because of what's sticking out of your bathing suit"? I just said I didn't think things were going to work out between us, and the entire time I was talking and telling her to leave, my eyes were riveted on that clump of hair. She left without ever knowing what was wrong.

And that's the kind of guy I was.

I, David Alan Meyer, was born thirty-three years ago in Lawrence, Long Island, the third child of Myron (Jewish) and Martha (Convert) Meyer. Myron Meyer had told his wife, even before they were married, that it was imperative he have a son. The plan, according to Myron, was to keep impregnating Martha until she produced a male child. (Myron's ideas were not unlike those of the Shah of Iran.) Two girls were born unto them and then me, the wanted one. Myron told Martha on the occasion of my birth, "It's a good thing it's a boy. We can stop now."

When I was four years old, I was playing with a pencil. My father said, "Put that down, David. You can lose an eye like that." My Aunt Joyce said, "He has such beautiful eyes. He's going to be a real lady-killer when he grows up." I thought that meant I was going to murder women.

When I was almost five, Grandma Meyer came for a visit around Halloween. She pretended to be frightened to death by my skeleton costume. Shortly afterward she passed on. I thought I caused her death because I was supposed to be a real lady-killer.

When I was five years old, my father took me to work with him. Mrs. Weld, my father's devoted secretary, spent the whole day spinning me around in a swivel chair, even though she had varicose veins and shouldn't be on her feet. My sisters stayed home. A few months later, my parents told me I was going to my father's work again. They took me to the hospital and had my tonsils taken out. How do you forgive a parent who lies to you?

When I was six years old, I brought home a spelling paper with a star on it. My father said, "So, we've got a regular Einstein."

When I was seven years old, I brought home a spelling paper with an "F" on it. My mother signed it so my father wouldn't know I wasn't a regular Einstein. I made it into an airplane and flew it across the room. My father said, "Stop that. You can lose an eye like that."

When I was about seven and a half, I saw a woman wearing a fur boa with the fox's head and feet hanging on her chest. I was happy that I wasn't going to grow up and be a woman and have to wear one of those.

When I was eight years old, my mother reprimanded me for leaving my underwear on the floor. Myron said, "Leave him alone. He's a boy." For twenty-five years I didn't pick up my underwear.

When I was nine years old, my father took me to work with him and I figured he was pretty rich because he had this big, rich-looking office in Manhattan. Mrs. Weld taught me how to use the mimeograph machine, even though she had arthritis in her hands. All the secretaries said I had beautiful eyes and would be a real lady-killer when I grew up. I knew what it meant by then.

When I was ten years old, the nurse in my orthodontist's office said she wished I was ten years older and she was ten years younger so that she could be my girlfriend. I smiled so broadly my bite plate fell out.

When I was eleven years old, my mortal enemy Stalin died. Lou, who owned the candy store near the school, said, "Death is too good for him." I agreed with Lou. I had spent time worrying about the Commies dropping bombs. I also spent time wondering what would have happened if my grandparents had never left the old country.

When I was twelve, Louise Lichtner invited me to my first boy-girl party. I didn't want to go to a party with girls and hated Louise for inviting me. I hated anyone with a vagina except for my mother and Mrs. Weld.

When I was twelve and a half, I took mambo and cha-cha lessons. Everyone did. Once my sister missed her lesson because she had "the curse." I wasn't ever going to get cursed in that way.

When I was thirteen, I was bar mitzvahed. Over three hundred gift-bearing guests came. Everyone said I would be a real lady-killer when my braces came off. I thought I was really hot shit.

When I was thirteen, *Playboy* was published for the first time. I dreamt about Miss February.

When I was thirteen, I got hurt in gym class and was sent to Miss Gleason, the school nurse. For some inexplicable reason this fifty-year-old woman gave me a hard-on. I ran to the boys' room and touched myself and came.

When I was thirteen, I thought about Miss February and got hard and touched myself and came. Had my father known, he would have said, "You can lose an eye like that."

When I was fourteen, they told me if I didn't apply myself in school I would ruin my life. I didn't apply myself and teachers told my parents I wasn't living up to my potential. I was more interested in pictures of boobs than the Civil War.

When I was fifteen and a half, I knew I was cute as hell and a real lady-killer. Bambi Siegel, a cheerleader, let me dump a whole container of milk on her and she didn't get mad. We French-kissed that same afternoon. I didn't mind her saliva.

When I was sixteen, I enjoyed bare tit more than anything

4

in the world. I got it off Louise Lichtner anytime I wanted in her finished basement. I never took her out.

When I was sixteen and a half, my father bought me a white Impala with a red interior. I could get bare tit off any girl in school by giving her a ride home. All I had to say was: "Put out or get out."

When I was sixteen and a half, I thought about the Rothschilds a lot. I couldn't believe how lucky they were, being Jewish *and* counts.

When I was seventeen, I had sexual intercourse with Louise Lichtner in the back seat of my Impala. I didn't even have to take her to the prom.

When I was seventeen, I applied to twenty-three colleges. I kept getting rejections. I was the first kid on my block to get an ulcer. I was finally accepted at Boston University Junior College. My father still thought I was a regular Einstein.

When I was seventeen and a half, I was voted the boy with the sexiest eyes in my high school yearbook. Shortly after, I took Bambi Siegel (voted peppiest) to a New Year's Eve party. I asked her if she would go "all the way" with me. She said no. I had her home by eleven-fifteen.

When I was eighteen, Myron sent me off to college with a checking account, a red Corvette and seven words: "Schtup all you want, but be careful."

When I was nineteen, I got into Phi Ep, the best fraternity. I also got into the best girls. All I had to do was tell them I loved them. All those people were right. I was a lady-killer.

When I was twenty, I was accepted into B.U., the real school, and didn't have to go to junior college anymore. I called my father, who said, "I thought that's where you were going."

When I was twenty-one, Judi Rosenberg quit college because I wouldn't marry her. She locked herself in her room and wouldn't let the maid come in and clean. Judi's mother was really pissed off.

When I was twenty-one, I married Frances Roache and made her convert to Judaism. I married Frances because I wanted a girl just like the girl who gave in to dear old Dad. Frances and my mother both came from the Midwest, had terrific noses and knew how to let their husbands take center stage.

When I was twenty-two, I joined Meyer and Meyer. Maybe I was no Einstein, but I could be rich as Rockefeller. I fucked the receptionist and thought that was what she was there for. I fucked my secretary and my cousin Ron's secretary. My uncle's secretary was a nice girl and didn't believe in fucking, so she gave blow jobs under the desk. I gave the three fuckers twenty-five-dollar gift certificates to Saks for Christmas and the blower one for fifteen. I gave old Mrs. Weld an umbrella and felt benevolent.

When I was twenty-four, I stopped sleeping with Frances. She annoyed me because she was still wearing the same clothes that she wore in college and because even though she converted, I had the feeling that she prayed to the Virgin Mary under her breath.

When I was twenty-five, I lost one point five million dollars for Meyer and Meyer. It drove Myron Meyer crazy. Not only was I not a regular Einstein, I was a dumb ass. I went to work in daytime television. I got the job through an old girlfriend because I was a hell of a cute guy.

When I was twenty-six, I told a girl that I would go to Israel and fight Arabs and probably lose my life if she didn't let me sleep with her. She let me. God forgive me. I'm sorry that I brought Israel into it.

When I was twenty-six, I was asked to transfer to the West Coast. I left my hi-fi and Frances behind. I bought her a fun fur and remembered that I paid for having her teeth fixed so that I wouldn't have guilt.

When I was twenty-six, I had a Mercedes 280 SEL, a Spanish

house, Gucci shoes, a job in prime-time television development, and I was a real lady-killer. They let me come in their mouths.

When I was twenty-seven, the world changed and the fun began to be over for me. Gloria Steinem and vibrators became household words.

This is the story of a cute Jewish boy who was raised to be a motherfucker.

This is the story of a motherfucker who could unhook a girl's bra with one hand in fifteen seconds, and how he couldn't survive when the girls stopped wearing bras.

This is the story of a man who couldn't survive the sexual revolution. Unfortunately, this is a story about me.

Ladies . . . persons . . . Gloria: my defense.

1

When I was thirty-two years old, after a lifetime of above-average sex I found myself having to pay for it. It's funny that the boy voted "the senior with the sexiest eyes" should have come to having to partake in the pleasures of a prostitute. I always thought that there were basically only two types of guys who seek out whores. First you have your seventeen-year-olds in quaint novels about growing up. Their first sexual experience is with an old hooker, who softens only momentarily when she says, "This is your first time, isn't it, sonny?" The kid always remembers her as being stretched out and having the map of the world on her face or some other part of her body. He throws up afterward.

Your second going-to-whorehouse type is the forty-five-year-old with the overhanging stomach and skinny legs. They're the guys whose wives have headaches or overhanging stomachs and fat legs. They can't get it off at home anymore or don't want to. (Occasionally they have a perversion like they enjoy making it while wearing stockings and their wives wouldn't understand, but headaches and flab are the norm.) These guys have too many bills to afford a high-class call girl and too many fears to pick up a hooker on the street. They come to the whorehouses for their weekly sex.

I, at thirty-two, having had my sexual awakening long

before, thanks to Louise Lichtner, and not yet into the hanging-stomach stage, was an unusual candidate for the whorehouse set. I am almost certain that all studies on the typical whorehouse customer did not include cute Jewish boys who worked out at the Beverly Hills Health Club three times a week. Why then did I go?: the question. The answer: Because the sexual revolution had begun and I was fighting on the wrong side. If I had been as rich as Rockefeller I wouldn't have had to face it. People with that kind of money can hire somebody to go through the sexual revolution for them.

Yeah, I got caught. Didn't think I was going to. I thought that women's liberation was something that was going to happen to the other guy. I figured it to be like white toilet paper. If everyone else bought it, I wouldn't have to. It didn't work that way. One minute they were letting me come in their mouths, the next they were all looking for multiple orgasms.

Monica Steinberg was the first girl to screw me (in the purest sense of the word). I had been seeing Monica about every other week for a couple of years when women's liberation hit the common woman. Monica, you could tell, was one of those girls who read *Love Without Fear* in college and had sex with the first guy who said he loved her even though she didn't enjoy one minute of it. Neither she nor the guy had a great time in bed because of her guilt and lack of movement. Miss Steinberg probably lay there motionless through the whole act and expected a thank you when it was over.

She was, at the time I met her, a twenty-eight-year-old college-graduate secretary at the William Morris Agency. She had learned how to put an outfit together and play tennis. She had moved three thousand miles away from her mother, who wanted her to get married already, but she still didn't move in bed. Why then did I sleep with Monica Steinberg about once every other week? For the same reason I put up with all those almost-virgins in college. For the same reason people climb mountains. I fucked Monica Steinberg because she was there.

I should have known things were going to change when Monica bought glasses like Gloria Steinem's and had her hair cut like Angela Davis's. One night when we were coming out of a movie, Monica turned to me and said, "Let's go back to my place tonight." I couldn't believe it. Her place? I hardly knew the girl. I didn't want to have to use her bathroom.

I had made it a rule never to go back to a girl's place. Why should I have to be on unfamiliar ground? Suppose I felt like having some Rocky Road ice cream afterward and she didn't have Rocky Road ice cream?

Monica was persistent, said I wasn't allowing an equal relationship if we always went back to my place. O.K., who am I to stand in the way of progress? We went to Monica's, a big mistake. She lived in a precious little apartment on Beverly Glen. She had a precious couch, not big enough for two, and a precious coffee table made out of a precious trunk, and flowers in back of the toilet. Monica's apartment was the kind of place with only diet soda to drink.

We're getting undressed and the conversation is unbelievable. "Are you a righty or a lefty?" asked Monica Steinberg. Two years, once every other week, and she didn't know what hand I wrote with.

"A righty."

"O.K. You take the right side of the bed." She knew I needed an explanation and went on, "That's so your right arm will be free."

Monica Steinberg expected me to work. I hadn't planned on working. Monica and I had a relationship that didn't include foreplay. It wasn't fair. She didn't tell me she wanted my working hand free when we came out of the movie.

"I won't go down on you anymore unless you go down on me." I forgot to mention that since college Monica had added "going down on" to her sex repertoire.

"Why not?" I wanted to go home. At this point I was willing to have no sex, just Rocky Road ice cream.

"I just don't think it's fair." I had the answer to that. I had been using it for years. I actually enjoyed using it.

"Look, Monica, what I produce for you, in the form of semen, is pure protein. It's actually good for you." I smiled.

"Yeah, I've heard that before. If that were true, I'd be the healthiest girl in the world."

"If God had wanted man to eat woman, he would have made man's head lower or her pussy higher." No response from Monica Steinberg. She was newly into the movement and taking herself very seriously.

As Monica undressed, I noticed for the first time that she was dedicating her body to growing hair. Under her arms, on her legs, every strand was standing there saying, "I'm a liberated woman. I don't have to shave." Fine, I'll pretend I'm in Israel, on the front line.

Monica pulled down the spread, revealing two pillows, a blanket and—get this—Snoopy sheets. Cute, Monica. We got into bed and the newly liberated Monica left the lights on. I can't truthfully say that I was impotent. It was more a case of total loss of desire to have sex. I wouldn't even think of making it with my ass in Snoopy's face or in front of Charlie Brown and Lucy. Christ, the whole gang was there. I didn't want to have sex! I wanted to play! I was goddamned embarrassed to fuck in front of Woodstock.

"What's the matter?" asked the new Monica.

"You." I said. I certainly wasn't going to blame it on Snoopy or myself.

"Can't get it up and you're blaming it on me. I'm going to tell my group about you." I made a mental note never to sleep with anybody in group therapy. Seven people are going to know about it.

"Don't want to get it up for you anymore, Monica. I don't care for your new attitude, your excess hair or your sheets," I said dramatically, dressing, putting on a piece of clothing with each insult.

"My sheets?" she said, completely ignoring that I had verbally attacked parts of her body.

"Your sheets suck. I don't want to have sex on them. I want to read them. They have all those adorable sayings coming out of their mouths. You've been upstaged by Charlie Brown, Ms. Steinberg."

With that I left, slamming the door, head held high. It was a perfect exit, except that I hadn't thought it necessary to put on my shorts. I'd stuffed them into my jacket pocket, making my departure as fast as possible. I was wearing suede pants. Snoopy was responsible for the worst ball rash man has ever known.

Kathleen Conway was the second one to turn on me. Kathleen had been my security fuck ever since I met her in an all-night supermarket. Making it with Kathleen wasn't exactly like drinking fine wine. It was more like Hawaiian punch—not great but always the same. (Maybe meeting in a supermarket gave the relationship the punchlike feeling.) I could call on Kathleen to make me feel good when I lost a hundred bucks on the Rams, at those times when I realized working in television programming meant shit and every time my father called to aggravate me. I could count on Kathleen to come over when my stomach was upset and I had a little gas. She didn't mind going to bed with a guy who had gas. And she was tall, had long legs and surfed. In how many supermarkets do you find a girl like this?

Shortly after the Monica Steinberg incident—it couldn't have been more than a few days: I still had the rash—Kathleen called and asked to come over. She said she had something she wanted to talk about. Trouble. A girl who surfs all of a sudden says she wants to talk, you got trouble. Naturally, I thought the worst—she either wanted me to marry her or she wanted five hundred dollars for an abortion. When someone like Kathleen wants to talk, you can expect tears.

"David, I really have been wanting to talk to you."

"Yeah?" Notice how I made it easy for someone to pour their heart out to me.

"My mother joined this consciousness-raising group." Jesus Christ.

"Your mother from Denver?" I couldn't picture her mother from Denver raising any consciousness. Her mother wore dresses with big flowers, her bust at her waist and a handkerchief stuffed in her sleeve.

"Yes, my mother from Denver. She said I shouldn't let you use me."

"You had a good time too." Good.

"Mother said I should come if you come."

"Yeah?" I was in shock.

"She also said I shouldn't have let you fart."

"You told your mother about that?"

"Yeah. Long distance."

"And your mother said I shouldn't fart?"

"Not exactly."

"I didn't think so."

"She said poo-poo."

"What?"

"She used the word 'poo-poo' instead of fart. She said you shouldn't poo-poo in bed." Poo-poo? That's some liberated woman.

"What else did your mother tell you, Kathleen?" Mrs. Conway was beginning to intrigue me.

"I shouldn't tell you this, but she said she and some of the other ladies were going to try to start an organization to get

13

back at men who have done bad things to women—a Women's Retaliation Committee, she called it. They're going to try to bring men to trial." Holy shit.

"I guess some men have done some pretty lousy things."

"Mom wants you and my daddy on the list." Terrific. I had a ladies' organization in Denver after me. "She said she'd put you on when I told her you don't care if I have an orgasm or not."

"That's not true." It was true, but I wasn't going to admit it to the daughter of the leader of a vigilante committee.

"She said I could have more than one orgasm—boy, was she surprised when I told her I didn't have any—so . . ." She stopped.

"So?" I urged her on. I was detached from this conversation, standing back, not believing it. Mrs. Conway entered bake-offs.

"So she's sending me a vibrator and I'm going to practice with it, so I won't be seeing you for a while." The year before, Mrs. Conway sent Kathleen a fruit cake.

"O.K." What could I say but O.K.? I was being replaced by some plastic and a couple of batteries. It's really great that Mrs. Conway's consciousness was raised. She taught her daughter to be one of the best masturbators in town. End of Kathleen.

2

After my unfortunate experiences with Monica and Kathleen, I thought my suffering was behind me. No, the sexual revolution was here—off the pages of the magazines and on to the sheets.

There was a Janet something, who told me, as we were undressing, that the last guy she slept with got it up for her five times in one night. There was a Lila Feffer, who told me, as we were undressing, that she takes nude Polaroid shots of all the guys she makes it with. No wonder Polaroid stock has taken a dive. There was a Helen Plotkin, who asked, while we were undressing, "Do you believe in kinky sex?" I graduated from high school in the late fifties. Helen, to me it's kinky if the girl gets on top. In each case, I repeated the Monica Steinberg trip. I bailed out before I had the chance to find out if I could make it with these girls. Trying to make it sound like their fault, I dressed quickly and always remembered to put on my shorts.

I tried to sort it out. Obviously, not every woman in the world (or Southern California) was going to be a problem. I had just come up against several within a very short time span and the whole situation was intensified. "You're a very nice, attractive guy," I told myself. "You were supposed to be a real lady-killer when you grew up. What happened?"

I also told myself that I really had nothing to worry about.

There were millions of women who were just sweet, old-fashioned girls and didn't care if they came or not. Every year *Playboy* has a new Miss January and a brand-new Miss April. There must be millions of girls who will tickle my back and never ask for anything in return. I didn't really want them, though. I wanted the new woman, like I wanted the new clothes and the new house and the new Mercedes and the *New York Times* delivered to my door. I'm a hip guy with a mustache. I don't wear undershirts. I can't all of a sudden start falling in love with Wacs. I left my wife Frances because she couldn't keep up. I want the girls with the long hair and loose tits and jeans. They just scare the shit out of me, that's all.

"What's the worst thing that can happen?" I asked myself.

"The worst thing that can happen is that I take one of these hip, beautiful, liberated women to bed and I can't get it up. I can't get it up! You hear me? She tells a few of her friends. Soon around every corner there's someone laughing at my failure. The whole world gets hysterical at my limpness because we live in hard times and people need something to laugh about. Then, as never before, everyone unites against me—men, women, blacks, whites, yellows, greens, people of all countries, all religions. Arab and Jew finally have a common cause—laughing at David Meyer's member. Everyone in the world chips in and takes out a full-page ad in the L.A. *Times.* It simply reads: DAVID MEYER CAN'T GET IT UP, and there's a black border around the page. That's the worst thing that can happen," I answered myself.

I would get into an elevator and be crushed against some busty stranger. If the stranger was fairly attractive, I would, by the time we got to the third floor, think some sexual thought, be it "Look at those knockers" or "I'd enjoy her under my desk." As I imagined it, by the seventh floor I'd tell her my name, she'd tell me hers, and she, not to lose out on me, would get off on my floor. I'd get her number. I'd call. We'd go to a movie. I'm still imagining. We'd end up at my place. As we're getting undressed, she'd tell me her grandmother reads *Ms.* magazine and has told her to beat the shit out of anyone who doesn't give her deep satisfaction. And that, as I imagined, would be the end of it. Why should I get it up for this woman who crushed against me, a perfect stranger in an elevator? Let her get another stud. By the time I'd get to my floor, I'd despise her and be ready to yell at my secretary because she had tits. (She probably hated me to begin with since she had an M.A. and all I had was a B.A., and she had to type and I didn't. I wondered if she could come. A secretary who could have a climax was equal to a lady executive who couldn't.)

Such hostility from a few bad sexual incidents. Yeah. You got it. Such hostility because up to now, everything had been just fine. All of a sudden it was the seventies, Gloria. All the lady novelists were writing books about how women were breaking through. How they had been wronged by men, how their marriages had ended, and how happy they were to be free. Books about how delighted they were that they had the guts to be single and be their own people. Housewives in New Jersey and secretaries in Hollywood read those books and applauded them, because guess what happened, folks. It was the seventies and before we realized it, men were "out" and women were "in."

In reality, it was still a male-dominated world and most women wanted to marry and have children and hoped that their husbands still wanted to make it with them after they were thirty-five. Most women. But there were your pacesetters. There were your Ms. Steinems, the new woman, whom many little girls and big girls looked up to. They bought her philosophy and they bought her glasses. She turned up as number one in polls of people they'd most like to be, replacing the First Lady.

Yeah. It was the seventies and men were "out." I know

because for about twenty-seven years of my life I enjoyed male supremacy. It was all a joke. Everyone knew it, and everyone laughed. Then one day Ms. Steinem and her friends sobered us all up. Now how the hell am I supposed to unhook her bra at the front door if she isn't the fuck wearing one? How am I supposed to get the thrill of ripping her clothes off if by the time I get out of the bathroom she's standing there naked looking through my record albums? How am I supposed to function in bed if she suggests we go back to her place and see her goddamn etchings? The ladies say that things should be equal now. O.K., that's fair. But it ain't fair to me. I'm not trained for equal. I was raised as a superior male child. Our fathers were raised as male chauvinists, only the rules didn't change on them.

People lived through the class revolution and the industrial revolution. They even lived through political revolutions. They came out O.K. because it didn't affect anybody's sex life. When you've been raised on spin the bottle and bare tit, how are you going to cope in today's world? How are you going to have the fun of copping a feel if she's going to give it to you anyway? And what if she cops a feel off me? I'm not prepared for it. They want multiple orgasms. I'm incapable of giving multiple orgasms, Gloria. I used to carry a Trojan in my wallet.

Equal pay for equal work. Yes. Equal jobs. Yes. Equal sex. Yes. I believe, Sister. I believe. Only I can't get it on with you, Sister. I want to and I can't. Help me: my body is two decades behind my good intentions.

In the world I was born in, things were different. Men killed Germans and women served doughnuts. Men drove the cars and could have premarital sex. (Women could participate too if they wanted to be ruined for life.) Boys ate the chicken legs, wore Yankee baseball jackets and had ant farms. Girls got left home when the boys went to the office with their fathers. "Boys will be boys" was the attitude at home and school. Boys will be men and men was a good thing to be. They went to work to make money so women could eat. And men got to be on top when they had sex. I learned that when I was eleven years old in the streets of Long Island in front of an eighty-thousand-dollar home. Richie Peretsky told me and then he showed me. We tiptoed up the stairs and peeked into his parents' room. Sure enough, Mr. Peretsky was on top and having a good time, it seemed. Mrs. Peretsky looked like she was in pain. I was going to be like Mr. Peretsky when I grew up.

If the women had stayed like Mrs. Peretsky, I wouldn't have been driven to a massage parlor, with no intention of being massaged.

3

One of the few good things about living in Los Angeles is that you have a lot open to you in the whore department. I, like the forty-five-year-old men with the overhanging stomachs, ruled out the classy call girl. Quite frankly, I was scared I was going to run into someone I knew. Two girls at the network picked up extra cash around Christmas time by call-girling and at least one receptionist I knew did more than reception. What if my own secretary was moonlighting?

"Why, David, I didn't know you had trouble getting it up."

"Don't be ridiculous, Ms. Hammerman. I knew you were the one who was coming here all along. Now take a letter."

I felt it was much safer going the massage parlor route. "GIRLS—GIRLS—GIRLS—in private rooms." One advertised: "The Art of Oral Love Preached Within." There was the College of the Religion of Love on Santa Monica Boulevard right next to a Clean Laundromat. One place directly across from a synagogue said: "Sexy Girls, Four Positions," and there was one that advertised: "Wrestle with a Naked Woman." (I didn't even consider that one. I figured if anything went wrong I'd be turned off wrestling.) I didn't even want to get into one that advertised "Simulated Sex Acts." (I had that in college.) There was one that was called Sexual Catharsis—need I tell you:

"GIRLS—GIRLS—GIRLS—in private rooms" ("We Guarantee Catharsis").

I don't know. It seems to me, and I may be crazy, that the whore business was the same for about five thousand years. Come the seventies, five thousand years of whoredom were shot to hell. All of a sudden the oldest profession in the world changes to the College of Religion of Love and ends up in a decent part of the city where your friends might see you going in.

I chose to go to a place that demonstrated waterbeds. If I panicked at the last minute or saw someone while I was going in, I could pretend to have come to buy a bed. I let my fingers do the walking and found my whorehouse in the Yellow Pages. It was the seventies. My house of ill repute was conveniently located on Melrose, between a car wash and a nursery school.

One sunny afternoon, after thinking about it for weeks, I put on sunglasses, drove down to Melrose, pretended to go to the car wash, pretended to go to the nursery school (what was I going to say if someone caught me at the nursery school?) and, like the best of spies, snuck into "Love-Able Waterbed Demonstrations, Private Rooms." Inside it looked like illicit business was going on. It was dark, the kind of dark where your pupils hurt when you walk in because they're dilating so fast. My eyes adjusted, revealing a simple desk and chair, a couple of rotten paintings of Spanish dancers on black velvet and your standard drab green everything else—a chair, rug, walls, a lamp, whores. No, no whores. They hadn't brought on the whores yet. There was, however, a drab green doorknob on the door. Some person in a free country, a country that has more colors than any country in the world, actually put this room together. I missed the red flocked wallpaper and ripped velvet couches and touches of gold that whorehouses are supposed to have. What did I expect on Melrose between a car wash and a nursery school—something out of a Visconti film?

My entrance into Love-Able had sounded off a buzzer in the rug. Then, I imagine, the Spanish dancer's eyes were mechanically moved aside and human eyes replaced them. They were possibly the eyes of Mr. Love-Able himself. I guess if I looked like a plainclothesman the girls would be ushered out the back door through the nursery school and into their red Pintos. Mr. Love-Able would then come out and try to sell me a waterbed. If I looked like a safe customer, the dancer's eyes would be replaced and someone would be coming forth to peddle bodies. My first instinct was to go, hope that no one saw me coming out, and make my escape into my Mercedes, where, even though I had a possibly nonfunctioning organ, I could feel like a man. I stayed. I told myself there was no sex for me in the outside world. I forced myself to think of the Snoopy sheets on Monica Steinberg's bed. I didn't want to take my eyes back into the bright light and I wanted to have sexual intercourse. There was a faint smell of vaginal jelly in the air. I knew there was pussy in the place.

A short middle-aged man wearing a suit and too-long sideburns came out of a door that seemed to lead to where the waterbeds were actually being demonstrated. I smiled at him, just in case he was the pimp. I'm sure pimps get smiled at more than people of any other profession. He wasn't the pimp. (I should have known by the overhanging stomach.) Obviously, the gentleman had picked out the waterbed he wanted and was on his way home. The buzzer sounded when he left. Suppose I was being trained like a Pavlovian dog? Every time a buzzer went off I would feel like having sex.

Another buzz, this time from within, brought the pimp. Call me old-fashioned, but I like my pimps to dress snazzy. I was actually looking forward to his outfit, expecting at least a bright pink satin suit, a carnation, a hat and spats, maybe not the spats, but I was entitled to a good look. This guy was wearing jeans and Gucci shoes and he looked Jewish. If I wanted to see that look I could have gone to the Polo Lounge or stayed home and looked in the mirror.

He lit a cigarette with a gold Dunhill lighter and sat on the edge of the desk.

"I have some terrific girls here, in case you want to have a complete demonstration of one of our beds," said the casual pimp.

"Sounds fine," I said. It did.

"In order to pay our girls for demonstrating, it is necessary to charge a nominal fee. It will cover the massage, which can be Greek, French or around the world, and the shower."

"Sounds fine." Christ, I was going to pay for it. Me, David Meyer, the kid who sent a girl home from a hotel because he didn't like her pubic hair sticking out.

"It'll be twenty-five dollars." That's some nominal fee. I should have got Charles Schulz to chip in.

"Sounds fine." Never argue with a pimp. He may flog you to death with the "G" on his belt.

Still sitting on the edge of the desk, he looked up at me. He seemed like a pretty nice guy. I thought maybe I should have bargained with him. *Listen, I might not even be able to get it up. Could I give you a deposit now of shall we say ten bucks, the second payment when I get hard and the third during climax?* He was looking at me for a reason.

"Are you David Meyer?" said the pimp. Jesus Christ! The fear of going to one of these places is being recognized. There are two major instances where one doesn't want to be seen— in a whorehouse and coming out of a Colonics Institute. Was it too late to say I was interested in buying a bed?

"Yeah, I'm David Meyer." My face said, "How the hell did you know?"

"My brother Hank was in your fraternity at B.U." I'm standing there talking fraternity with a pimp in a whorehouse.

23

"Oh, yeah, I remember Hank." I didn't, but I wanted this discussion ended. If you don't remember them, people always go into long descriptions of the person.

"Hank remembers you too. He mentioned you only a few weeks ago. He was one pledge class behind you and he said you gave him hell." Oh, my God, Hank's brother was going to take revenge. Everyone at the network would know I "accidentally" drowned in a waterbed demonstration.

"Oh, yeah, well, we were kids then." Don't hurt me. "So what's ol' Hank doing?" Ol' Hank made us sound close. Maybe he'd give ol' Hank's friend the best whore in the place and maybe he wouldn't hurt me. I'd sure hate to be kicked in the head by a Gucci loafer.

"Hank is a lawyer back in New York, works for the state." The old brother story—one a cop, the other a hoodlum. One day they come face to face, brother against brother. Does the cop give it to his own brother? No. It's really a yogurt commercial.

"A lawyer, huh? That's great for good ol' Hank." I'm standing and chatting in a whorehouse. "Did he ever get married?"

"Sure, married with two kids. He married a girl from B.U. You might know her. Judi Rosenberg." Know her? I laid her. I felt sorry for Hank. The girl was one of those who never moved a muscle in bed. Maybe Hank's brother got him wholesale whores.

"I don't think I knew her." You don't tell a pimp you slept with his sister-in-law.

"So what do you do, David?" Enough questions. I'm here to see waterbeds demonstrated, not to reminisce.

"I'm in television programming." We both deal with whores.

"Great. . . . What exactly is television programming?" Good question. I wished I could answer it. I couldn't. Like all people

24

in television programming, I didn't really know what I did.

"I work at a network and writers and producers come to me with ideas and I develop them and decide what ultimately gets on." Almost the truth. I submitted projects to the head of television programming and he ultimately decided what gets on. I lied because I figured if God was going to punish me on this particular day, it would be for cavorting with whores, not for fibbing.

"Well, David, I'll tell Hank I saw you." No, don't, schmuck. Don't tell Hank you saw me. I was the big scorer of the frat house. I was the one who found Desiree Goldblum, the fraternity punchboard. Hank might not understand that everything has changed since women's lib, especially since he's married. Married men don't feel the pinch.

"That would be great." No more talk. I'm begging.

"Let me ask you a question," said Hank's brother, leading me to believe that pimps have all the time in the world.

"Sure." Please don't ask why I came here.

"Why'd you come here? Do you mind my asking?"

"Not at all." Fuck.

"As I remember, you were a real ladies' man. Hank told me about how some girl's mother kept calling you, begging you to at least see her daughter." Christ, that was Judi Rosenberg, who left school in her senior year because I wouldn't marry her.

"To answer your question," I said with dignity, "I came here because all of a sudden you can't get good sex out there. They want our jobs and they want our dicks," I said, feeling I had been the first man to verbalize the situation.

"You know, you're the third guy this week who's come in here with that problem." Columbus thought he was the first to discover America. "I think women's liberation is great. Sure has picked up business."

"Great."

"I didn't know the other two guys, so I just let them get showered and massaged."

"Really just massaged?"

"Sure. What do you think we do in these places?" It was not a rhetorical question.

"I thought . . . I thought . . . You know what I thought." He had to know what I thought.

"That's what everyone thinks. Most guys who walk through that door expect to fuck, but they get a shower, towel dry and a massage. We have little holes in the doors to see that the men don't do anything funny."

"I just had a shower," I said feebly.

"Hey, I wasn't going to rip you off, buddy. Special customers, guys I know, they get the real thing. I won't even peek through the hole."

"Thank you," I said politely. I was very grateful.

"It will cost thirty-five, ten more than the shower and massage."

"Of course," I said, making it sound like he was the fairest person in the world.

"Hank's buddy is going to get the best chick in the place." What does that mean? Who you think is the best chick or who I think is the best chick? I don't believe one man should choose another man's best chick.

He stepped on some sort of mechanical device that opened up the back door. Since I am Jewish, I don't know how the device works because it is mechanical and nice Jewish boys don't know from mechanical. They can hardly turn on their televisions, and when their stereos break down they've been known to cry.

We went through the door and into a small back room. Sitting there were three whores. One was reading. The other two were playing chess. Hey, everybody, whores don't read and play chess. They lie around in torn satin robes eating chocolates. If anything can turn a man off, it's a reading whore.

Do I have to tell you none of the girls looked like they were supposed to? Any one of them could have passed for a close friend of Mary Tyler Moore. They wore slacks and sweaters. Their hair wasn't dyed and they had no flab. And get this—one (the reader) was Jewish, wore the Star of David around her neck. (*"What's a nice Jewish girl like you doing in a place like this?"* *"Well, I went back to school to get my master's and I'm going to Europe with my parents this summer and I didn't have anything to do in the meantime, so I figured I might as well whore."*)

A Jewish whore is a lot to take. I remember once there was a Jewish Playmate of the Month and there was a lot of talk about it. She lived in Queens and was shown eating breakfast (probably bagels and lox) with her Jewish family. She was one of the very few playmates who didn't scuba dive or ride horses. If I can remember correctly, her big hobby was collecting dolls of all nations, perfectly correct for a Jewish Princess Playmate.

My father was personally offended that there was a Jewish Playmate. He related her to Julius and Ethel Rosenberg. He didn't know whether they were guilty or not, but he could never stand the idea that a Jewish person could do something criminal. When Jack Ruby shot Lee Harvey Oswald, Myron nearly went crazy. He kept repeating over and over again, "Why did he have to be a Jew? Why a Jew?" At one point he said, "I don't think he did it," even though the entire country saw it happen on television. He still brings it up sometimes, Jack Ruby and the Jewish Playmate.

I was hoping that good ol' Hank's brother had the Jewish girl in mind for me. I had a feeling that I could get it on with her. She was a thirty-year-old version of Sandy Weiss, queen of my senior prom. If there was anybody I needed to fuck at this time in my life, it was the Queen of the Prom. Sandy, it was a known fact, didn't go all the way at the time she was crowned and now I had the chance of schtuping her, if Hank's brother gave her to me.

He gave her to me. "Honey," he said to her, "this is a friend of mine, David Meyer." (Pimps shouldn't give names. I was David Meyer. She was "honey.") "I want you to treat him real good. He can have anything he wants." I was on my way back to the fifties with Sandy Weiss. I said, "Hi." She said, "Hi." Hank's brother stepped on another mechanical thing and another door opened. She motioned for me to come and I followed her into another office-type room, bare but for a metal desk and two metal office chairs. All of Love-Able could be moved out in the back of a ten-dollar U-Haul.

Sandy (I liked to think of her as Sandy, Queen of the Prom) sat at the desk and motioned me to the chair. What the hell was going on? Was she going to interview me?

"Tell me, Mr. Meyer, do you think you are really qualified to sleep with me?"

"Well, yes, I guess so."

"Do you have any references?"

"No." I would have to say no. There was not one woman in the world who would admit to enjoying having sex with me.

"I'll have to think it over. I'll get back to you before the weekend. Don't ball us. We'll ball you."

Actually, she looked straight into my eyes and said, "Would you like me to show you the waterbed?"

"Yes," I answered, a bit confused.

"Is there anything else you'd like?" I understood. I had heard about this approach on an eleven-o'clock news in-depth report on massage parlors. It was done to save the girls from being accused of soliciting. The customer had to ask for it, another embarrassment of modern society.

"Yeah, well . . . I'd . . . I'd like to make it with you. You know." She knew.

Sandy, Queen of the Prom, explained, as any saleswomen

28

would, that I had to pay in advance and guess what, folks, the whole world has gone crazy. *You can pay for whores by Master Charge. All major oil company cards are accepted.* Am I the only one living who thinks this is strange? Jezebel didn't take credit cards. Whores are supposed to be slipped the cash, crumpled bills left on a dresser or stuffed into bras or, for a little drama and flair, dropped on the floor so that they would know what they were doing was dirty. I wouldn't do that, mind you. I saw it in a movie once. All I'm saying is I was born too late. I don't want to pay for whores by credit cards. There's nothing seamy about credit cards.

I handed Sandy my Shell Oil card. What do married men do? They've got to pay cash. What if the little woman opens the Shell Oil bill and finds three gas receipts, a bill for replacing a taillight and a thirty-five-dollar receipt from Love-Able?

"What the hell is this, Larry?" She shows her hubby the receipt.

"Love-Able?" He doesn't know at first and then he pretends not to know. "Love-Able? I don't know." (He thinks quickly, as men who have been with whores often do.) "Wait a minute. I think it's a garage on Melrose. I took the car there to get the transmission fixed."

"Love-Able is a garage? Sure, Larry. I'll bet it's a whorehouse, Larry. I'll bet you took you there to get your transmission fixed. That's what I think, Larry."

Sandy slipped my card into the holder, slid the slider across, had me sign and handed me my receipt and my card. She put the card too close to the edge of the desk and it slipped to the floor. Symbolic enough? She was most apologetic, but I was the one down there on the floor feeling dirty about the whole thing. I shouldn't have felt that way. Jesus forgave the whore, not the man who partook of her pleasures. Whores are arrested, not the men who are found with them. People say naughty lady, not naughty man.

"I'll bet I'm not your typical customer," I felt I had to say, after retrieving my card.

"No, you're not. Most people pay by Master Charge."

Sandy led me to a narrow room with a waterbed, just a waterbed with a fake-fur throw. Thank God she talked as we got ready.

"You from Los Angeles?" she asked, slipping out of her jeans. She wore no underwear.

"Yeah . . . well, I am now." I felt what I said was too noncommittal and then I realized I shouldn't be worried about conversation with a whore. I should be worried about getting it up.

"I thought you might have heard of us through one of the airlines."

I always thought that airlines were for flying people from one destination to another, so I said, "Airlines?" and worried a little more about my performance. Suppose nothing happened and she told Hank's brother and he told Hank and Hank told Judi Rosenberg and their two lovely children. I had to get it up for the kids' sake.

"Yeah, at least one of the airlines gives their passengers a sightseeing guide and we're on it."

Oh, my God, the airlines are pimping. How am I ever going to fly again? You figure an airline that goes to the trouble of finding whorehouses for its customers might not take the time to check the landing gear.

Sandy got down on the bed and motioned for me to join her. I went to her, talking all the way. "Listen, it's been a long time . . . that's very interesting about the airlines . . . the problem is I've come across several feminists, one with Charlie Brown on her sheets . . . so where're you from . . . I might have this problem. I don't know if I actually do. There's no one I really want to get it up for, present company excepted."

"Is there anything you want in particular?" she said, like a waitress. I was ordering sex.

"I'll have sexual intercourse, hold the mayo." She got the

30

joke but just smiled; a queenly smile like Sandy Weiss had all through the prom.

"So nothing in particular?" my whore said.

"Nothing in particular, just good clean fun, ha-ha-ha." She didn't ha-ha-ha with me.

Why I said "Nothing in particular" I'll never know. I didn't want nothing in particular. I wanted sex like I had it in the late fifties. I wanted it not on a waterbed, Ms., but in the back seat of a 1957 Impala like I had it with Louise Lichtner in broad daylight on the school hockey field. I wanted to French-kiss until our tongues got tired. I wanted you to be careful of your new nose job and scared that a hockey puck might come near the car and you would get caught. I would sneak my arm around over your cashmere, stretching my fingers down toward your new breast. I'd have you remove my hand. I'd put it back. You'd sigh and leave it there. I'd forget for the moment that I'd applied to twenty-three colleges and had got rejections from seventeen so far. Despite your worried protests, I'd get my hand inside your bra, feeling part bust, part padding. You'd be worried as hell that everyone would know you gave bare tit, but you'd resign yourself to this too because I'd be telling you at this point that I'd vote for you for Victory Queen. Before you knew what I was doing, I'd get your bra unhooked; not off, just unhooked. I'd fondle your breasts for about two and a half hours. Eventually, but not before the hockey team was finished for the day, my other hand would work its way up your skirt and into your cotton pants.

"Please don't," I would have you say.

"Come on, I love you." And my hand would get to stay.

"Please don't. I'm not that kind of girl." Music to my ears, so much more stimulating than anything Monica Steinberg could ever say.

I would get your pants down because I was stronger than

you, once again not off, just down around your ankles. I would be pressing you firmly onto the seat at the same time I was putting on a scum bag. The zipper on my Bermuda shorts would get in my way but not pinch.

"Please, David, no more." You'd be worried, knowing the real thing was coming.

"I really love you. I'm going to drop out of school so I can get a job so we can get married." I would be working my way into your body.

"No, don't."

"Don't what?"

"Don't drop out of school." Which meant I could fuck you and I would.

The minute it was over you would pull up your underpants, completing the act. You asked what I want in particular? I know my raised consciousness shouldn't allow it, but this is the kind of sex I want once more in my lifetime.

Sandy motioned me to the bed. The last thing I said before going to her was: "I'm in television programming." As if knowing that, she would be kind.

The whore knew her stuff. She knew her stuff so well and I was thinking of Sandy Weiss so hard that the whole thing was over in seconds. I hardly got the benefit of being on a waterbed. I hardly got the benefit of being on a woman. Since an airline was involved, I wondered if the whole thing could be tax-deductible. I could say it was transportation costs and in a way it was.

"Listen, I'm sorry I was so fast." I really wasn't that sorry. I was fast in the back seat of cars too.

"I don't care if you were fast." She didn't say it bitchy. She really didn't care. Why should she care? The faster I was, the more credit cards she could take in in a day.

"I just felt bad that it was no fun for you." She looked at me like I was crazy. We are living in an age of liberation so I am actually worried that my whore didn't have a good time. What did I expect? Did I want her to run and get her Shell Oil card and pay me? I doubt if I'll ever again be able to go to bed with a girl without thinking about whether she got it off too. Perhaps the airlines could help me with my problem.

Dear Sir:

I used one of your recommended whorehouses and I came ahead of schedule [I figured they'd understand schedules] and I felt badly for the whore, which made me realize that I can no longer be selfish in bed. What should I do?

Sincerely,
David Meyer

Dear Mr. Meyer:

Sorry for the delay, but your letter has been shifted from department to department until it finally came across my desk. I suggest you take our flight 121A to London and change to flight 315 to Lisbon, arriving 7:15 P.M. every day but Sundays and holidays. Follow the map we provide on board, which will take you to Señorita Gustaf. She comes faster than any whore in the world, and we remind you that we are a worldwide airline. Thank you for flying and fucking with us.

Sincerely,
Señor Gustaf

As we dressed, I asked the whore out. Maybe to repay her for my speed. Maybe because I wanted to schtup her for nothing. Probably because it's always good for your ego when the whore wants to spend time with you. Also, there was the desire to show this girl the path to decent living. With a lot of work and care, love and attention, I could get her to stop sleeping with men for money and do what everyone else did—sleep with men because if you don't, they won't take you out again. She didn't date clients, in the same way psychiatrists don't accept dinner invitations. But I'm David Meyer. Girls leave college because I won't marry them. They cry and go into analysis because of me. I'm the one with the sexiest eyes.

"Well, if you won't go out with me, I'll have to come back and see you." Once or twice a week I could be back in the fifties.

"Fine." Fine? If you were going to use one word, Sandy, the word could have been "Great." "Fine" is a very nebulous term and it makes me insecure. If I ever relate this story I'm going to have to change "Fine" to "Great." Why not great? Thirty-five bucks for sixty seconds' work.

I felt good. Left Love-Able and went straight to the network. For the first time in months I was able to clear off my desk, return calls and do the *New York Times* crossword puzzle—not the whole thing, but there were ten blank spaces less than there had been in previous days. Doing the *New York Times* crossword puzzle is definitely related to sexual activity.

I was also able to make decisions for the first time in a long time. I said no to three pilots about liberated women. They dealt with a lady doctor, lawyer and detective. I gave the go-ahead to a script on an idea about a guy who was both a doctor and a lawyer and in his spare time was an amateur detective.

I was able to take calls from agents. Spinning around in my desk chair, I had the ability to tell them that the network was not interested in their stars. "She's old news," I said. "Her TVQ is nothing. Let me double-check. . . . Yeah, eighty-three percent of the people know who she is. Eleven percent like her." Or "Hi ya, Bernie. Look, you deliver Liza for me and I'll see to it that you get the show as a package." I got a hot team of writers to do a half-hour pilot for seventeen five, even though their going price was twenty thousand. I was able to wheel and deal as I had in the days when Kathleen Conway was at my disposal. (Wheeling and dealing must also be related to sexual activity. I'll bet some of our best secretaries of state have been great in bed.)

I was able to stay late and read pilot scripts. It was always hard for me to get through scripts and there were always a dozen on my desk. They were in a dozen different-colored folders, all bearing hopeful writers' names. I'd get through a couple and a couple more would appear. I hated that pile. It represented staying late at the office, and if I stayed late at the office I might miss dinner or sex. On this particular night, I wasn't hungry sexually or otherwise. That little girl from Love-Able got me through all those scripts. I was even able to write fairly intelligent notes in the margins. (Would Shakespeare have appreciated my notes? I probably would have written "Punch this up" in the margin of *Macbeth*.)

Yeah. I felt good, so good I had the guts to call my father.

"To what do I owe the honor of this?" Myron Meyer said that every time I initiated the call.

"Just thought I'd call to say hello, Pop."

"What time is it there?" He always asked the time, never got used to the simple three-hour difference.

"It's nine o'clock there, right? So it's six o'clock here. Still three hours difference, Pop."

"It's nine-fifteen here, so it must be six-fifteen there."

"Right, Pop." I should have known not to round out the time with a man who proudly wore a Patek Philippe watch.

"So what's new?"

"Nothing much." I thought of telling him I had found a wonderful whore, but quickly decided against it. I'm sure the man would have been devastated that his only son was laying out credit cards for his pleasure.

"So how's work?"

"Fine. Fine. But I could leave with two weeks notice if you want me to come back to the business. Ha. Ha." There was silence. He would never forgive me for losing one point five million for Meyer and Meyer. *I wouldn't have come back, Pop. I just wanted to hear you would have me. You wouldn't have me. You would change the subject.*

"So, are you seeing anyone?" said my father, changing the subject.

"Sort of." I don't know why I said that. I wasn't sort of seeing anyone. I had just paid thirty-five bucks to get it off with a whore. She was nothing to me. I went back to the office and she admitted the next man to her body.

"So, what's she like?"

"Long legs, brown hair, green eyes, very tall . . . Remember Sandy Weiss, the girl who was Queen of the Prom?"

"Her father was in textiles?"

"Yeah, I think so. This girl looks like an older version of Sandy Weiss."

"The Weisses moved to Florida. I heard they bought a condominium for over a hundred thousand. They're all moving down there."

"Yeah, well, this girl looks like Sandy Weiss."

"Don't rush into anything. You have your community property laws out there. She gets half of everything you got." I've never seen the girl in daylight. My father already has me divorced.

"I'm not rushing into anything. Bye, Pop." Pop, can a Jewish whore give you a social disease?

Just as I was about to leave, at seven-fifteen, Alan Milner called me into his office. I knew what those seven-fifteen meetings meant. They meant that Alan had no place to go that night and rather than go home and play with his Sony playback and all his illegal tapes (Alan Milner could see *The Exorcist* anytime he wanted), he'd call people into his office and pretend that he had something of great consequence on his mind. He'd keep you until he was tired enough to sleep. Funny, you would think an asexual wouldn't mind being alone.

"You wanted to see me, Alan?" Gave him the same smile I gave the pimp, slid into one of his uncomfortable modern chairs. Alan's office was chrome, glass and too clean. It was the type of room where you felt guilty standing on the rug.

"I'd like to get some relevant product going for next year." Yep, Alan didn't want to go home. We were just getting pilots filmed and taped for this year. Nobody but Alan, who didn't want to go home, was getting into next year. People who don't want to go home make great heads of departments. (Asexuals also make great heads of departments. They never take time out to fantasize.)

"We should get some relevant product going for next year," I agreed. I was wearing jeans but I was the man in the gray flannel suit. I got my job in the first place by showing Alan how well I could agree with him. We both ordered salmon during the interview at the Polo Lounge, both drove Mercedeses, and I agreed with him.

"People aren't watching just cute shows anymore and they're not going for Wasps this year. We need to latch on to some minority that hasn't been done."

"Chinese," I volunteered because I was hungry all of a sudden and thinking of lemon chicken. If Alan had thought I had come up with a great idea, forty million people would be watching a show about a Chinese family because I was thinking lemon chicken.

"I don't think the public will buy Chinese."

"It could take place at this restaurant." I could take place at this restaurant.

"They won't buy it. They won't relate."

"Japanese?" I said, into teriyaki.

"Same thing." said Alan. Chinese and Japanese were the same thing. No wonder he had not chosen a sex to love.

"Puerto Rican?" I said, hoping to have hit on it.

I wasn't thinking Puerto Rican cuisine.

"Nah," said Alan, dismissing a people.

"Greek?" I guessed again.

"Not minority enough."

"Excuse me?" Not minority enough?

"People don't think of Greeks as underdogs. That goes for Jews too." You can know a person for years and not mind them. One day they call your people Jews in a way that you'll never be able to like them again.

"Well, we're probably not going to come up with it tonight," I said, standing to let Alan know the meeting should be over. I was getting his rug dirty.

"Sit down," said Alan with no charm. A Rose Kennedy he wasn't.

"Polish?" I said, falling back into my chair, relieved to get off the rug.

"Too funny," said Alan.

"What?" Too funny?

"People will be expecting a lot of Polish jokes. I don't want to give it to them."

"We could always do blacks again." Now that all the networks had their token shows, I figured it might be time for a second round.

"We can't do another black show. All the black shows have been done, thanks to goddamn Norman Lear. Thanks to goddamn Norman Lear, everything relevant's been done."

"Hungarian?" I tried.

Hungarian was dismissed, as was Yugoslavian, Norwegian, Dutch and the people of Iceland. Two television executives were sitting in a Hollywood office thinking of an unused minority group that could sell Tide. We were up to Egyptians when Alan first showed signs of getting tired.

"Too topical." Egyptians have only been around forever.

"Ethiopians?"

That made Alan sleepy and he brought the meeting to an abrupt close. "This is getting silly," he said, like the whole thing was my idea. He yawned in my face just as I was about to suggest Eskimos.

"Well, I'll keep thinking," I said as I backed out the door.

"I am going to count on you to bring in a relevant series this year." Me, sir? Oh, thank you, sir, for the opportunity. You won't be disappointed that you've chosen me for this great task, sir. How about a series, sir, about the American Indian and his hardships and really do it right, showing poverty . . . What? Too relevant, you say? Of course, sir. I understand. You want a series that is relevant, involving an identifiable minority that isn't so realistic or so much of a minority it will be a turn-off. And if I succeed, you and I can go on second-guessing for another year. You've come to the right person, sir.

"I'll come up with something great," I said, hoping to hear an "I know you will."

"I'll bet," said Alan Milner.

I went back to Love-Able, one, two, three times a week, always requesting and getting my whore. I knew she was the prostitute and I was the customer. I knew I had to pay for her favors. I knew she gave to other men the same charms she gave me, and yet somehow I managed to think of her as my girl. I didn't know her name, never once saw her off the premises, but I believed we were a couple. We just happened to see each other at a waterbed demonstration establishment.

Furthermore, I considered it a perfect relationship. We didn't talk much, but talking was not what I needed at this time of my life. Even at thirty-five dollars a shot, she was less expensive than a wife. She was not demanding like a woman wanting a relationship and more comfortable than a first date. My girl didn't bother me with late-night telephone calls dialed because she wanted to know where she stood, and I never had to tell her what working in television development really meant. She never cried or asked to be satisfied. All she ever wanted was my Shell Oil card and I loved her for it. We would grow old together, I'd be a steady customer for the next forty years and I'd see to it that she was the oldest working whore in the business. At seventy, she would still be the Queen of the Prom.

"Yeah, Pop. I'm still seeing the same girl," I said smilingly into the phone.

"You know I have some property for you in your name. If you marry her, she gets half."

"Don't worry, Pop. We're not thinking of getting married." She's not even thinking of walking out the door with me.

"What time is it there?"

"Pop, did you ever go to a whorehouse?"

"Don't be crazy. It's six-thirty here."

"It's three-thirty": me.

"Why did you ask?": my pop.

"Ask what?": me.

"If I ever went to a whorehouse": my pop.

"No reason": me.

"Stay away from those places. You'll get diseases. Find a nice Jewish girl. What's the matter—the girl you're seeing won't schtup?"

"Yeah . . . she schtups."

"Atta boy": my pop.

Atta boy. Atta boy was paying for it.

I had a couple of good months. I went to the gym Tuesdays and Thursdays, my whore Mondays, Wednesdays and Fridays.

On Saturdays I shopped. It was during this period that I was able to acquire Ava Gardner's shoes from *The Barefoot Contessa* at a studio auction.

My output at work continued to be better than usual although I hadn't come up with that relevant series yet. "Do you have any further thoughts?" Alan would say if we got into an elevator together by mistake. I would hush the topic up quickly, indicating that what I had was such hot stuff it shouldn't be discussed in an elevator. Once I got a memo from A. Milner re: Relevant Series. I sent back a memo from D. Meyer re: Delay in Relevant Series. "You wouldn't believe it," it said, "but I was just about to hand in my complete thoughts on what I considered to be a *hell* of a series. Fortunately, I found out a series just like it was developed by Screen Gems and that they're pitching it all over town. Naturally, I burned the whole thing."

"I am expecting that series," said A. Milner after a Wednesday-morning department meeting.

"I'm expecting to give it to you," replied D. Meyer, who had four different writers working on it, none of whom could tune in to the inherent humor of the common man from their Beverly Hills homes.

Despite the "relevant series" intrusions, I did have a couple of good months. Then one night Myron Meyer called.

"We're coming out," he said, ruining my life.

I knew it had to happen eventually. I knew that sooner or later my father would tell me that he and Mom were coming out to California. He might pretend it was a business trip. He might say it was a stopover on his way to Hawaii or Japan. For whatever reason, Myron Meyer would be out.

I didn't want him to come, in the same way I didn't want him to visit me up at college. He would show up at school and instead of being my father, he would go out of his way to become one of the gang—using words like "crap," sitting around the frat house putting everything down like we put everything down, going to the game, whatever the hell the game was, and yelling his kishkes out for old B.U. I didn't want him to yell his kishkes out for old B.U. What the fuck did he have to do with old B.U.? After the game, he took about ten guys out for "a good steak." They put up with his old jokes because no matter how rich your father is, when you're in college you never feel you can afford to go out for steak.

The real trouble with my father was he didn't come to visit. He came to get involved in my life. He was caught with us once in a sorority house after hours. You don't want your father caught anywhere with you, especially when there are Jewish coeds with boobs around and you can't grab one, like all the other guys, because your father is there.

And now Myron was coming to get involved in California. I knew him. He'd be yelling his kishkes out for the network. He'd ask Alan Milner out for a good steak. He wouldn't be content to go on a Universal tour, he'd want to meet Lucille Ball because he heard that she had offices at Universal. He'd tell Lucy that she shouldn't have given up her weekly show and that I was a hell of a good kid. He'd be looking for my new girlfriend. I had to stop him.

"Dad, I don't think you should come. . . ."

"We have to come. Your mother would be so disappointed. She's been looking forward to this trip." Like hell she would be disappointed. It was him. He couldn't wait to come out and buy steaks for everyone so everyone would like him. He couldn't wait to help me and Lucy career-wise.

"I just don't think it's a good time to come. . . . They think there may be a major earthquake soon." Good thinking. When the hell has a major earthquake ever been announced? Einstein would have come up with a good excuse.

I tried to stop him. I said I'd go to New York. No. I said I had to go to New York. No. I said it was the rainy season. No.

I said I didn't want them to fly because I feared they'd be hijacked. No. Myron would rather risk his life or end up in Cuba just to see his David and make a pain in the ass of himself.

I wanted them to stay in a hotel, even though I was comfortably ensconced in a two-bedroom-and-den house. I didn't want him breathing down my neck, suggesting I get up earlier and telling me things like to be good to my feet. I didn't want him to know what I really lost every Sunday to the bookie.

"Pop, you can stay with me if you want." It was a half-assed offer and I said it in a half-assed way.

"I don't know. We'll be in the way." It was a half-assed refusal.

"Look, I have a big house." My tone didn't change. I was still half-assing it.

"I don't know . . . we can stay at a hotel." He wasn't really fighting me. He seemed . . . I don't know—half-assed.

"I insist." I got strong because he was timid. I wanted them in a hotel, any hotel, preferably one in Puerto Rico.

"Well, if you insist . . ."

"Great, Pop."

"And we can't wait to meet the girl."

"Great, Pop."

They couldn't wait to meet the girl, huh? O.K., there were two possibilities. Either I could take my parents to meet the girl. O.K., there was one possibility. I had to get the girl out.

As we undressed at Love-Able:

"Hey, did you know my parents are coming out?" How was she supposed to know? Was our Ms. Rona writing about it?

"I didn't know that," she said pleasantly enough, considering the question.

"It's going to be terrible. My father is going to blame me if it rains. You know what I mean?"

"I know what you mean." She smiled. My whore smiled at

me and everything was going to be fine except, of course, my father coming to visit.

"They'd like to meet you."

"They would?" She was surprised. I guess the girl wasn't used to being taken home to Mother.

"Yeah, I told them all about you . . . not exactly all about you. I . . . uh . . . told my father I was seeing you, which is not entirely untrue. You've got to admit that, right?"

"Right."

"So I was wondering if we could enter into a bit of a business proposition—you know, I'd pay for your time and . . ."

"Sorry, I couldn't."

Why couldn't she? Did Hank's brother have her chained to Love-Able after hours? Did he force her to take heroin so she'd be dependent on him? Perhaps he beat her, threatening her with death if she ever told the coppers. On the other hand, maybe she had a boyfriend, someone she was putting through law school. She had to earn money as a whore because she never took typing in high school. I bet Sandy Weiss never took typing either.

"Is there no way that I can get you to do it?" I thought of offering her a fur coat but negated the idea. I gave my ex-wife Frances a fun fur when I left her. I was a one-fun-fur man.

"Really, I can't," my whore said. I searched her arms for needle holes but saw none.

We made fifties love and even though I was depressed and worried from her refusal, she managed to make the sex work. Bless you my child, for you have sinned . . . and you did it great.

Where was I going to find a girl who would pose as my girlfriend and looked like Sandy Weiss in balmy California? Shit. Why did I have to tell my father who she looked like? I could only hope he'd forget what the Weiss daughter looked like. It wasn't going to be easy. The man remembered what they paid for their condominium.

213–9178: M. Steinberg.

"Hello."

"Hello, Monica, this is David Meyer."

"Oh, yeah?" It wasn't going to be a friendly call.

"I was wondering what you were doing tonight." (And from May third to the seventeenth.)

"I'm sleeping with someone who can get it up, you bastard."

"Well, then, maybe some other night." We hung up together.

613–6549: K. Conway.

"Hello."

"Hello, Kathleen. David Meyer here."

"Oh, hi. My mom mentioned you the other day. She's really getting that Women's Retaliation thing going." A bit friendlier than Monica, but distant.

"Great. I was wondering what you were doing tonight."

"Having a three-way."

"Excuse me?"

"I'm sleeping with this guy and girl I know, a great couple. Mother said bisexuality is in."

"Yeah, well . . . maybe I could join you."

"Don't be silly, David. If you joined us it wouldn't be a three-way anymore." The girl could count.

"Listen, my parents are coming into town. They'd like to meet you."

"Oh, gee, David. I couldn't. I couldn't do it with your parents. I have some morals."

Goodbye, Kathleen Conway.

As I was undressing at Love-Able:

"So you're absolutely sure you wouldn't want to pose as my girlfriend and meet my parents?"

"I'm absolutely sure."

46

"Marry me." I was proposing to a prostitute because my father was coming to California. If she did marry me, would she turn our sexual relationship into the old joke? Question: How do you get a Jewish girl to stop fucking? Answer: Marry her. Question: How do you get a prostitute to stop prostituting herself? Answer: Lose your Shell Oil card.

"I'm going to have to turn down your proposal."

"You wouldn't have to give up your job or anything." I am a liberated male. If we were married would she charge me thirty-five bucks a night?

My whore had just turned down my marriage proposal and the sex was still good. She was the Hank Aaron of prostitution.

Alan Milner is not an easy man to talk to. If you've had a hell of a night, he doesn't care to know about it. If you start bleeding during a meeting, that's your business. If two doctors were carrying me past his office on a stretcher, he wouldn't ask what happened.

During the whole time that I had been working with Alan, we never got into personal relationships. I knew he was asexual because everyone knew he was asexual. (Actually, it's hard to actually confirm that anyone is asexual. There are no witnesses. It's more a feeling in the air.) He knew I was Jewish. I knew his address and telephone number and he knew mine. The last time he asked me any questions about myself was when he interviewed me. It wasn't going to be easy going to Alan with a problem, but I knew he could help.

As head of prime-time programming, Alan Milner was required to go to show business functions. At each one of these affairs, he had a lovely female companion. He took different girls, but they were all lovely, each one knowing how to dress and be affectionate enough so that Alan came off looking good. The girl, I am sure, was dropped off immediately afterward, and Alan went home to his empty asexual bed. What I needed from my boss was just one of his shills.

"Alan, I'd like to ask you a favor."

"Think of anything yet?"

"I'm working on something and by the way, the Manning script is great. Very funny, a lot of laughs. A few too many midget jokes and a line about a shepherd I don't understand, but it's got good yuks. Alan, I'd like to ask you a favor." He heard me this time. He had a shocked look on his face like no one ever asked him a favor before.

"A favor?" His whole body withdrew from me. Perhaps he thought the favor was asking for his house, car, job, toupee. Maybe he thought I wanted to put my arm around him. One didn't touch Alan.

"You know that girl that you took to the affiliates dinner, the one with no tits?" I was embarrassed that I had said the word "tits" in front of someone without sex.

"Jeannie Harbinger?"

"Yeah. That's the one. She does commercials about never having to clean your oven again, right?"

"Right. . . . What's the favor?" He was still frigid.

"Well, it's hard to explain, Alan. I'll skip the details." (People always skipped the details for Alan.) "I was just wondering if I could, you know, have her number."

"No."

"Excuse me?" He was saying no?

"I don't want you going out with Jeannie."

"Yeah, well, I understand." I didn't. "How about one of your other ones? Who was that one that you went to the Christmas party with?"

"Eve Leslie. No."

"No?"

"No. I suggest you don't call her."

"Marilyn. How about your friend Marilyn?"

"Stay away from Marilyn."

Alan wasn't going to let me play with any of his girls. Richie, my best friend when I was a kid, was a selfish bastard, wouldn't even give you a chance to try on his waxed teeth, even if you promised not to suck the green liquid out. There is, however, a major difference between Alan's and Richie's attitudes. Richie played with his toys, Alan dropped them off.

"So I gather, Alan, that you don't . . . uh . . . ha, ha . . . want me to go out with any of the girls you know. Please, Alan, let me have just one of them. My parents are coming and I told them that I had this girl and . . ." You know those little beads of sweat that appear on your forehead when you're begging? They were there.

"You say the Manning script is funny?" said Alan Milner.

I hope one of these days, Alan, that you need a woman draped on your arm for some function. I hope that you can find no one and have to resort to taking a transvestite to a major film opening. I hope, as you're getting out of the car, your transvestite gets his boobs caught on your sleeve and you end up with a stuffed bra hanging from you. I hope Rex Reed is there to report the whole thing.

O.K., I had to find a girl. Writers would come into my office to discuss a script and I would ask if they had ex-wives who would like to earn a little extra money. Agents would call and I'd make it clear that their clients wouldn't get the job unless they found a shill for me. I even went as far as telling an actress that I would get her work in a pilot if she would do a little extra acting for me—say around two weeks. The Screen Actors Guild caught me on that one. I got a very threatening phone call from those people. They were ready to picket my house during my parents' visit.

My secretary said that even though she loved me very much and would do anything in the world for me, she couldn't possibly pose as my girlfriend because her analyst felt that during this period of her treatment, she shouldn't take on anything that involved role-playing.

"I'd really love to do it but I'm all fucked up and I've got to get my head straight and find out what space I'm in," she said.

"Fine. While you're finding your space, could you bring me a cup of coffee and my Rolodex?"

213–7474.

"Hi, you might not remember me. My name is David Meyer and my parents are coming into town and I was wondering if you would like to be my girlfriend for a couple of weeks."

"What did you say your name was?"

"David Meyer."

"Fuck off."

"Does that mean no?"

Click.

613–2893.

"Hi, you might not remember me. My name is David Meyer and my parents are coming into town and I was wondering if you would like to be my girlfriend for a couple of weeks."

"David Meyer, huh? Don't you remember what you did to me?"

"No. I am terribly sorry. I don't."

"You fell asleep on me."

"I do beg your pardon, but a lot of gentlemen fall asleep after sex."

"This wasn't after, schmuck. This was during."

"Yes, well, I was wondering . . ."

Click.

713–5896.

"Hi, you might not remember me. My name is David Meyer and my parents are coming into town and I was wondering if you'd like to be my girlfriend for a couple of weeks."

"Oh, hello, David." A friendly voice.

"Hi."

"I want you to know I have no malice toward you."

"Excuse me, but I don't seem to remember what I did to you."

"It was because of you that I became a dyke."

"You're sure it was because of me? Maybe it was a deep-rooted . . ."

"It was you, but I don't want you to worry about me. I have a very nice girlfriend. She's gentle."

"Uh . . . would either one of you care to pose as my girlfriend for a couple of weeks?"

"Gee, I know I wouldn't and if Karen did you a favor I would bust her head in."

516–8696.

After the I'm David Meyer and would like you to pose as my girlfriend push: "You bastard, don't you remember what happened?"

Another one? I had forgotten how I'd got around before my whore.

"I'm afraid I don't remember." How often I would have to say that while going through my Rolodex.

"We went out several times. You seemed to like me. We had sex on many occasions. Although it turns my stomach to think about it now, I did enjoy it then. I was, by the way, somewhat overweight. Do you remember what you called me?"

"It's coming back to me. I think I called you . . . my little butterball."

"That's right, David, and do you remember what you asked me to do?"

"Lose weight?"

"Right again. I lost twenty-five pounds, starved myself for four months. Do you know what you said after I got thin?"

"That you looked good?"

"Nope. After all that dieting you said I'd look good as a

blonde. I bleached my hair that very afternoon."

"It was very attractive."

"Do you have any recollection of what you said to me the next time we went out?"

"I'm afraid I don't remember."

"I'm afraid I do. You said I was too tall, David. I am not a very tall person, but for you I was too tall. I was a thin, blond person with too much height. I cried that night. The next morning I went to an orthopedic surgeon to see if I could be made shorter."

"You didn't do it, did you?"

"No, Mr. Meyer. I didn't cut off my legs for you. Disappointed?"

An entire Rolodex overflowing and not one understanding woman.

As we were undressing at Love-Able:

"Why don't you be my girlfriend for a couple of weeks?" David Meyer begging his prostitute.

"You know why." I didn't know why, but I didn't want her to think me dumb before having sexual intercourse.

My hair had been falling out for some time. It's just that the added pressure of finding a girl seemed to be making my hair stampede out of my head. I went to Paul the expensive hair stylist because he made my hair look thicker, or I thought he did.

"Paul, it may be my imagination, but I think my hairline receded an inch this week."

"It's hard to know whether these things are imagination or not," said my hair stylist, like he was the West Coast's leading psychiatrist. He was far more successful than any shrink: forty dollars a shot and he could do two cuts and an expensive treatment in an hour.

"I'm under a lot of stress, Paul."

"That could be doing it," he said, looking for causes through a magnifying glass.

"You don't know any girls who would be willing to pose as my girlfriend for a couple of weeks?"

"No, but I know a couple of guys who would," Paul the expensive barber chided. He yanked about fourteen hairs that I couldn't afford to lose out of my head.

"Really, I need a girl," I said, in an anxiety-ridden state.

"Hey, you better calm down, David. When you tense up like that, it sets off chemicals that aren't good for the hair follicles."

O.K. Myron Meyer was due in less than a week. I could tell him that the girl and I had broken up and be rid of the whole situation. I couldn't tell Myron that the girl and I had broken up. He would want to talk to the girl and patch things up. My father was coming to interfere and a broken-hearted son was something he would love to meddle with. I wasn't going to let him. I was going to use my ace in the hole. Yeah, it was time to call Barbara Hirsh.

5

I first heard about Barbara Hirsh in the men's room. I was still
working in daytime television then and I went to take a pee.
There was no executive men's room at the network so you had
your herds of nebbishes next to stars of shows next to office
boys next to the new head of programming, all in one big
happy row.

Some guys talk in men's rooms. Office boys would tell each
other who was getting fired because they read mail marked
confidential. Executives admitted to affairs, moaned about
their tax bills and let on what they really thought of the current
season. I guess it really takes a good pee to get you in that
frame of mind. I also guess that the plot to kill Julius Caesar
was developed in front of a urinal.

Whenever I was in the men's room, I just kept my mouth
shut and listened, and since it was a good place to pick up
information, I was in there a lot. It's amazing that the entire
network didn't think I had a bladder condition. One fine day
in February . . . That's the real problem with California, there
are fine days in February. (If you ask me, the weather sucks.
Who can appreciate spring when you're having Christmas in
the pool?) One fine day in February, I'm standing there and
I hear that they're going to fire my boss of four years, the man
who brought me to California, good old Barry. I really felt

sorry for the guy, forty-five, divorced, trying desperately to grow sideburns.

As I was zipping up, I heard the really bad news. Good old Barry was being replaced as Head of Daytime Television by a woman. A woman. My first reaction was to get in the toilet and flush. I didn't want her. I wanted someone I could grow sideburns with. I wanted to pee next to my boss.

O.K., if I were born today I would be growing up in a world where there is such a thing as a female surgeon and a female jockey and a female boss. There were no female jockeys when I was born, Gloria. Look, I know that was wrong, but for the first twenty-seven years of my life, I didn't see a woman win a horse race or even enter one. So adjust, you say. Take it like a man. Yeah, O.K., I'll try . . . but I couldn't stand having a woman boss for the same reason that I'm scared shitless to go to a woman doctor. I'm sure she's just as good as her fellow man—her fellow person—but I'm scared to go to a woman doctor because right there in the middle of the examination I might get a hard-on and she might be just looking at my throat.

The real difference between a woman and a man is that women are never standing there or lying there with a part of their bodies popping up when they don't want it to. Equal? We won't be equal until they can find the cure for the unwanted hard-on. What would happen if right in the middle of discussing with my woman boss whether we should put Quacky Duck on Saturday mornings, I got hard and had to sidestep out of the room with my hands in my pockets? You're fifteen years old and you're in English class and the teacher is talking about Eustacia Vye and you're getting turned on. Good old Barry wouldn't give me problems like that.

A lady boss? Myron Meyer never had to have a lady boss. Why me? Me because I was in daytime programming and somebody high up in the network ranks had a sudden awakening that more women than men watch daytime television. This same somebody had also been accused by an equal rights committee of not having one woman in an executive position. They picked on us, good old Barry and me.

Barbara Hirsh became Head of Daytime Television and good old Barry shaved his sideburns, put on a suit and went back to his wife so he could stop paying alimony. (His wife made it clear she preferred the alimony to him but she'd take him back if he promised to relate to her as a person.) Ms. Hirsh was not only my boss, but taller than I was. A tall Jewish girl with a B.A. from Brooklyn College was going to tell me what to do.

After a week, I realized that there were only two ways to handle the situation. I could work at my maximum ability and treat her like any superior, forget she was a woman and give her the respect, admiration and devotion she deserved—or I could schtup her. I chose to schtup. My instincts told me that I had to make her insecure and the only way I knew to really make this girl insecure was to take her to bed. Sure, you're all going to accuse me of using my boss as a sex object. Let me remind you that it takes two to schtup. (Whereas it is actually possible to tango alone. I'll bet Alan Milner does.)

Here was my plan: I would ask her up to the house. She would come, she being tall and lonely, me being male. I'd get her into bed, she being new in town, me being male. The following morning, I would make no mention of the night before. I would never bring up the incident or invite her home again. I have found from experience that if you lay a girl once and never mention it again it drives her crazy. She wonders what's wrong with her, which makes her insecure. Insecurity always gives the other person the upper hand. The person with the upper hand is boss. It may not say so on the door, but everyone in the office knows. I knew it would work. Barbara Hirsh is the type of girl who never had a nickname.

I asked her up to the house and schtuped her. (Sex with

Barbara was like watching daytime television. You could do something else while you were doing it.) I took her home, walked into the office bright and cheerful the next morning with an idea for a new game show called *The Magic Box*, which was a rip-off of *Let's Make a Deal*. I talked business straight through, shook her hand when I left and knew that everything was going to be just fine. The head of the network might have thought she was the boss, but I was the boss. I had the penis.

I saw Barbara Hirsh deteriorate. She asked me to accompany her to screenings and parties, which I did, but I never laid a hand on her. I was charming, polite and willing to be her friend, but you could tell she was wondering what the hell was wrong with her. I guarantee she thought there was something wrong with her personality or her feminine hygiene spray.

After a while, Barbara went into therapy. I don't think I was solely responsible. Many single girls go into therapy once they start making over seventeen thousand a year. I'll take part of the blame, but I think she would have ended up on the couch even if I hadn't come along. If a girl is tall and successful, she's got to seek help sooner or later.

Not long after Barbara started with her analyst, she asked me to have lunch with her. I should have known her analysis was going to be a problem for me. Obviously, her doctor would encourage her to deal with her problems, and since I was at least part of her problems I was to be dealt with.

We went to King's Four-in-Hand—Chinese and dark. We talked for close to two hours. (People in analysis talk a lot, using words like "sublimate" and "project.") Two hours and it boiled down to this: David, if you want to keep your job then you better put out.

I was the sex object.

It was the casting couch and I was on it.

I related to Tuesday Weld.

Is this what women did the minute they were liberated? Yes.

They ran right out to perform the injustices that were performed on them. Gloria, whatever happened to "Turn the other cheek"? Whatever happened to the Geneva Convention? It was the Romans all over again, not only conquering their victims, but raping them besides. Why must every victor stay around for the spoils? . . . Look, I'm not saying you're all the same. I'm one of those guys who doesn't even think you're all the same in the dark. Some of you gals must realize how hard it is on us guys. I'm sure some of the Romans didn't rape.

Why waste time? Right there in the King's Four-in-Hand I asked Barbara over, making it sound like it was my idea in the first place. After she demanded I fuck her I said something like: "Barbara, let's stop beating around the bush. Come on over tonight and we'll get it together." Translation: "Come on over and we'll have sex because I'm Jewish and I don't want to give up one job until I have another even if it means fucking my brains out." When I left my father's business, I had an anxiety attack every day of my life until I got another job. I'd stick with Barbara until something else came up. In the meantime, the only something that had to come up was my own little pecker. (Little it was not. That's just an expression—I don't know why I had to clarify that. I'm too mature to have to tell anyone the size of my penis. It's so unimportant—and it's not little. Funny, I have no idea why I felt I had to say I'm not small.)

At about five o'clock, there was a memo from the desk of B. Hirsh, saying, "Pick me up at eight?" It ain't fair. They want to be liberated. They want to make more money. They want to make advances and ultimatums and they still want to be picked up. Ms. Hirsh lived up on Mulholland, a twenty-minute drive, and once you got there you couldn't turn around and come down without scratching your car in her driveway. She wants to be liberated, let her scratch her own car. Let her know what it's like to get out of bed and drive yourself home after sex. Come on, Barbara, you want to play with the guys. Some of us don't want girls on our team, but if you force us, you're gonna have to play like the rest of us and you and your car might get dented.

From the desk of D. Meyer: "I'll meet you at my place at eight."

From the desk of B. Hirsh: "Can't you pick me up? I hate driving at night."

From the desk of D. Meyer: "No, I can't pick you up. I never told you before, but since we're being honest I feel I can let you know. I hate your driveway."

From the desk of B. Hirsh: "Fuck you."

From the desk of D. Meyer: "Yes, I always thought that was our intention in getting together."

There were no more memos. Interoffice memos remind me of when I was a kid. I'd fight with another kid and when it was over but not settled, one of us would run up at top speed and sock the other one in the back, screaming gleefully, "I got you last!" Then the other would have to retaliate and so on. This would go on until somebody's mother called or some girl got accidentally hurt and screamed. Interoffice memos are "Got you last."

I knew Barbara would show up, mainly because she couldn't tell her shrink that she copped out. The doorbell rang at eight-oh-five even though the car pulled up at five to. Didn't want to seem so anxious, Barbara, ol' girl?

We small-talked about the office, all the stuff that I had heard in the men's room, and smoked a joint. Barbara smoked but you could tell she'd never be comfortable around grass. She made you feel like the cops were going to arrive any minute. We drank wine and prepared ourselves for sexual activity. We were both from the fifties so we couldn't get right to it. If you hit puberty in the fifties, I don't care how many shrinks you go to, you've got to put in time before.

It was awkward as hell. The eleven-o'clock news was over and it was obvious that we had to get down to business. The basic problem was that Barbara had made the first advance hours ago in the restaurant but couldn't follow it up. The way I read it, this afternoon she had demanded that I have sex with her and was now waiting to be ravaged. She wanted to take advantage of me *and* have me ravage her *and* drive her back and forth. Girls don't play fair. Not yet they don't.

Barbara was wearing a long dress with about a hundred tiny buttons—the kind you put on little kids' sweaters. All of a sudden she's playing hard to get. Big-mouth from the restaurant is standing there in a dress that might as well have been a chastity belt. Why, Barbara? If you wanted to make it (and you did; you drove yourself to my door), why didn't you arrive naked under a trench coat? Or you could have worn jeans and a polo shirt—isn't that what you always wore when we went out as friends? What was with all those baby buttons? Do you begin at the bottom and work your way up to erogenous zones? Do you begin at the top and work your way down? Or do you merely open the ten buttons covering the snatch, pop it in and send her home with a "See you in the office, boss"?

Barbara's buttons took both hands, and she kept her attention on what I was doing because she feared I was stretching her best knit. She was on her back on the bed, letting me unbutton, but watching to make sure I didn't pull a thread. Her hands would take over only when mine had failed. Remember that button game—Doctor, Lawyer, Indian Chief? I was playing that game—Doctor, Lawyer, Assistant to Daytime Television.

Ms. Hirsh looked pretty good by the light of the television. I liked making love with the television on. It gave off just enough light. It made the whole thing seem more casual, and if things got boring you could have sex and Johnny Carson at the same time. (Since the *Tonight Show* is taped at six in the evening, even Carson could have sex and Carson at the same time.) The only problem is if you get too involved in the show, you might laugh at a joke while you're supposed to be caressing private parts.

We had fair sex—nothing Masters and Johnson or *Cosmopolitan* would want to know about, not too different from our first go. I fell asleep right afterward. Ladies, listen, it's not an insult, it's not that I don't want to look at you, or talk to you, or hug you. It's just that I get fucking tired (or tired fucking) and it's totally impossible to keep awake. Frances, my ex-wife, was the only woman I know who let me sleep after sex. I know it's insulting, but I can't help it. The curtain comes down, we've taken the final bows and it's time to rest. I bet that's the one advantage of being homosexual. They probably both fall asleep.

Barbara woke me up. They all wake you up. (Except for Frances, and I thank you for that, Fran.)

"David . . . David . . . *David*": Barbara Hirsh.

She woke me to ask if I minded if she spent the night. "No, suh, boss. I don't mind, boss, suh. You do what you think right, boss." Next thing you know, I thought as I lay there, she'll be asking me to give her blow jobs under the desk.

I didn't want Ms. Hirsh to spend the night. I didn't want to have to do cute after-sex things like taking a shower and washing her back or having a pillow fight or holding hands and singing "Yesterday" at 2 A.M. I didn't want her wearing my robe and I didn't want to walk in on her on the toilet. I didn't want to have to kiss her in the morning before she brushed her teeth. I let her spend the night.

There was no way of knowing. Even Einstein couldn't have predicted it. Barbara Hirsh had chosen the worst night possible to demand compulsory love. It is a night I'll never forget and, may I add, it is a night the total population of Southern

California won't forget. Barbara Hirsh had demanded that I be her lover the night of the big earthquake.

Forgetting Barbara Hirsh for a moment, I would like at this time to get into my feeling about living in Southern California. It is a stupid, asinine place to live. Why would anybody want to live over faults? Because show business is here? We don't mind sitting on something that might kill us because we get to see our names on television? And what about the doctors and the lawyers and the people who own clothing stores? They live here because they get to be in close proximity to stars. Sure the weather is O.K., if you like constant hot spring, but we might die.

I remember in school, it must have been in about the fifth grade, we learned about volcanoes. I couldn't believe that people actually lived near volcanoes, knowing that they might erupt. But those people were uneducated and poor. They didn't have TWA to fly them to another home. I knew this, and yet I kept thinking how dumb it was to live near hot lava. I couldn't get it out of my mind.

"Why don't they move from there?" I asked teachers and parents.

"Because they don't know any better," was their reply.

And here I am in Hollywood, California, sitting on ground that might move, among all those rumors from psychics that we are going to fall into the Pacific. We don't know any better.

I think six thirty-two was the exact time of the Big Quake, as we Los Angelinos affectionately call it. I was awakened, not by the noise of the rattling windows, nor by the jerking ground under me, but by Barbara's hysterical shrieking. Perhaps she thought God was punishing her for forcing a man into bed. Maybe that's what really did happen. God made this earthquake happen because he was really pissed off with the way Barbara Hirsh behaved. I'd like to believe that, but my sense of logic won't let me. If God really felt that way, the center of the Big Quake would have been my house and not Sylmar.

Barbara shrieked in fright. I don't blame her; it was a pretty violent experience and I had a heavy wrought-iron chandelier hanging over the bed, which was threatening to crush us. You could lose an eye like that.

Barbara's shrieks turned into screaming confessions: "Oh, David, I love you. . . . Oh, David, please! . . . David, never leave me. . . . Please, David, I'm too tall. . . . You can be the Head of Daytime Television if you say you love me. . . . Please, David!"

Obviously, the earthquake had shaken Barbara loose and she was verbalizing everything before the chandelier crushed us both. At the height of her hysterics, after pouring her heart out, Barbara, out of nervousness, peed in the bed. Not a lot, just a little leak, but enough for us both to notice.

Unfortunately, the chandelier didn't get us, and I had a post-hysterical woman on my hands. Barbara faced total embarrassment. She had uttered her last words only to find that those weren't going to be her last words.

The ground stopped moving, the chandelier swayed rhythmically. We heard the sounds of sirens in the distance. Barbara turned toward the wall and said, "Maybe it's better if you don't come back to work." Poor Barbara, you're thinking. Poor girl spoke too soon and, as a result, humiliated her tall self. Poor David: that's what you should be thinking. Poor David obviously couldn't go back to work for poor Barbara because it was too embarrassing for poor Barbara to have David around as a reminder of the morning she let herself go, confessed her love and peed in his bed. People lost their lives in the earthquake, they lost their homes. I don't know anybody else who got pissed on. Never think that sleeping with your boss will insure your job, especially in earthquake country.

It probably happened:

FROM: The Desk of B. Hirsh
TO: Mrs. Conway, Chairman,
          The Women's Retaliation Committee,
          Denver, Colorado

It has come to my attention that you are forming a Women's Retaliation Committee. I heard about you through a friend of a friend. I understand that you are just in the beginning stages, but I just wanted to get my vote in early. One *David Meyer* got me crazy by sleeping with me and never mentioning it again. It was because of him that I had to go into analysis and it was also because of this same *David Meyer* that I said things during an earthquake. I'm not holding a grudge, but I would very much appreciate it if you would cut off his balls.

Sincerely,
Ms. Barbara Hirsh

I hadn't seen Barbara since then. I swore that I would never speak to her again. Men do strange things under pressure. I'm sure Nixon would have called Ms. Hirsh during his last days in the White House if his father was coming to visit and he needed a girlfriend. 513–6378. She picked up at exactly two rings, the single girl.

"Hello." Hadn't spoken to her in ages, but I knew immediately that was the voice from the earthquake.

"Hey, Barbara, it's David," casually, although the last time we spoke we were thinking life was over.

"David who?" She knew who.

"David, the one you said you loved." Let her have some more insecurity.

"How are you, David? I've been meaning to call you for months and months and months, ever since I heard you got a job in prime time."

"It worked out great that you fired me."

"I didn't fire you."

"You said something like: 'It would be better if you didn't come back to work.' Maybe I'm crazy, but I felt that you didn't want me to go back to work."

"I'm sorry." Good. Now she owed me something.

"Barbara, I'm going to give you a chance to make it up to me."

"You are?" She was happy. I was absolving her guilt. Say three Hail Marys and pose as my girlfriend.

"My parents are coming for a couple of weeks and . . . and I'm not actually going with anyone . . ."

"And you want me to masquerade as your girl." She was quick. No wonder she was the Head of Daytime Television.

"Listen, if you don't want to, there are a million girls who do." I could go through the Yellow Pages.

"I'll do it if you take me to the Emmys." We were into negotiations.

"I'll take you to the Emmys and provide my own tuxedo, if I can have you on twenty-four-hour call."

"You can call me at four in the morning if I can have you on and off for a month. There are a slew of parties coming up."

She was a tough lady, knew she had me. I said fine. A gentlemen's (-persons') agreement and Barbara and I were into a relationship of using each other. Many single people get this type of thing going. The guys have girls for functions. The girls get exposure and some free movies. They are each other's convenience. I just had to hope that my father didn't notice that my convenience looked nothing like Sandy Weiss.

As we were undressing at Love-Able:

"I got someone to pose as my girlfriend." I said that for an unbelievable reason. I wanted to make my whore jealous. I know I love her now. I must have loved her then.

65

"That's good," said the prostitute.

"I wish it were you," said the customer.

"No, you don't," she said.

Yes, I did.

I must have loved her.

Myron Meyer is the type of person who doesn't know what he's like, a man with no self-realization. Like the old ladies with sagging stockings and shopping bags, he doesn't begin to know he is a stereotype.

Myron was the third child (the first died at four months) born to Abe and Lily Meyer. Abe was a scholar from Rumania, a boy who packed his suitcases only with books when he left the old country and went to Philadelphia. The trouble with Abe was he didn't want to do anything but study and would have liked to be paid for going to the library. Lily, an enterprising young woman, also from Rumania, got enough cash together, opened Abe's Luncheonette and ran the whole thing herself while Abe sat in the back booth and read.

Myron and his brother Herman grew up in the luncheonette. As babies, their cribs were behind the counter. As little boys, they went straight to the store after school, where they both sat at the counter and ate until they were the fattest little boys in school. Lily also grew. It would have been a very strong person who could oversee all those daily specials of meat loaf and mashed potatoes and not partake. Abe stayed thin, as a scholar should be. The story goes that Lily would put a cheese sandwich in front of him at noon and he'd still be eating it at dinnertime. Scholars tend to chew slowly.

When World War II broke out, Myron enlisted, against his mother's wishes. Abe felt it was all right for the boy to go. It wasn't until years later that the family found out that Abe, who could read three languages, didn't know there was a war on. Myron came back from the war, not a hero but slim. Lily took one look at him and cried her eyes out. Being thin meant Lily had lost him. He could now fit into the back booth and read with his father, and that's exactly what Myron did. He went to the Wharton School, sweeping the floor for his mother and studying with his father. After graduation he decided to go to New York to make his fortune. Lily begged Myron to take his brother Herman with him and to let Herman be part of his business—whatever business it was. After all, Herman didn't have the advantages Myron had had. He didn't get to fight a war and get thin, which meant he didn't get to study with Abe, which meant either Myron should take him or he would spend the rest of his life eating meat loaf. Lily won and although no mother wants her children to move ninety miles from home, she smiled the day they left. Lily's big push begat Meyer and Meyer, a successful business dealing in providing important machines for those who needed them. They were the only ones in the New York area who had the important machines, so they made a lot of money. Lily was happy. They're not sure if Abe ever knew the boys left Philly.

Both boys got married the same year. Herman married a fat wife and had a fat daughter and a fat son. (My cousin Ron went into Meyer and Meyer, my cousin Gail became a receptionist for a wholesale jeweler, and she was the smart one.) Myron married Martha Douglas, a shy girl from the Midwest who came to New York to live with her aunt for a year. Her aunt lived in the same building as Myron and Herman and, as in a Doris Day–Rock Hudson movie, Myron and Martha met in a stuck elevator.

Why Martha Douglas? What makes anybody's father fall in

love with anybody's mother? He saw in Martha a wife, a mother, a servant, someone to see that his bagels were fresh, someone who would lower her eyes when sex was mentioned, someone who would never ask for a life of her own.

When Myron told Lily he was marrying Martha, she was so upset she couldn't finish her tuna on rye.

"She's not Jewish," Lily cried.

"She is. She converted," said a romantic Myron.

"We don't believe in converts."

"Yes, we do. The rabbi converted her."

"They convert because they know that Jewish boys make the best husbands, but they never stop praying to Jesus under their breath."

I had a good solid heritage and should have inherited Abe's desire for knowledge, Lily's insatiable drive for survival, Myron's combination of them both and Martha's ability to bend. I didn't. Only one thing leaked through to me. Like Abe, I am able to sit in the back booth.

As we were undressing at Love-Able:

"My parents are coming today."

"Great."

"It's not great. It's terrible. I may not be able to see you on a regular basis. I'm going to try to, but it is not going to be easy sneaking out of the house."

I wanted her to say, "Oh, my God, David, darling, what am I going to do without you? The others I just take credit cards from but you . . . to you I give my heart."

She said, "I'll be here. Come when you can." A little flat for a star-crossed lover.

I met my parents at the gate. He looked balder, his pot was bigger, a vision of what I would be if I didn't go faithfully to Paul the expensive barber and the gym. She looked like her mother, not only because she had her mother's features, but because she was my grandmother's age—my grandmother's age from my earliest recollections. Both of my sisters had children. My mother was a grandmother. I just didn't expect to see Myron and my nana coming off the plane. I had a picture of my parents on the boardwalk in Atlantic City, taken during the thirties. These were not the same people. He bought six suits at once and she memorized soap operas.

The ride home from the airport was not fun. I drove and I listened. Three people, some related by blood, one had been in one of the other's womb, two had made love on at least three occasions. We hadn't seen each other in ages. Were we getting into each other's heads? Were we relatives relating? We were talking about how tough the steak was on the plane —and in first class yet.

"I'm going to write a letter to them. That was the worst steak I've ever had, the robbers": him.

"Your father was very upset. He tried to get something else, but all they had left was a kosher meal": her.

"Gee, Dad, I'm sorry." I was trying to communicate and project, trying to feel my father's pain over the rotten steak. (Actually, I was happy that he didn't get on a flight where they recommended whorehouses.)

"Ah, look, it happens. Every steak in the world can't be great. But in first class . . . I don't want to talk about it anymore."

He doesn't want to talk about it anymore, so we don't talk about it anymore. He is not only king of his home and king of his business, he is king of all the conversation that goes on about him. He left his steak and went on to my car.

"How long have you had the Mercedes?"

"I got it soon after I came out. It's a great car. I got a good deal."

"You got a good deal?" He leaned back and drew on his cigar. "You got a good deal on a German car?" I knew what was coming. "Six million Jews were murdered, did you know that, David? You got a good deal from people who killed six million Jews?"

"Pop, I bought the car in Beverly Hills from people who had nothing to do with . . ."

"It's a German car, made by Germans. The money goes into German hands."

"When we went to Europe last year your father wouldn't go to Germany," said my mother.

"Pop, we have to forgive and forget. The people who made this car were not even born during the war."

"You know that? You know for a fact that the people who make this car didn't kill Jews? It's the car Hitler drove."

"Pop, I get great mileage."

"Hitler got great mileage too. I never thought when you moved to California that you'd forget your religion."

I didn't answer. We drove past pumping oil wells and billboards in silence. I would never enjoy the car again.

"Everyone seems to be dying," said my mother, trying to cheer us up.

"What's that supposed to mean, Martha?" said Myron, off the car and into his wife.

"I don't know if I wrote and told you, David, but your friend Richie's mother died and Louise Lichtner's father passed on too. She wasn't close to him. And do you remember the Morganthals, they lived right near the *shul?*" She said *shul* like a convert. "They both passed away, first her, after being sick for about two years, and then him about six months later. They said he died of a broken heart."

Nice, Mother, very nice. You got it all out without even taking a breath. The thing that got me was that she actually enjoyed being a human obituary column. No, she was better than just obituary. She hit sickness, both mental and physical, and all personal tragedy.

71

"A terrible thing happened to Linda Ferguson," she barreled on. "She left her baby for just a second outside the bakery and this group of kids came along and dumped over the carriage. That little nine-month-old baby has a broken toe and they had to take her to a free clinic because Bob is out of work." And right on. "And did I tell you about your Aunt Celia? She got mugged in both arms last month."

She was a soap opera, my mother, only she wasn't over in half an hour and you don't want to tune in tomorrow. She spilled bad news all over you until it soaked into your guts and depressed you for about a year and a half. And when she stopped, he started, like a team of vaudevillians, only they weren't performing to make you laugh. They were there to make you unfit for a normal life. There they are, folks, Myron and Martha Meyer, the hottest act in town. Step right up, step right up and enter the Mercedes. Never in your life will you hear such hardship or experience such pain, and it's one big continuous show. . . .

As we got off the freeway, she tapered off and began looking for stars and he, so as not to fill the car with silence, started up again.

"In your job, you decide about new television shows, like what's going to be on television?"

"Yeah, Pop." Sort of.

"I have an idea for a television show."

No, Pop. Don't you realize that the whole world has an idea for a television show? The lady in the cleaners had an idea about a kooky lady in the cleaners. She has a different problem each week with different stains. I tell her it's a good idea, because I want the spaghetti sauce out of my silk shirt. The man who cleans my pool has an idea about a kooky man who cleans pools. Each week he would get involved with different hazards of pool cleaning, like leaves stuck in the drain. He visualizes a large pool onstage and everything revolving around him. He will be willing to give up cleaning pools to star in the series. I tell him it's a good idea, because I don't want slime in my pool. There's a girl, there's ten of them, who told me about a series about a kooky girl who lives in the city. I wanted to make it with them so I told them great, kid, great. Then here's Myron. I have to listen. It's only fair. He listened when I lost his firm one point five million.

"A lot of people don't know how interesting leasing business machines is." They all begin like that, only you substitute cleaning, pool maintenance, manufacturing seat belts. "You could do a show about a guy who leases business machines. Each week he gets involved in different problems—the machines break down, someone is late paying their bill. You know, stuff like that." I thought he was through and this was the part where I was supposed to say it was a good idea.

"It's a cute idea, Pop."

"I'm not finished." He's not finished? What's more to say about a guy who leases business machines? Maybe there's a kooky son who buys a Mercedes. My father went on. "This guy had a war injury." Of course. They all have war injuries, even the cleaning lady. "He hurt his face and had to have plastic surgery. The surgery had to be done in the jungle someplace and it came out crazy. The gimmick is this man ended up with a puttylike face and he can change his whole face around. He can remold his nose, cheeks, mouth, so that he can actually look completely different every time you see him." I was hoping he'd go on; not that I was interested in what he was saying: I just didn't want him to stop for fear my mother would start listing tragedies again.

Myron continued. "Changing his face gives him a terrific advantage in leasing machines. He could get a deal up by bidding against himself and he could always save face." My father laughed at his own joke. Obviously, he had thought through his idea. What impressed me was not that his idea was good, but that he was thinking. My father was trying to be creative. I liked him for a while.

"I'd like to call it 'The Man with a Thousand Faces' or 'The Man of a Thousand Faces.' How soon do you think it could be on television, David?"

If I wasn't driving, I would have stared at him—you know, the kind of look when your mouth is open and your whole face is slack. The look you see in bad movies and in good college productions.

"Well, Pop, the season for . . . uh . . . giving ideas is over now. The network has made all its commitments for pilots this year. Maybe . . ." God was with me: I turned into my street. We could, thank you, God, stop talking.

"Mom, Pop, we're here." I pointed to my house. They both squinted, trying to take it all in. I knew the pseudo-Spanish quality about it would be foreign to them.

"Which one?" asked my mom.

"The one with the stained-glass windows," said I, proudly pulling into the driveway.

"It looks so dark and small. You paid seventy-two five for that?" said my father, who was not yet out of the car and already knocking the home I love.

"Something about this reminds me of my cousin Loretta's place in Florida. Did I tell you, David, that Loretta's beautiful little granddaughter died of a brain hemorrhage?" Good, Mom.

They came in, looked around. Everything was strange to them. I had modern graphics on the wall. They had pastoral scenes and sconces. I had what you call your eclectic look—a few antiques, a little modern. They had what I call "listen to the decorator"—expensive and dull. I had books all over the place—not that I read them, but you know, coffee table books. My parents had books too, none published after 1952, when they gave up their membership in the Book-of-the-Month

Club. I had plants. They had dried flower arrangements. Their walls were white, mine shrieked color. They weren't going to be comfortable in my home. And there was the problem of the waterbed.

Having fallen for my whore on a waterbed, I found myself purchasing one. (To be delivered in a plain brown wrapper.) I put it in the guest room for the purposes of illicit sex. I guess it was there in case I could convince the Queen of the Prom to come home with me. The only other bed in the house was my bed. *My* bed. The thing I go to sleep on. The only thing I could sleep on—my security thing. I don't know when it happened, but a few years ago I was no longer able to sleep anywhere but on my very own bed.

A miracle. My parents, in a moment of not wanting to be any trouble for me—their expression, not mine—tried the waterbed and liked it. Myron's back never felt better and I was left to wonder if they had sex on a bed that was bought for that purpose. All I know is they were both smiling in the morning.

They were still smiling by the time I got home from work that night. They spent a wonderful day, they said. Know what they did their first day, their first time in Los Angeles? They didn't go to a movie studio, or Disneyland, or to Grauman's to match their footprints with Rita Hayworth's. They went shopping for groceries, stocking my house with foods they could relate to. I was hoping that, having survived the waterbed, they could palate things like avocado, honey granola bread and organic apricot-apple juice. They couldn't.

"We got Bumble Bee tuna. You know, it's cheaper out here. Always buy the best tuna, David. Did you read about the ladies who were killed from that bad tuna?" said my mother. Terrific. Not many people could relate tuna fish to death.

"We found a place with good rye, but there isn't one place in this whole town that has a good bagel," said my father, who would refuse a kosher meal on a plane but would search the city for a bagel. He was a closet Jewish eater.

"The oranges were twelve for a dollar. I pay ten for a dollar." My mother was caressing every orange she washed in preparation for the refrigerator, a refrigerator which up to now never had more than two bottles of wine and a few rotten organic things in it.

"What about the steak?" I knew he'd get to the steak. "Where can you get a good steak out here?"

"I don't know, Pop." I wouldn't dare suggest a steak restaurant to my father. I had seen how he had berated the airline that brought him here.

Of course, to Myron, if I didn't know where to find a good steak, it meant that I didn't eat steak, which meant that I couldn't afford steak. Nobody would just not want steak.

"Well, David, tonight I'll take you out for a good steak. Invite some of your friends." Like in college. Let me grow up, Dad. I make money. I can take you to dinner, Pop. I can even pay for Mom.

"Why don't we take your girlfriend?" My girlfriend, Pop, is busy tonight. She works at this waterbed demonstration place, Pop. I saw her for a quickie on my way home from work, Pop.

I got Barbara Hirsh to go for a good steak with us and felt she played the part of girlfriend very well, looking at me over her wineglass, holding hands when it was necessary to hold hands. No one would ever know we severed our relationship because she peed in my bed. My parents would never know I was pining for a prostitute.

Myron and Martha seemed to be having a hell of a good time. They slept on the waterbed. They kept buying food. They were in pursuit of the perfect bagel. In their spare time, they straightened up my whole house, even my underwear drawer. "My drawers are so neat you could blindfold me and I could find anything," said my father. I snuck out to Love-

Able, trying desperately to stick to my Monday, Wednesday, Friday schedule. (I missed one Friday night and couldn't sleep all weekend.) My mother called every second cousin of hers in the state, and my father got to meet his first homosexual. I introduced him to everyone in program development when he came by to see where his little boy worked, and to take his little boy, lest he starve, to lunch. When I introduced him to one guy, Myron picked up on something—he wasn't quite sure what.

"There's something strange about that boy," and he ordered corned beef on rye, "make sure it's lean." My father told a waiter in the Polo Lounge to make sure it's lean.

"He's a homosexual, Pop." I thought I'd lay it right out.

"You mean a homo?" Yes, Pop. "Homo" is a short, disgusting form of "homosexual," taken from the Latin, meaning "even though you're a man and I'm a man I'd like to give it to you."

"Yes."

"He sleeps with men?" my father asked.

"Yes."

"I never met one before." The man was sixty-four years old. It's hard to believe he never came across a homosexual.

"I'm sure you have. You just didn't realize it. You can't always tell. Some even marry."

"You're not, are you?"

"No, Pop." But I have to pay for sex.

"Good. I wouldn't want a sissy for a son."

"I'm not." I'm a great kid, Pop, except for one silly mistake that cost you a small fortune.

"They know at the network that this boy is a homo?" My father wouldn't drop it, pursuing it almost as hard as the bagel.

"It's common knowledge, I guess."

"Only in America, I tell you. You kids knock this country and I tell you this is the only country in the world where they'll let a homosexual work at a network. In other countries they'd kill him."

What did you say? Did you say in other countries they kill homosexuals? In your head they kill homosexuals, Pop. I can't understand my father and I can't change him, so I change the subject.

"What do you think of Barbara?"

"She doesn't look like the Weiss kid."

"Around the eyes. Didn't you notice right around the eyes she looks just like Sandy?"

"I don't know where you got she looked like Harry Weiss's daughter."

"I'm telling you around the eyes. They could be twins around the eyes."

"Yeah? . . . Don't rush into anything."

"I'm not rushing. She . . ." She isn't the one I think about while I'm doing push-ups.

"I rushed into marrying your mother."

No, don't tell me, Pop. I don't want to hear. I want to think you loved my mother so much that you couldn't bear to live without her. I want to think that if you didn't marry her, both your hearts would break because you were destined to be together till death do you part—no, even after death. I want to think of the two of you in heaven on a waterbed. I don't want to hear about rushing into things. Don't think I'm old enough to know the truth now. Please, Pop, don't get deep in the Polo Lounge. Nothing deep is supposed to come anywhere in the vicinity of the Beverly Hills Hotel. That's why they have plastic plants.

"I was young. Your mother was a beautiful girl but . . ." Don't say but, Pop. There shouldn't be a but. She was the love of your life. "I married her without thinking the whole thing out. We were young. I was just starting out. I guess I was a bit of a rebel. In those days you married your own kind." What about love, Pop? You're not talking about love. "I guess I love her. She's been very good to me, David."

Oh, Pop, no. Don't tell me over a corned beef sandwich that you never loved my mother. My generation doesn't know what love is. You people knew. You're the ones who heard bells and danced holding each other and took pictures on the boardwalk. You went on roller coasters. You had movies where people walked off into the sunset together. You had Vivien Leigh and Katharine Hepburn and Rita Hayworth falling in love over and over again. You had a chance to start out poor and live on love. Please, Pop, don't tell me you don't know if you love my mother and in the same breath say, "Pass the mustard."

That was some lunch. First he tells me he rushed into marrying my mother, then he got into my entire life.

Myron's talk with his son:

1. Don't rush into marriage. Don't forget the California community property laws.

2. When I'm no longer here—and these things have to be talked about, David—I want you to look after your mother. The girls will comfort her, but she'll need a man in her life. If she's visiting or living with you when she dies, God forbid, I have provided a fund for shipping her body back to New York.

3. Get a good tax man. It's worth every penny.

4. Don't bring home any black babies.

5. Don't hang around with homos. The girls will think you're that way too.

6. Don't forget you're Jewish. A lot of people come out to California and forget they're Jewish.

7. Don't smoke marijuana. They have proof it deteriorates the brain.

8. Get yourself a haircut and some nice clothes. Nobody is going to give you a promotion if you look like that.

9. Watch out for those crazy women who go for the women's

79

liberation bit. They're no good, David. They have crazy ideas that are just going to hurt you.

Gee, thanks for lunch, Pop, and thanks for the great pointers. I especially like the one about black babies, but the "get yourself a haircut and some nice clothes" was mighty fine too. And, Pop, thanks again for telling me you didn't really love Mom. Gosh, gee, Pop. I hope you didn't tell her.

The two weeks were a year, slowly moving along from dinner to dinner. We went to a different restaurant each night, my father alternating between steak and roast beef, rare, and if it's not rare it goes back. My mother told tragedies and searched for stars. Barbara Hirsh showed up in a different outfit nightly, holding my hand as if she really meant it. I had the feeling that Barbara was no longer business-dealing with me and was trying to slide back into my life, imagining that we once had something. All we had was a couple of fucks and a couple of fuck-ups, Barbara.

My parents were supposed to leave on Friday so that my father could rest up over the weekend before going back to work. "I need a rest after this vacation," he said a hundred times, and always managed to add, "I'm still on New York time." The Emmys were going to be on Sunday night, two days after their departure. Barbara Hirsh got her grubby little hands on two extra tickets and invited her two best friends, Myron and Martha, who all of a sudden could extend their trip by a few days. I couldn't say "Go home." During the first week, they had got tickets to *Let's Make a Deal,* left the house dressed as chipmunks and failed to get on the trading floor. The Emmys would make up for that.

Myron rented a tuxedo and looked all wrong. Somehow he decided that wearing a lavender ruffled shirt would be hip. He was a conservative dresser, but in California he wanted to be "in." He would have been "in" in a South American band. My mother borrowed a dress from one of her cousins who lives in

L.A., and looked like she was wearing her cousin's dress. I loved them, but they just didn't look like the type of people you want to introduce as your parents. They looked short—not that tall matters. It's just that they looked short and somehow looking short is not a good look for the Emmys. It's fine for a wedding in New Jersey.

I had a big problem with my mother. She stared at stars from the minute we got there. I know that may not seem like a big problem, but my mother really stared, mouth open, mesmerized. When I introduced her to Tim Conway she couldn't talk. I had to extend her limp arm myself. She practically fainted in front of Robert Young and told Carol Burnett how much she loved her, over and over again, until I backed her away, making a tiny rip in her cousin's dress. Lucille Ball was in our row and my mother looked at her while everyone else was looking at the stage. When Johnny Carson appeared, I had the feeling that she would float unconsciously up to the stage and tell him she had stayed up to see him a couple of times.

My father was quiet. Awed. It made me uncomfortable. I was used to seeing my father in control, the boss. On this night, he looked at me for approval every time he made a move, his cigar bitten like a bullet.

Then there were the questions. He wanted to know everything. Were the cameras on? Should he wave? What happens if Johnny Carson makes a mistake? How does Ann-Margret's dress stay up? Who was going to win, as if I knew. When the program started, Myron, for the first time in his life, was hard of hearing. He missed the nominees. I had to repeat them. He missed the winners. I had to repeat each winner as he/she was running up the aisle. He missed every one of Carson's jokes. I had to repeat them and he laughed alone. I was sure the entire industry was looking at the man in the lavender shirt who was laughing late and I was sure they all knew it was David Meyer's father. I shouldn't have cared. The man's a good man.

He gets up at six in the morning, even on weekends. He gives all his old suits to the maid's husband. He can find things in his drawers blindfolded. This man should have the right to laugh when he wants to. I just wanted to die, that's all.

The topper of the whole night was my mother's pocket camera. I didn't even know she had it until the actual presentations started and she began to take pictures, her flash cubes flashing away.

"Mom, I don't think you're supposed to take pictures in here."

"Why not?" And she took one of John Davidson.

"I just don't think you're supposed to, and they're not going to come out anyway. It's too dark in here." Please, Mom, put the fucking camera away.

"I want to show your sisters where I was." And she leaned over and took one of Lucy.

I was the one who saw the usher coming toward us. "Mom, someone's coming to tell you to stop taking pictures." We were in the middle of the row and he had a hell of a time getting to us, crawling over people's feet.

"You're not allowed to take pictures in here, ma'am," said the young usher, just doing his job.

"Why not?" Please, Mom, give up the camera.

"It's a rule. My boss told me to tell you." Martha wasn't listening. She was so excited to see Mary Tyler Moore on stage that she took a picture of her right in front of the usher. He crawled out of our row and his boss, I assume he was, crawled in.

"I'm afraid I'm going to have to take that camera from you," said the boss.

"This is my son. He works in television," said my mother. I had no idea what that was supposed to mean. Because I worked in television, the man was supposed to let my mother take pictures at the Emmys?

"I don't care who he is. You're not allowed to take pictures in here." By this time, about three rows of people were pissed off at us. My mother and the boss of the ushers were talking in whispers but they're yelling at each other, you know what I'm telling you?

"I'm not bothering anyone," my mother said, clutching her camera. She looked at me, angry with her only son for not defending her.

"Ma'am, I am going to have to ask you to give me the camera. If you don't, I'm going to have to ask you to leave." The showdown.

My mother turned toward the boss of the ushers and, aiming her camera two inches away from his eyeballs, took a picture of his furious face. That was the first time I saw my mother in an act of defiance. I don't know what the Emmys do to people, but it made my father scared and my mother strong. She actually shot the guy with her camera. (I was sure Mary Tyler Moore noticed and knew whose mother was out of order.) The usher boss was totally enraged and ready to drag my mother from her seat when Barbara Hirsh intervened.

"I'll see to it that she doesn't take any more pictures. Mrs. Meyer, give me the camera, I'll keep it for you." Martha handed over the camera to Barbara. I have a feeling she was shocked at what she had done. The boss, semi-satisfied, crawled out of the row, seeing spots, no doubt. I don't think my mother forgave me for not defending her.

It was the longest night of my life, ending with Barbara wanting to go to bed with me. I knew she was trying to sneak back in there. Ms. Hirsh was searching for a relationship. No, thank you. I had a relationship with a very nice whore. I smiled and told Barbara I was tired. I didn't have to sleep with her. My parents were leaving the next day. The masquerade was over.

My father had got me at lunch. My mother got me in the car. I had picked her up from the house of one of her endless cousins. You have to realize that my mother and I talked maybe twice in my life. Once was when I had to make a map of the entire world for citizenship (history in the old days). You were supposed to be able to mix flour and water and get this wonderful substance that could be molded into continents and carried into school proudly, if the kids in the car pool let you rest it on their legs. The girls all came in with great maps, consistently perfect. The guys all came in with a world that flaked.

I figured if I was going to be able to wow my citizenship teacher, a nice lady with hairy legs ahead of the times, that I was going to have to incorporate Martha's help. If my mother could make cookies, surely she could make the world. Myron's world would have been flaky.

We put our heads together, bought the construction board, mixed the flour, argued the size of Australia, talked about the poor, poor people of India, smiled at each other. She drove me to school so there was no chance of a kid in the car pool ruining our work. The hairy-legged teacher gave us an A and displayed our world on open-school night, even though Florida chipped. That was the closest I ever got to my mother. My next project was pasting pictures of Brazil on colored paper and, hell, I could do that alone.

Somewhere along the way, I tuned my mother out completely. Even when her mother died I couldn't say anything. "I'm sorry, Mom. I know how much you loved her. We all did." I couldn't say that to my own mother. I just pretended I didn't have to say anything and cried for Nana in my room. I've been warmer to strangers. My bookie has received more warmth from me. Alan Milner, the asexual, has received more of my smiles.

So now, after a lifetime of my not hearing her, my mother

was in my Mercedes, looking straight ahead, delivering her mother-son talk. I was nine again and she was Mommy, the only mommy in the whole temple who had a nose like Debbie Reynolds. It was more than just the nose. My mother had a whole profile like Debbie Reynolds.

"David," she said, "sometimes your father can be grouchy, but he's a good man. I . . . I want you to know that . . . you may not think so, but . . . he's been good to me." You lie, Mother! You lie and you know you're lying. You want me to send him back to New York in dry ice if he dies in California, only you're not saying that. He hasn't been good to you. He's been rotten to you. That's my whole problem, Mom, and I don't need a psychiatrist to tell me that I am all fucked up because my father was rotten to my mother. He didn't beat you or make you eat on the floor, but he made you denounce Jesus, whom you were taught to love and who you believed loved you. He made you go to the movies he wanted to see and have the dinners that he wanted to eat. Do you realize, Mom, that you ate your whole life what he wanted to eat?

And what about vacations? He likes the sun, so you go to Puerto Rico and he gets the sun, while you find the biggest hat possible and find some shade to read in. Mom, you never got to drive the car you really wanted, or wear your hair the way you wanted to. You both led his life. Don't tell me he's been good to you. He's been good to himself. My God, no wonder we're fucked up. We cute Jewish guys are trying to live in a world like father, like son. We know like-father is wrong but we too like vacations in the sun.

And the sexual revolution. You want to talk about the sexual revolution, Mom? You had to know about it because you subscribed to the *Ladies' Home Journal* and even the *Ladies' Home Journal* has articles about the new sexual freedom. I knew you must have known that women were entitled to sexual satisfaction. The whole world was into the joy of sex and they were telling you any woman can. It had to touch you somewhere, maybe in the supermarket. You glanced across the magazine rack and saw a dozen articles in a dozen magazines whose titles told you that everyone in the world was having a hell of a time in bed or could have. Did you ever think, Mom, that you might have missed all the fun? God forgive me, I've wondered if my mother ever had an orgasm.

I drove my parents to the airport.

"We don't want you to miss work. We'll take a cab if it's inconvenient," they said.

"Don't be silly. It's not inconvenient." I always enjoy a stimulating drive to the airport during the rush hour.

Father in front, mother in back among the luggage. They chatted away and with each mile I felt more relief. I was driving my parents to an airplane which would carry them three thousand miles out of my life. I had guilt from feeling such happiness.

"You shouldn't feel guilty," I told myself.

"I whistled when I gave their luggage to the porter," I continued.

"You whistled? Maybe you should feel a little guilty," I answered myself.

I kissed my mother, just enough passion, just enough son. She walked to the terminal with tears, wiping them with a fresh handkerchief. My father had to get a last word in.

"Have a good time, kid. Keep schtuping."

Advice from Myron Meyer—keep schtuping. What happened to the times when fathers, upon departing, gave their sons real advice and revealed the true meaning of life? What happened to the times when fathers told sons, "Neither a borrower nor a lender be"? Now, that's something to tell your kid. Keep schtuping? Is it any surprise that I was a male chauvinist pig? No wonder Kathleen Conway's mother had me on her list. My father didn't tell me to go out and have an equal relationship with a woman. I didn't have to listen to the man, you say? True. Look, the man was leaving town. If he had told me not to be a borrower or a lender, I would probably have listened. I would probably listen to "keep schtuping" too. He's my father, Gloria.

7

The only good thing that happened as a result of my parents' trip was that I no longer worried about my performance at Love-Able. I could walk out not wondering if my whore had a good time.

"Obviously your father's presence gave you reaffirmation of your masculinity." That was me, talking to myself, driving through the hills. Ms. Barbra Streisand was blasting from my car tape deck. As they say on New York subway walls, "Barbra Streisand Will Inherit the Earth."

I rode around the hills a lot. That's because in Southern California, if you don't feel like swimming, schtuping, or shopping, the only thing you can do is drive through the hills.

"Mr. Meyer, I'm afraid your son will never walk again."

"Was it an accident?"

"No, he moved to Los Angeles."

It's a strange place, this land they call California. You don't feel like you're going to get mugged, but you don't feel like you might run into Zubin Mehta either. The palm trees don't replace the Met or the Mets—not that I ever went to the Met or saw the Mets in person. The eleven-o'clock news here is different. There could be war, but the headline story is Mae West was seen in Westwood. When you move to California you have the feeling that you're never going to write a symphony, even if you can't play "Heart and Soul" on the piano. Everything is clean, but you're not going to find an old copy of Dickens, not that you ever looked for an old copy of Dickens, and somehow the subway that you never went on because you couldn't stand it is missed. In California, you can play tennis practically anytime you want to, but you have the feeling that you'll never again run into great graffiti.

And no great operas have been originated in the Hollywood area.

And you miss the slums because the slums are a reminder that you're doing well.

And you resent the people. You have your twenty-three-year-old kids who went to Beverly Hills High and U.C.L.A. and for graduation their daddies gave them the car of their choice and the rights to this year's best seller so that the little tykes can go right into producing big hit movies.

The streets are clean and there are no crowds, but it's not Fifth Avenue; it's Alta Loma and La Cienega. And you stop walking.

I spent a hell of a lot of time in my car. My life consisted of driving to and from work, to stores where I could buy good pants that fit exactly right, including forty-dollar jeans, to Paul the expensive hair stylist, to Pips or whatever private restaurant I joined that year in order to keep up with the Warners and the Goldwyns, to the gym because I had fears of middle-age spread (mainly because I was approaching middle age and beginning to spread) and to my prostitute.

And one day I went to Love-Able, to find my whore was gone. Just gone. No goodbye, no note, no remorse. Gone. There was a new girl there, who told me that my girl had left to take guitar lessons. She would be a great guitarist. She was terrific with her hands. Sandy, please, I beg of you, give up the guitar. Play me. I love you. You're the only person in the world who can take me back to that red-and-white Impala.

The end of an era. I used to wonder how people knew eras were over, and now I knew. We were to grow old together, but she left me. In an emotional fog, I walked out into the bright, sunlit street only to bump into Barbara Hirsh, who was trying to see in the window. Why was I caught in the act on the day I didn't even perform the act? Like Barbara in the earthquake, you were pissing on me, God.

"I was looking for a waterbed," I feebly explained. She didn't buy it, but what could she say? "You were not. You were cavorting with whores." Then I would have to say, "Who are you to call them whores? Let he who is innocent be the first to live in a glass house. You know not what you talk of when you call my love a whore. She is not a whore. She takes guitar lessons. You are the whore, because you sleep with men although you are not wed in the eyes of the Lord, and you are the whore because you work in daytime television. Remember, Barbara Hirsh, that Jesus forgave the prostitute. Do ye consider thyself better than Jesus?" It would have been a terrific speech out there in the middle of the day on Melrose. I might have got a few of the kids from the nursery school listening.

Barbara asked if I wanted to go for coffee. I said, "No, thank you." I remember thinking: How can people drink coffee? I've lost my beautiful whore. Only once before in my life had I felt such a hole inside me. It was when I lost all that money for Meyer and Meyer.

From the trial of the Women's Retaliation Committee versus David Meyer, as imagined by David Meyer:

"You said you had the same feeling when you lost your whore that you had when you lost your father's money. Are you equating your loss of a woman with the loss of money, Mr. Meyer?": the prosecuting attorney.

"I don't know. The hole was there."

90

"Will you tell the ladies of the jury what happened when you worked for your father?"

"I went into my father's business because my father had always expected me to. And because I didn't feel like looking for a job. Would a prince not take over a kingdom? At first it was fun; secretaries and receptionists to play with, decorating the office. They put in new carpeting for me and took me out to lunch every day. After a couple of years, I wanted to prove to my father that I could be a great asset to the company. They were looking for ways to diversify, and after much research I came up with a few ideas. I suggested Meyer and Meyer go into toilets for dogs, which was rejected, a cap-your-own-teeth mail-order program, which was also rejected, and taco stands in the East, which was finally accepted because I proved to my father, my uncle and my cousin that we could not lose. One year later Meyer and Meyer had lost one point five million dollars on taco stands in the East. My father turned gray and talked about retiring and moving to Florida. I left Meyer and Meyer and the color returned to my old man's face and hair. Because I was cute and had a faithful old girlfriend from college, I got a job working on a daytime soap opera within a month. I will never forget the feeling of all that money lost. We should have gone into toilets for dogs."

"And, Mr. Meyer, you equate losing a woman you loved with losing the money?"

"Yes . . . I'm afraid so."

"Your witness."

So my whore was lost to me. I loved her and she left no forwarding address. After leaving Barbara Hirsh to go get coffee by herself, I walked back to my car, got in and bowed my head over the wheel. An idea came to me because ideas come when you are bowing your head over a wheel. I decided that I would immortalize my woman. Not in a painting, not in a poem, nor in song. I would make her the subject of a relevant half-hour television show. She would be immortalized until she was canceled.

I sped back to the office and ran breathlessly into Alan Milner's office, bursting on the scene with all the energy and enthusiasm a young lover should have. I should have been wearing a tunic.

"Alan, listen, hear me out. I've got a great idea for a relevant half hour. It's about a young Jewish girl who plays the guitar. She's a free spirit, today's woman . . . did I mention Jewish? Now here's the gimmick . . . you're gonna eat it up, Alan. The gimmick is . . . the thing that makes this half-hour sit-com different from all other half-hour sit-coms is that the girl is a hooker. . . . I know goddamn Norman Lear did hookers, but this is different. Each week this girl solves a different man's sexual problem. Like, for example, one week the man could be asexual, or another he could have this problem about making it through the sexual revolution. Whadda you think, Alan? Great, huh? It's new, revolutionary. It's what television should be doing today." No lover has ever pitched harder.

Alan Milner looked at me the way I deserved to be looked at. His look never killed. It merely placed you on a rack, your arms and feet bound in leather. It then whipped you until you screamed, "Mother!"

"Maybe it's a rotten idea," I said. No lover has ever dropped an immortalization faster.

"Dad, I'm going to quit my job to take piano lessons so that I can write a symphony for my whore."

"Don't ever quit a job, David. Jobs don't grow on trees. Whores do."

After taking a phone call, reading his mail and giving a script go-ahead on yet another *Bonnie and Clyde* rip-off, Alan turned to me and said, "There's something in your idea."

I was staring out the window, having turned to poetry, trying to think of words that rhymed with prostitute. "Huh?" the newly turned poet said.

"There's something in your idea."

I was, at this point, shocked that there was a possibility that the head of prime-time programming was thinking that there was an idea in a series about a guitar-playing prostitute. "You like it?" I was no longer staring out the window. My glazed eyes were on Alan, but we were both out of real life and into a Fellini movie. Soon, I thought, Alan would become six naked old ladies with breasts dangling to their knees. They would all be cackling at me, only you wouldn't see me. The next time the camera panned to the spot I had been standing in, a Roman paperweight would be in my place.

"There's something about doing a series about today's woman," said Alan. "I've been wanting to do a series about a really independent, free-spirited girl of today."

"What about the whore part?" I asked. If you're in the immortalizing business, you can't lose sight of the immortalizee. If only the tacos had worked out, I could have named a stand after my love. "My idea was that the girl was independent, today's woman and all, but the gimmick was she was a whore and each week solved a different man's sexual problems." I knew, as I said it, I was suggesting taco stands in the East.

"Surely you are jesting." He didn't say that. He said something along the lines of: "What're you, an asshole?" "Surely you are jesting" would have suited the occasion better.

"She wouldn't actually have to be a whore, exactly." I was backing away already. Had I been pitching *Macbeth*, I would have said at this point, "Well, actually, all those people don't have to die." On Oedipus: "Well, actually, he doesn't have to love his mother, he could like her a lot." And so goes the television process. We are in the business of dissipating. We water down so much that by the time our product is viewed, it is moldy, like a sneaker that has been left out in the rain. That's what the public has to watch four, five hours a night—wet sneakers.

"Can you make her a nurse?" Alan Milner continuing to water.

Can my whore be a nurse? Can she heal the sick instead of healing the well? She is a whore, not a nurse! Ha! I'll spit on anybody who dares to call my whore a nurse.

"Yeah, I guess she could be a nurse," I said. You say things like that in television development. Had Herman Melville come up against Alan Milner, *Moby Dick* would have been the story of Captain Ahab and his fight with a big white nurse.

I should have quit. I should have spit in Alan's face and said, "How dare you change my whore into a kooky nurse? You shall find my resignation on your desk in the morning, sir." Should have done it. Couldn't. It could have been done in the forties, fifties, sixties. If you're a Jewish male living in the seventies, you don't spit in people's faces. You change whores to nurses and you do it with a smile. (If I had been a Rockefeller, none of this would have happened. Myron wanted me to be a regular Einstein. Being a Rockefeller was good enough for me. Rockefellers don't have to change whores to nurses. Rockefellers have boats where no one gets seasick.)

Besides, the thought of leaving my job panicked me. I wasn't a twenty-two-year-old kid looking for work. I was thirty-two, too late to be a young genius. Twenty-five-year-olds were the heads of entire studios. Nobody ever said, "And he's only thirty-two."

It was the seventies and everyone was out to give minorities a chance. The *Wall Street Journal* ran an article on how white males were being discriminated against. WHITE MALES COMPLAIN THEY ARE NOW VICTIMS OF JOB DISCRIMINATION was the headline. I was driving along one day, top down, radio on.

Some guy was talking about an organization to help Jewish boys get jobs in advertising. An organization. You hear, Gloria? An organization. It seems Jewish boys were being discriminated against in the advertising world. By the time they hired their token black, their woman, their Spanish-speaking person (Puerto Rican on the East Coast, Mexican on the West) and maybe an Indian, there was no room for your Jewish boy. But the Jewish boys had their chance, you say? No, the Jewish fathers had the chance. It never again will be equal for your run-of-the-mill male.

I never did pursue the series about the independent nurse. It hurt. I missed my whore too much to see her distorted. Days or weeks passed. I don't remember which. I don't think I knew at the time. Unread scripts were piled high on my desk. Unwashed dishes were piled high in the sink. Maybe there were dishes on the desk and scripts in the sink. Maybe Alan Milner wouldn't fire me and my Mexican maid, who came in twice a week, wouldn't quit. Or was it the maid who would fire me and Alan who came in once a week? The maid called me señor and Alan called me asshole. Or did Alan call me . . . No, that I remember: Alan called me asshole. They probably both called me asshole.

I lived for the weekends, because on the weekends I searched for my woman. Hank's brother, the owner of Love-Able, did not know where she was. His girls never kept in touch. At first he wasn't sure who I was talking about. There is a pretty big turnover in the waterbed demonstration business. I had to bring in my high school yearbook to show him Sandy Weiss's picture.

"Oh, yeah, that one. A few guys have been asking about her."

Could other men be in love with my whore? I decided no. They wanted to use her for illicit sex. Now that I had lost her, I wanted more than that. I wanted to hear her play the guitar

95

and have breakfast with her. I wanted to know her sign. I wanted at least to know her name.

"I'm sorry. We don't give the girls' names out," said Hank's brother.

"I'm sure she'd want me to know," was my feeble argument.

"Sorry, pal, I promise the girls. It's their protection." Whatever happened to "the customer is always right"?

"I'll find out from the airlines," I said vehemently.

Since I was at Love-Able, not to waste a trip, I had a whore. She was black. Since I first laid eyes on *National Geographic*, I had been turned on to black women, but that was the first time I had sex with one. It was no fun. The girl had so much pride and dignity, there was no room for fun.

On my way out, one of the other girls (a chess player) pulled me aside and told me she thought the girl I was looking for lived in Westwood. In any movie or television show, this is enough of a clue. Some police sergeant or estranged lover spends a few hours stalking Westwood and finds his prey. I spent entire weekends there, roaming around, knocking on apartment doors, showing people my yearbook. I came up with nothing. A woman in a garden apartment said a girl who looked like Sandy Weiss used to live across the way, but she thought she moved to Malibu. I said, "Thank you, ma'am," and would have tipped my hat if I had one.

I searched Malibu, found nothing, but got a pretty good tan on my face. The trouble was that practically every girl out there, with the exception of the blondes, fit the description—tall, thin, long legs, looks good in a bikini. Searching is, by the way, a great way to meet someone. All you have to do is wear a raincoat out on the beach on a sunny day and immediately everyone figures you're working for the FBI. I almost gave myself away with the suntan lotion, but most people were cooperative. I would go up to someone, my Gucci loafers leaving a trail across the sand, and say, "Excuse me, ma'am"

—I used the "ma'am" a lot ever since it worked well in Westwood—"but we're"—I used "we're" instead of "I" because it sounded like I had the whole country behind me—"looking for a girl about thirty years old, tall, looks like this girl here." I'd show them a picture of Sandy Weiss. "We're interested in her whereabouts. She's a very nice girl." Thinking back, I shouldn't have added the "very nice girl" part. Detectives don't say "very nice girl." Jewish fathers do.

They would either know somebody of that description or not, but I was treated with the utmost respect. Take my advice. You want to be respected, go down to Malibu on a sunny day, fully dressed, suit and tie, raincoat. You're gonna feel like Peter Falk. Peter Falk, of course, got his girl in an hour. I wasted six months getting sand in my cuffs.

The first big clue came in Schwab's. I was standing there at the magazine rack, as I often did, thumbing through what I thought was *Playboy* and turned out to be *Playgirl*. It's not nice to rip off a national institution, girls.

When I was about thirteen years old, one Friday on my way home from school, pocket full of twenty-five cents allowance, I stopped at Lou's candy store. Richie, who was with me, saw *Playboy* first. You couldn't miss it. There were stacks of them, higher stacks than *Time* and *Newsweek* had. *Playboy* compelled us and we bought a copy. Lots of little male chauvinists like Richie and me were willing to forgo the Yo-Yos, the Hi-Bouncers, the baseball cards and the egg creams for a look at tushies and tits. We were willing to pool our money so that two or three boys chipped in for one issue. We were the ones who made Hugh Hefner a millionaire, because this is what all we little boys were waiting for . . . clean pornography. There had never been anything like this—boobs all over the place and it was acceptable in our homes because there was literature in it. Even the naked girls weren't bad people. Wasn't the Playmate of the Month, although she was standing there naked, except for a carefully placed golf club, a nice person? Her father, who sat there with her right in her own dinette, said she was. And she had hobbies. She went horseback riding and collected seashells. I was crazy about seashells. If I touched myself and looked at her tits and seashells, wonderful things happened.

Before *Playboy*, all the world had were magazines like *Titter* and *Wink* and the girls in *Titter* and *Wink* were disgusting. They showed beaver. They looked like they really wanted something from you and they didn't have hobbies. Not one of them had seashells. They attacked little boys in their free time.

I would say that *Playboy* magazine was the biggest single influence in my life. I believed in the Playboy Advisor more than I believed in my parents, teachers and religious leaders. S.W. from Arkansas wanted to know whether it was wrong to tell a girl he loved her just because he wanted to sleep with her. And guess what? It was all right. In so many words, *Playboy* said it was O.K., or that's the way I interpreted it. After all, the whole thing was her problem and she didn't have a magazine that she could write in to.

Playboy is in my subconscious and I can't get it out. I still buy the hi-fi equipment they suggest. I still want to visit the mansion before I die. I still look at the centerfold, but even Hugh Hefner has turned on me. Just recently there's been a major change in the magazine. There's no more airbrushing and they're showing all the girls' pubic hair. I sent a girl home because I saw her pubic hair sticking out of her bathing suit. Pop, Hef, what's left?

It's the seventies, so now there is *Playgirl*, for little girls to have dreams with. There I was in the middle of Schwab's looking for tits, and the centerfold was a guy with his cock in some tree. Just as I was about to put the magazine down and thumb through what I had intended to thumb through in the first place, an article caught my eye. "I Worked in a Massage Parlor" was the title, and it was written by Linda Minsk. There was a picture of Linda Minsk. She was my whore.

I bought *Playgirl*, trying to hide it in between *Esquire* and *Penthouse* so the lady at the cash register wouldn't think I was interested in looking at men's members in among the flowers. I think I mumbled something like: *"Esquire* and *Penthouse* for me . . . *Playgirl* for the little woman."

Didn't wait to get home. I read the article in Schwab's parking lot. Remember, Gloria, when you posed as a *Playboy* bunny so you could write an exposé? Linda Minsk had posed as a whore for almost six months and now she was telling all—about the working conditions, the boss, the other girls, me. Yeah, me. The name was changed to protect the innocent and to keep the innocent from suing, but it was me. She called me Cecil (Cecil?) and I was the guy who came to the massage parlor because of trouble adjusting to liberated sex. Cecil had fantasies about fucking in the fifties. She had me down.

I was really pissed off. Not the pissed off you get at a member of your family nor the anger you felt when Jackie Kennedy wasn't at Onassis' bedside when he died. It was the kind of pissed off you got when Ford pardoned Nixon. Linda Minsk was the enemy. She made me love her and then she called me Cecil.

I went home. Got drunk. Threw up. Slept. Got drunk. Slept. Ate. Threw up and screamed. Oh, God, I gave her the best five months of my life! She was the woman I loved and I was research material to her. Pop, help me. I started out life being a real lady-killer but they're killing me now, Pop. They're writing about me and laughing at me and saying my sexual consciousness is twenty years behind the times. I can't keep schtuping like you told me to, Pop. They don't schtup like they used to and when they do, they write about it.

Time passed, which is the thing time does best. I guess my heart began to heal. My soul never would. If the soul lives on after we die, my soul would still be pissed off at women who write exposés. If there is such a thing as reincarnation, a little baby would be born into this world hating exposés and not knowing why.

"You still seeing the girl?" asked my father.

"No."

"So, what happened?"

"I found out she was a whore," I said, ruining Barbara Hirsh's reputation on the East Coast.

"A Jewish whore? Go on." Yeah, that's what I was trying to do—go on.

"What time is it there, Pop?"

"Mr. Milner would like to see you in his office," said my secretary.

"Tell him I'll be there in a minute."

I panicked. There was no reason why Alan had to see me. We had spent the last few days making final decisions on what scripts, among those I had put into development, should go to pilot. I didn't expect to be in Alan's office until it was time to talk about casting, at which time I would say who I wanted and Alan would suggest who he wanted and we would make offers to the people Alan wanted. Until that time, our paths would not cross. So why did Alan want to see me? To tell me I was doing a great job? Nah. I wasn't doing a great job. I read the scripts, but I didn't know what was funny, sad, moving, dramatic, bad or good. He didn't want to see me about a relevant-series idea. Two days before, I had run into Alan at a screening and whispered, just as the movie started, "How about a series about a couple who adopt kids of all different nationalities." In the dark, Alan whispered back, "That stinks." Perhaps Alan wanted to see me because he found out that as a kid I ordered greeting cards to sell from the back of Captain Marvel comics. They promised boys bikes and guns just for selling easy-to-sell cards for all occasions. I sold two boxes to Myron and hid the money and the unsold cards in my dresser drawer. I knew the bikes and guns would go to other boys and I lived in fear that Captain Marvel or someone from the card company would come to get me. Maybe the card company tracked me down after all these years and had contacted my boss. Alan Milner would inform me that I owed the company one point five million dollars: pay up or go to jail. Nah. Maybe Alan realized I really didn't know what I was doing and he was calling me in to fire me. "David," he would say, "I finally realized you're full of shit. You don't know what the hell you're doing." "Alan," I would have to say, "please don't fire me. Sure I don't know my ass from yours, but who are you going to find who's better than me? Nobody knows anything when it comes to television . . . except for you, sir." He would have to say, "Look, David. I guess you know by now I hired you because I thought you were cute." Asexuals enjoy beauty around them. They surround themselves with sex and then don't partake. I'd blush and add, "I know that. I was voted the boy with the sexiest eyes in high school." He'd look into my eyes and soften. It's a hell of a secure feeling knowing your eyes got you the job.

"Mr. Milner has to leave his office and wants to see you immediately," said my secretary, sticking the top half of her body into my office. They teach them that in secretarial school, sticking the top half of their bodies into offices.

I got up and walked slowly to Alan's office, the prisoner going to his execution, priest behind reading from the Bible, director behind the priest trying to get it on one take.

"Hi, Alan, you wanted to see me?" I said, trying to make my eyes work for me.

"I'm having a party Saturday night. I expect you to be there."

"Sure." Sure, Alan. I'd be happy to come to your party, Alan. You wouldn't believe what I had to do to try to keep my last job. Going to a party is easy compared to sleeping with Barbara Hirsh. Sure, Alan, I'll be there.

I never liked parties. As a little kid, I used to refuse to go to birthday parties. I didn't like the feeling of another kid getting all the presents. Louise Lichtner's boy-girl fiasco put me off parties altogether. In college I disliked fraternizing with the fraternity because I'd rather be schtuping Desiree Goldblum than participating in Greek night or something else equally cute. When I was married, parties depressed me. I had to show up with Frances, and anyplace I had to show up with Frances depressed me.

My first year in California, I went to party after party, not enjoying myself but scared I was missing something. Word got around that I would come where invited and friends and friends of friends would call and invite me to anything from dinner for six to their kids' bar mitzvahs. You could count on David Meyer. He was the extra man you've been looking for. He'll even come and sit by your cousin Hilda.

After a year, I figured I had to reciprocate. I had my secretary call and invite everyone, which must have been painful, since her name was not on the list. My guests arrived, the food was served, the music played, there were some laughs, but I had a rotten time. End of party-going, except of course when the boss beckoned.

I drove up to Alan's expensive, light and airy home at about eight-thirty. There was, of course, valet parking. From out of the bushes came guys in red jackets, ready to take your car. Ninety-five bucks so that your friends shouldn't have to walk a hill. Hollywood.

Alan, the perfect host, greeted me at the door.

"There are people here from the other networks and every studio in town. Be sure not to say anything about any of our projects."

"You mean including the relevant one I'm working on about the albinos?" I kidded. Alan didn't laugh. He just walked away, seeing to it that his guests had a glass of wine in one hand, well-rolled joints in the other. Alan didn't smoke but he was a magnificent host.

The house was already crowded, people obstructing Alan's magnificent modern furniture and his worth-a-small-fortune art collection. There were, at a single glance, enough names in any corner to get mention in Joyce Haber. Tatum O'Neal was there, waiting to grow up. Groucho Marx was there, staring at Tatum, wondering what that was all about. It didn't seem fair to expose him to her youth. The two should never have been in the same living room or lifetime. Guests included writers, producers, television stars and an occasional well-bred secretary, but there was not one dentist or architect or simple scientist. Hollywood.

Everyone at Alan's that night had a chance of having their name on a billboard on Sunset Boulevard at any given moment. The women wore Indian jewelry and the men had tax shelters. The men wore Indian jewelry and the women sheltered their taxes too. (I'll bet Karen Valentine, at one time in her life, was advised to buy cattle.) Hollywood's leading homosexuals were there. They wore Indian jewelry, had tax shelters and checked their images in Alan's mirrors. (Alan had a lot of mirrors in his home. What does an asexual need mirrors for?) The grand old people of movies were there. Well, not all the grand old people of movies, just the ones who had consented in recent years to work in television. Some music people, the new nouveau riche, were there. They, of course, had Indian jewelry, tax shelters, looked in mirrors and had all the sex they wanted while they were on the charts. People in the music business didn't have to go through the sexual revolution. They just had to sing about it.

All these people came to Alan Milner's to stand on his stained hardwood floors, sit on his custom couches, wipe with his cushy toilet paper, because they hoped to be Alan's friend. If they ever needed to be on television, he could make it happen.

I wandered around for a while, overhearing. At least six guests were talking about what a great view Alan had. Good filler. One girl, in short, short jeans with her bottom hanging out, came over and asked me if I could be any person in the world, living or dead, who I would want to be.

"Golda Meir," I said. Which is the only correct answer to the question.

"Why is everyone I meet out here gay?" She sighed and took her tush away.

I took my tush away too, into the back yard, where I figured I'd be alone and could reflect into Alan's pool. A girl in a lot of makeup was out there trying very hard to look like Cher.

"What's your sign?" she asked.

"I'm on the cusp between Aquarius and Leo." Good day.

When Mickey Spillane went to parties, all the dames stood around with a throbbing between their legs. At the parties I went to they wanted to know your sign and who you wanted to be. The throbbing might have been there, but these girls wanted to see you the next morning.

By nine-thirty, there were over a hundred and fifty people (and just as many plants; asexuals have time to water) packed into three rooms, one of them a dining room loaded with food, catered, hot and Oriental. Nine hundred bucks, easy. I know. I had been to this exact same party dozens of times. I had had this exact same party. There were the same guys with the same expensive leather jackets, the same girls with backless dresses asking opening questions you don't want to answer, fifty-dollar books on the coffee tables and Elton John singing from speakers in every room. I had answered the questions and tasted the food and worn the expensive leather jackets. I wanted the man in a red jacket to bring my car.

"Great party, Alan," I said, when I got his momentary attention. I would probably have thanked my host for a wonderful time at the Last Supper.

"You're not really developing something about albinos, are you?" said Alan, so that a hundred of the over a hundred and fifty people could hear and think me dumb.

I saw my whore from the back first. No, she was not my whore. She was Linda Minsk, the revealer. There was no way that it wasn't her. I knew that back. She was standing in the corner, talking to a guy, a glass of wine in a hand that had touched my erogenous zones. I forgave her immediately.

O.K. I had to have her. Suddenly I didn't care that I was Cecil to be written about instead of David to be loved. I wanted Linda Minsk, whore or writer. I would walk over and say a casual "Hi." She would faint from delight and surprise in my arms. I'd drag her home unconscious with some excuse to the valet parking guys. "Too many chemicals in the food," I would say, and . . . the rest sounds a lot like Snow White. My kiss would revive her and the whole fairy tale would end with my schtuping her in the back seat of a 1957 Impala.

I stood there staring at her back, unable to make my move. I was offered an egg roll on a silver platter and couldn't say "No, thank you." The waiter got the idea and left. Christ! How could he offer me egg rolls? My whore-writer was fifteen feet away.

After two false starts, I took a deep breath, threw my shoulders back, walked over and forced myself to say a casual "Hi." Her "Hi" was even more casual than mine. She didn't know who the hell I was.

"Hi": me again. She was supposed to faint in my arms.

"Hi": her again. She didn't remember and wasn't trying to. I didn't exist in her life. I had been inside her but that was months ago and this was the seventies.

"Hi," said the guy she was with. He didn't look as if he was going to faint either.

"I'm David Meyer." Still no recognition of name or face. Would I have to schtup for her to remember me, or call myself Cecil? She would have remembered a Rockefeller or an Einstein.

"I'm Linda Minsk and this is Duane Sommers." We all said "Hi" again.

"So what's your sign?" That was me. Dumb on two counts. It was dumb to ask anyone their sign. It was especially dumb to ask two people at once.

"I'm a Pisces," said Linda, nicely, charmingly. She made me feel I hadn't just said, "So what's your sign?" Duane rolled his eyes upward and sighed. The great Duane Sommers couldn't stand that people were talking about astrology around him.

"You know, you look familiar," said Linda, remembering. You have a difficult situation here. I can't help her out and say, "Don't you remember, we met at Love-Able when I was horny and you were whoring?"

"You look familiar too," I said. I was so turned on to the girl, I wanted to take her right then and there on the Oriental buffet. I didn't care if soy sauce would eat into the leather of my jacket.

"I'm a Scorpio," said Duane, who decided he wanted to be part of the conversation.

"You're not a friend of Henry Berman's, are you?" Christ. She was guessing. Stop guessing, Linda.

"Wait a minute," she said, smiling, snapping fingers. It was coming to her. Not now, my love. Please, let's not figure it out in front of the Scorpio. "You were one of my customers."

"Right." Let's drop it, darling. We'll talk later, right after my kiss revives you.

"When I was working in that massage parlor." Shit, Linda. Snow White would have stopped.

Duane looked at me like I was crazy, stupid and sexually inadequate. I would like to know, Duane, why Linda didn't get a look. She was the one who got paid for performing sexual acts.

"That's right. I remember now." I tried to make it light and final before she got to the Cecil part. I knew I was never going to discuss the massage parlor with her. Never, now that she was a civilian.

"So what have you been doing—anything new?" said Linda, head tilted, lips smiling. God damn it. She was looking right into my face. She really wanted to know what I was doing. I wasn't going to tell her I was still in television programming in front of Duane. He looked like the type who said things like: "I wouldn't own a television" or "I only watch channel 28."

"I'm . . . I'm trying to put this movie together. I'm . . . sort of producing." That would be my screen credit: "This Movie Sort of Produced by David Meyer."

"When you've got it together, why don't you come and see me. I'm at Paramount," said Duane. He wasn't trying to help me. It was his way of telling Linda that he was better than me because I had to get it together and he was the person I had to get it together for.

"I'm interested in doing this one independently": me telling him that I'm not interested in his help, which I thought would impress Linda, but was a stupid thing for me to do. I had turned down help from a major studio.

"Why would you do a dumb thing like that?": Myron Meyer.

"Because, Pop, for once in my life I was more interested in the woman than the deal."

"Women grow on trees. It's hard to get deals."

"This woman is different, Pop. She doesn't care if I live or die. I love her."

Duane got bored with our conversation and, seeing that I wasn't going to give up, excused himself and made his way to the food and the tush. I was alone with my whore, only she wasn't my whore. She was Linda Minsk, a woman I hardly knew, not Sandy, Queen of the Prom, the girl who sent me to heaven, or at least back to 1958. The whore I knew and the Linda who was standing before me were two decades apart. The former was a high school slut, just a girl with a bad rep; the latter a writer and exposé artist of the seventies. I could see her nipples against the thin material of her dress. I still wanted her and that, pal, was the problem. How was I going to get the Linda Minsk in Alan Milner's overly decorated living room back to the Sandy Weiss in Love-Able? Would any prince have wanted anything more or less from his concubine?

"I'm sorry if I interrupted anything," I said, indicating Duane of Paramount.

"I'm glad you did. I really couldn't stand him. You know what he said? He actually said that he understood why Great Britain needs a monarch."

"No kidding."

"I could never go to bed with a man who sees the sense in having the Queen of England."

"You were planning to go to bed with him?"—my darling.

"Until he brought up Queen Elizabeth." I was going to be very careful about who I brought up.

"Listen, why don't you come back to my place? I think the Queen is a terrible person." I lied. I don't even know the Queen.

"That's not the point. The point is poor people having to support royalty. Why? Just because they're born into it?"

"I agree. You are absolutely right. Why don't you come back to my place?"

"No, thanks," she said, and I could sense that she was starting to drift away. Maybe I didn't put down the Queen enough. Maybe I should have said I know for a fact that she has bad table manners.

"Listen, if you don't want to get together tonight, why don't I take your number and give you a call sometime?" I said, fearing that I would lose her again.

"I am the most impossible to reach. Why don't you give me your number?" she said.

I gave her my number and watched her write it down on a little piece of cardboard torn from a matchbook cover. I had this awful feeling she'd lose it. How many times had I lost the scrap with some girl's number on it?

I left the party shortly after our encounter, went home and sat by my phone, waiting for her to call. What the hell was this? I was supposed to take her number. Miss Minsk was supposed to wait by her phone for me to call. I am David Meyer, the son. I am the fucker, not the fuckee! The day she wrote my number down was the beginning of the end, Gloria.

9

From the trial of the Women's Retaliation Committee versus David Meyer, as imagined by David Meyer:

"Your Honor, with your permission, I would like, at this time, to call Myron Meyer to the stand."

My father walked slowly to the front. He looked old and gray and very potbellied. Everyone said he looked awful due to the strain of his son's being on trial. They said it almost killed him.

"Do you, Myron Meyer, swear to tell the whole truth and nothing but the truth, so help you God?"

"I do." This worn-out version of my father took the stand.

"Mr. Meyer, are you aware of why your son has been brought before the Women's Retaliation Committee?"

"So he schtuped a few girls. So what?" said my father, trying to defend me.

"And you condoned this schtuping?"

The prosecuting lawyeress was on her feet. "Your Honoress, I object to this line of questioning. It is not Myron Meyer who is on trial here. It's his son."

My lawyer wouldn't give up. "I am trying to show the court how the father's attitudes had a major effect on the son. By doing so, I think I can make the court understand that due to his upbringing, David Meyer could be nothing but a male chauvinist pig and that his actions were not directly his fault.

111

He was merely carrying out his destiny."

"Objection overruled." And there was a shot of Perry Mason smiling, because there always is.

"Mr. Meyer, would you tell the court and ladies of the jury how badly you wanted a son?"

"Very badly. I prayed to God that I'd have a boy."

"Why, Mr. Meyer?"

"Every man wants a son, to go to ball games with, to . . . uh . . . to take into the business, to . . . to teach to go to the bathroom standing up."

"So you wanted a son . . ."

"I had to have one! I warned my wife . . . I mean, if she hadn't produced a male child I wasn't going to get rid of her or anything."

"Yes, of course. . . . Mr. Meyer, would you tell the court, as briefly as possible, what you taught your son David about being a man?"

There were beads of perspiration on my father's forehead. Those beads were seen in millions of homes via the miracle of television.

"I taught my son what I knew. I taught him that men must go to work so that they can support their wives and children. I taught him not to cry. I taught him not to pee all over the bathroom floor. I taught him to be a man."

"Did you teach him to be king of his castle?"

"Yes."

"Did you teach him to eat the turkey leg while you taught his sisters to eat wings and breasts?"

"Yes."

"Did you teach him that it is better to be a man than a woman, Mr. Meyer?"

"Yes. Yes!"

The court went crazy. Not because they didn't expect this attitude from Myron Meyer, but because they couldn't stand

112

hearing what he was saying. One woman down front covered her ears. CBS got a close-up of her.

"Mr. Meyer, I have one final question. How would you say you treat women?"

"I put them on a pedestal."

"So you can worship them?"

"No . . . so I can look up their dresses."

Nobody laughed. It had been said with too much conviction. Oh, Pop, you're a grandfather. Don't tell me you're still trying to catch beaver.

"No further questions. Your witness."

"I have just one question, Mr. Meyer. I know what I am going to ask is not in the usual line of questioning, but I would like you to, if you would, make a value judgment. Would you say it is your fault that your son has abused women the way he has?" The prosecuting attorneyess.

"What abused women? He schtuped a few. So what?"

"No further questions."

My father returned to his seat, thinking he had helped. I guess he had. It was proved that Myron Meyer's son didn't have too many alternatives.

"Oh, come on, David, you can't live your whole life blaming your father for what you are. You're a grown man. You make your own alternatives": the world.

"Yes, except when things directly relate to my male organ": David Meyer.

Myron Meyer could take only part of the blame for my being a male bastard. I would have to take part for nurturing it and hanging on to it and some would have to go to Louise Lichtner and her mother. Louise Lichtner was the first girl in the seventh grade to need a bra, have bad breath and throw a party for boys and girls. She also had large pores.

I got invited to the Lichtner party by written invitation. I was twelve years old. I didn't want to go. What did I want with people who needed bras? They say kids in the ghettos grow up fast. Ghetto kids never had to deal with Louise Lichtner and her mother. Those two gave the entire seventh grade their sexual awareness.

Probably from David Meyer's file, on record at the Women's Retaliation Committee (transcript of an audio tape), the voice of Louise Lichtner:

Well, I . . . uh . . . actually first met David in the third grade, but I never really spoke to him. In the fifth grade I gave him a valentine and I sort of watched his face when he opened it. I . . . uh . . . I never should. He opened it, dropped it on the floor, never bothered to pick it up and eventually stepped on it. I threw up my lunch.

When I was about nine or ten, people used to pinch my fat cheeks and ask me who my boyfriend was. I said . . . I said David Meyer. I don't know why. Maybe every little girl makes believe she has a real boyfriend. Maybe it's because grownups force us to have those fantasies by asking those questions. I don't know. I do know that it's not easy for a ten-year-old to have boobs.

In the seventh grade my mother told me I could have a party with boys. I didn't even want a party with boys, but my mother made it sound like this great thing. Naturally, I invited David. He came over to me in the middle of the party and I thought it was to talk. I smiled. He let punch dribble out of the side of his mouth all over my dress. I continued to smile. And that was only the beginning. I gave him B.T. for years and finally my virginity. He never even took me out. He was the guy with the sexiest eyes and I was voted "most giving." Hah!

I haven't thought about this incident in years, but then I read about your organization and how you've helped other women to get back at the men who destroyed them, and I was hoping that you would do the same for me, if at all possible. Of course, I hold

114

no resentment, but it would make me feel better if David was
. . . you know . . . castrated.

My father drove me to the party. There I sat, no seat belts
then, in a little red sports jacket and tie, hair flattened with
water, almost parted, almost staying down. Myron talked his
"Cheer up, kid" talk, which can only depress a boy of twelve
who doesn't know why he's on the way to Louise Lichtner's
house.

"So, you're a big shot now. Going to parties with girls." I
didn't say anything, just tried to look precious, as they always
told me I did in my little red sports jacket. "Going to parties
with girls, a little pisher like you. Tell me, do you have a
girlfriend or are you playing the field? If you're smart you'll
play the field. Love 'em and leave 'em. Don't get hooked," said
Myron to his son.

I didn't say anything because I didn't know how to say,
"Pop, I'm not ready for this. Suppose there's kissing. I don't
want to kiss girls. I have a bite plate in my mouth. Turn the
car around and go home. Pop, I'm not ready to go."

No wonder I spit punch all night.

It was after Louise's party that the seventh-grade social life
was born. It was mothered by mothers of the girls, who were
tired of sex and trying to get the next generation started. It was
fathered by no one. I understand in Scandinavian countries
there is none of this. Boys and girls grow up, all the way up,
being friends. I can only imagine, under these circumstances,
that little boys do not have the same hostility for little girls that
we did. Of course, in Scandinavian countries, everyone looks
good, even during puberty.

Myron Meyer's twelve-year-old pisher learned how to treat
the seventh-grade women. He opened their looseleafs and let

their papers fly under car wheels and they let him copy the answers on the true-false tests. He stole their lunches and threw them around the cafeteria, letting tuna fish salad fall in their hair, and they asked him to their parties. He pushed them into the street while waiting for the car pool and tore pages from their math workbooks, and any one of them would go with him to the seventh-grade spring fiesta. He learned to be a prick.

When he was all grown up he would find himself waiting for a phone call from a Linda Minsk. He would hate himself for caring.

After two weeks of not hearing from Linda, I felt an insatiable desire to talk. I called Barbara Hirsh and told her everything—about the massage parlor, how I had searched for my love, how I found out who she was, how I had run into her at Alan's, how I was devastated that she didn't call. I called Barbara at about two o'clock in the morning because Linda Minsk had fixed it so I couldn't sleep. Barbara was happy to hear from me.

"You're too good for her," Barbara concluded.

I'm too good for her? Why? Because any man is too good for any woman? She was telling me that an ineffectual-at-work, scared-to-be-impotent man, who comes in a minute and a half, was too good for Linda Minsk. How does a person come to this conclusion?

"I'm not too good for her. She's too good for me. That's why she didn't call." Give me sympathy over the wires.

"Maybe you're right," she said. Thanks a lot.

"I love her," I said with the intensity you put into saying you love someone at 2 A.M.

"How can you possibly love her? You don't even know her," said a perceptive Barbara Hirsh.

"I love her. My heart falls out when I think about her. I met

116

her at my most vulnerable and my response to this girl is purely emotional. I loved her before I knew her name."

"You love someone you haven't even really talked to?"

"I've talked to her . . . sort of . . . not really. I haven't really talked to her."

"So you can't love her."

"I do. I always seem to love the ones I don't talk to." Unfortunately true. The ones I talked to became platonic. I'm sure Barbara was thrilled at my new revelation. I was, after all, able to talk to her.

"You love her because you can't have her," she went on. "You're shocked because up to now you have always gotten everything you wanted."

"I haven't always gotten everything I wanted."

"Name one thing you wanted that you didn't get," said Barbara Hirsh at about 3:10 A.M.

"I didn't get into the first nineteen colleges of my choice."

"Gee, that's a shame," said Barbara Hirsh, yawning.

Two more weeks went by. I don't know why, but I told Alan Milner everything. We were in the office late, having just finished a three-hour session with two comedy writers, who were so insecure they couldn't be serious for two minutes straight. My head hurt from them. My heart hurt from her.

"So why do you think she hasn't called?" Alan asked with frozen eyes. The man hated asking questions almost as much as answering them.

"She could have lost my telephone number . . . or forgotten . . . or gone on a trip . . . or she can't stand me and just took my number to be polite."

"Let's say she just took your number to be polite." Why couldn't we just say she went on a trip? It would have made me feel much better, Alan. I could probably have begun breathing again. Eventually I could have led a normal life.

"O.K., let's say she took my number to be polite." The blood stopped pumping to my heart and my hairline receded once more.

"What bothers you most about this?" Alan asked, pissed off because he was getting involved in my life.

"I don't know."

"Think. She took your number. She hasn't called. What bothers you about the situation?"

"That . . . that a woman can get the best of me," I revealed.

"You feel she's gotten the best of you?"

"Yes." And I breathed for the first time in weeks. The hair didn't come back.

"And that's all that's bothering you?"

"No. I'm dying because there's nothing I can do about it." I stopped breathing again.

"There isn't a person in the world who could do anything in your position," said Alan, softening for the first time, probably the first time in his life.

"Myron Meyer could."

"You really think so?"

"Yes." And the sad part was I really thought he could. My dad's better than Superman. My dad can defy Kryptonite. He could defy the armed forces of the United States of America.

When I was in my senior year at B.U., Myron started worrying about his little boy's going into the Army. Uncle Sam may have wanted me. There was no way that Myron was going to let me go. I would say that Jewish fathers did more to undermine the military of this country than any foreign power.

I was summoned home one weekend to meet the best lawyer in the country for keeping Jewish boys out of the Army. His name was Craig Kelly and I can't imagine how he got into any form of draft evasion. He looked like a man who loved the Army and everything it stood for. He had a crew cut and wore

118

terry-cloth socks. His wife waited in the car, even though she was invited in about three dozen times. People who leave their wives waiting in cars generally like the Army.

"Pleased to meet you, David," and one of those handshakes that go beyond firm and into pain.

"Yes, sir." I felt like saluting this man who looked like an undercover agent.

"Mr. Kelly has it all figured out," said my father.

Mr. Kelly did have it all figured out. He had kept over seventy-five boys out of the United States Army and had managed to do so without any convictions whatsoever. And this was in peacetime. We're talking about keeping a boy out of Fort Dix, New Jersey, for six months.

"Your father tells me, David, that you're interested in staying out of the Army," Mr. Kelly said, in a tone like doctors on television.

"Yeah . . . not exactly . . . well, I guess so." I vacillated for two reasons. One, the country was still in a patriotic mood. It was unpopular to actually say you wanted to skip selective service. Two, suppose Mr. Kelly was from the CIA, or whatever organization is out to catch boys whose fathers hire lawyers.

"Good," said Mr. Kelly, missing my intended indecision.

"Yeah, well, I really want to stay out." Might as well pee or get off Mr. Kelly's pot.

"I like to ask the boys, because sometimes it's the father's idea and the boys really want to join up," he explained to my father. He didn't have to. My father knew I was scared shitless.

Mr. Kelly had an attack plan. First we would bring up the ulcer that I had developed as a senior in high school as a result of getting nineteen rejections from the finest schools in the country. If this didn't work—and it probably wouldn't, because we only had one doctor's opinion and you can't tell the Army that Louise Lichtner's letting me fuck her made it go away—we would invent a history of lower-back problems. Mr. Kelly knew an orthopedic surgeon's nurse who would phony up some old records, making it look like I had back problems for years. All we had to do was cross her palm with silver, this Florence Nightingale. Back problems, Mr. Kelly explained, were terrific because nobody could prove you didn't have them. You just had to moan when the Army doctor poked.

If that didn't work—and sometimes it didn't: every once in a while they drafted some poor youth with an imaginary physical defect—we could say I had migraine headaches. (You had to moan when the Army doctor poked your head.) If that didn't work, we would have to go to Dr. Lewis, Mr. Kelly's friendly orthodontist. Dr. Lewis, for a nominal fee of several thousand dollars, would put braces on my teeth. I had had braces on my teeth and said my Haftorah at my bar mitzvah with a shiny mouth. I had lost two bite plates in the lake at Camp Ver-Mont. Mr. Kelly calmly explained that Dr. Lewis didn't care how straight your teeth were. He had fitted over twenty boys with braces and all of them were able to get out of the service. Uncle Sam wants you, but not with braces on your teeth.

"What did you do in the war, Daddy?"

"Well, son, I had braces on my teeth."

"Has anybody been drafted with braces?" asked Myron, who was sick over the idea of having to pay for orthodontics twice for one kid. One of his all-time-favorite remarks was: "No one put braces on my mouth when I was a kid." He said that almost as much as "No one sent me to college with a red Corvette."

"Not exactly," said Mr. Kelly, ready for any of Myron's questions.

"What do you mean—not exactly?"

"Two of my boys had such perfect teeth that the Army saw through our little ruse. I just had to keep working with them."

"How?" we both asked.

"One boy I trained to react as a homosexual. Actually, I didn't do it all myself. I work with an associate of mine, Rudi Fox. It took us over a month, but our boy fooled an Army psychiatrist and came through with flying colors." Mr. Kelly laughed at his own joke. The only one among us who did, unless Mrs. Kelly was laughing in the car.

"With the other boy, we went for high blood pressure," Mr. Kelly continued. "We kept him up for three nights before his physical and then had him run a mile and a half. No problem. Besides having high blood pressure, the lack of sleep made him appear unbalanced. We kept him out on two counts, but I didn't charge extra."

This Mr. Kelly seemed to know his stuff. He even had pictures of his successful clients. Most of them were smiling. Some were even waving from Cadillacs. "If you let Mr. Kelly keep you out of the Army, you'll be happy and rich," I guess was the message. Mr. Kelly left my home that afternoon with a check for twenty-five hundred dollars. First payment. I'll bet Mr. Kelly did a lot of smiling from his Cadillac.

About a month after seeing the lawyer, I met Frances Roache, a plain sophomore. I know Judi Rosenberg and her friends didn't know what I saw in Frances. And neither did I. I imagine I married Frances for three main reasons. She would provide a husband-centered marriage for me, allow me to be the star of our relationship. She was a virgin when we met and I liked that no man had preceded me. And most of all, I was attracted to Frances's Protestantness. Like my father before me, I saw the advantage of marrying a girl who would prove her love by converting. The girl renounced Jesus Christ for me. It felt very good to me at the time.

We'll never know if Mr. Kelly would have kept me out of the Army, because Frances Roache did. Uncle Sam wasn't drafting married men that year. Mr. Kelly didn't refund advances and I knew in my heart that Myron was pissed about the twenty-five hundred. He gave us a smaller wedding gift than I would have expected.

10

"I'm really tired of hearing about this Linda Minsk who hasn't called," said Alan Milner and Barbara Hirsh in different conversations.

"It helps me to talk about it," I said.

"It's boring already," they replied independently.

"Either I talk about it or I'll have to suppress it," I said.

"Suppress it," they said.

"It's not healthy to suppress it," I said.

"Well, do something. You're boring," said my good friends and the lady in the cleaners. By now I had told her everything.

After a number of weeks, I was finally able to put Linda Minsk in that part of my brain that suppresses. Ms. Minsk no longer existed for me, along with Nazi atrocities, the execution of Julius and Ethel Rosenberg, starving children who appear in ads on the pages of the *New York Times*, cancer, poor Indians, migrant farm workers, flood victims and the Getty boy who had his ear cut off. If any of these things emerge into my consciousness I turn them off and, like Peter Pan, try to think of pleasant thoughts so that I can fly. I will say to myself that I really ought to be doing something about the world and that maybe I should become some fatherless boy's big brother. The thought will not stay with me long enough for me to take positive action. I'm one of the ones who turns the page in *The*

New York Times Magazine quickly to avoid dwelling on the hungry child who needs just fifteen dollars a month from me to live. In my entire adult life, I only did one thing for my fellow man: I listened to Cesar Chavez and didn't buy grapes. History will prove me to be one of the biggest non-grape-buyers the world has ever known. There will be a picture in the Encyclopaedia Britannica showing me in Safeway, forcefully pushing my shopping cart past the grapes and on to the tangerines. It was the seventies, and we latched on to easy things. Why should I have to be a big brother when I was helping Chavez? I can't do everything, I convinced myself.

She called.

"Hello."

"Hello, David, this is Linda Minsk." My heart skipped a beat, my eyes rolled back, my cheeks flushed. I had seen this reaction on my sisters when one of their boyfriends, who they were praying would call, called. I had heard this reaction in a girl's voice when I called. I would hear a slight revealing catch in the voice, which said, "Thank God, you called. I can function again." Now the catch was in my voice and I hated it because it had never been there before.

"Oh, hi." That was me, trying to sound casual. I had heard that tone too and seen through it as clearly as one would see through a brand-new Mercedes windshield.

"Listen, I'm sorry I didn't call before. I really didn't feel like it. The whole mess the government is in has really gotten me down. Today I felt like it so I picked up the phone and hi." She wasn't playing games. I was all ready to play and she was being honest.

"I'm surprised you called after all this time": me.

"Why? I said I was going to": her.

"Yeah . . . well . . . great." That was the best I could come up with. The golden tongue of David Meyer had tarnished and was lying green within his mouth.

"David, how'd you like to go out to dinner tonight?"

I had been asked out before by women, but not so casually. The girls that asked me out before sounded like they'd rehearsed asking me out.

"Yeah, well, I'd like that. Maybe I could," I answered, being vague because I didn't know any other way to be. There was no way I wasn't going to make it. I would have canceled a trip to Europe to be there. I loved her.

"Is that yes or no?" She wasn't going to let me get away with being vague.

"Yes, sure, I'd love to." I was a fucking Connie Stevens accepting a date with Eddie Fisher.

"We'll go to The Garden of Life, O.K.? Where do you live?" We had made it on a waterbed but she didn't know where I lived. It's strange what we learn about each other. She knew the size of my penis but not my address.

"I'm on Harold Way, 8495, off Kings, above the Continental Hyatt House."

"Don't worry. I'll find it."

"I could pick you up," the male pig said.

"Nah, you'd never find me." How dare she say that. She can find me but I can't find her. That was a little bitchy, Linda Minsk, especially since you knew the catch was in my voice.

"So you'll pick me up. Great! How about seven-thirty?" She had made the call, chosen the restaurant and decided who's picking up who. I wanted to choose the time. I had to. It meant everything to me.

"I'm sorry. I can't. I'll be there at eight." Shit, Linda. I'm the man. Puncture my balls, shoot Paul, my expensive hair stylist, but let me at least choose the time.

"Eight is fine," I said, continuing to be Connie. The score was: Boy–nothing; Girl–all.

Goodbyes and see you later. I hung up and was walking on

air. Me, David Meyer, who had spit punch and left a permanent stain on Louise Lichtner's dress. Me, David Meyer, who made Judi Rosenberg quit college and lock herself in her room, crying. Me, David Meyer, who farted in bed occasionally and never got one complaint. That was the David Meyer who was walking on air, spinning around the house—Scarlett O'Hara waiting for Rhett Butler to show up.

I twirled my way to the phone.

"Hello, this is David Meyer. I'd like to make an appointment with Paul [the expensive hair stylist] late this afternoon."

"I'm sorry, but Paul is booked up the rest of the day. How about Wednesday at two?" said the expensive English girl who sat at Paul's expensive antique desk behind his expensive stained-glass partitions, next to his expensive cash register with all the large bills inside.

"He has to see me. This is David Meyer." Linda Minsk called and asked me out. I needed to be fluffed and dried.

"I'm sorry, Mr. Meyer, but he's booked." She was trained to kill, but she had also got worse and more protective since Barbra Streisand started going out with a hairdresser and Warren Beatty played one in *Shampoo*.

"Please . . . please, can't you squeeze me in?" Please, miss, this girl I'm going out with might not love me if my hair is not shiny and nice.

"I'm afraid he can't," said the cool English bitch.

"I'd like to speak to Paul," sternly.

"I'm afraid he can't come to the phone," just as sternly. I died because Paul was making someone else look terrific while my hair lay limp.

"Well, you tell him that David Meyer wants to talk to him. I saved his life when we were in the Army together. I'm sure he'll want to come to the phone." The English understood wartime relationships, and within seconds Paul the expensive hair stylist was on the phone. The girl never stopped to wonder why the Army had let Paul in.

"Hey, old buddy," said Paul, even when he realized who he was talking to. Sure he called me old buddy. I dropped about forty bucks a week in his antique cash register.

"I've got to have my hair washed and dried." Paul, please come through for me. Would Natalie Wood have gone out without a shampoo and set?

"Tell you what, ol' buddy. Come at around seven. I'll stay open late."

"Oh, thank you . . . I'll be there." Bless you, Paul.

He'd stay open late. That meant I'd have to bring Paul the expensive hair stylist a little present . . . like a car or a house. Ol' buddy. Remember when you used to walk off the street and into a regular barbershop? Remember when I used to have hair growing all over my head, even the front?

Of course, Paul the expensive hair stylist was running late and didn't start blow-drying me until seven-twenty. Of course, he had a million funny stories to tell about all his famous customers. Of course, he stops drying when he starts talking. I got out at a quarter to eight, running like crazy, worried that I didn't praise Paul enough for staying late. I think I blew him a kiss at the door.

I raced home and dressed quickly but carefully, washing in every possible place, deodorant everywhere. I pictured Linda washing and dressing and hoped that when she finished she'd end up smelling like a woman. On the question of deodorant, I'm with the new feminists in every way. I want a woman to smell like a woman. What's with stuff like raspberry-and-champagne douche? I especially enjoy the smell of pussy, if I may be frank. At the end of my senior year in high school, after having had the real thing, thanks to Louise, I tried to recreate the smell. And succeeded. You take a couple of ounces of lox, regular as opposed to Nova Scotia, just because it's cheaper, and add—you have to use some judgment here—about four drops of ammonia. That's all there is to it and you get instant "smell of a woman." If I had been an enterprising young man, I could have bottled it. It probably would have done a lot better than taco stands.

Linda wasn't there by eight and had anyone been on Harold Way that night they would have seen me peeking through the drapes—Judy Garland waiting for her young man in *Meet Me in St. Louis.* At eight-seventeen, after several hundred peeks, she arrived in an old Porsche and honked. My father wouldn't have liked that. He used to get pissed when my sisters' beaus didn't come to the door. Of course, there was nothing I could do about it. I had to run to the car and get in, letting Linda drive—Audrey Hepburn in *Roman Holiday:* a motorcycle there, but same thing.

She drove, her hair flying, too much noise from the car for a real conversation, to The Garden of Life, and the minute we got there I knew I wasn't going to have an easy time. The owner knew her, which meant she frequented the place, which meant she was on home ground and I was not. How many times had I done that to a date? A great way to make someone insecure is to take them to your favorite restaurant where you know the owner, the waiters and the menu and she doesn't even know where the ladies' room is. Here I was, Gloria: she knew it all and I didn't even know where the ladies' room was.

The Garden of Life is one of those places in Los Angeles that are all of a sudden "in." Los Angelinos are very cruel to their restaurants and this week's favorite is likely to be next week's trash. One year we tend to like dark and cozy and the next it's light and airy with a lot of plants. The Garden of Life was of the light and airy school of restaurants and it was a joke. That's another thing Los Angeles has—funny restaurants. They tried to make The Garden, as we "in" people who bought forty-dollar jeans called it, a religious eating experience. You had the feeling, as you sat there eating every possible grain, that in the kitchen they were praying to alfalfa sprouts. The owner and all the waiters and waitresses dressed in flowing white and whispered. The only time they stopped smiling was when I once asked if they had ever had pepperoni pizza. Leave it to Los Angeles to come up with the first Church of Good Food. The big sin is eating an Oreo.

Our waiter was a great friend of Linda's. It seems they were both into pyramids, whatever that is. (I know what pyramids are. I just didn't know how they related to modern Hollywood, like the two of them did. I had just recently gotten Rolfing and est defined.) Fine. It was obvious she respected the waiter more than she respected me. Fine. I could take it. Maybe. Linda was at home. The owner brought her favorite juice without having to ask. She didn't even have to look at the menu. I had to suffer with the menu. The waiter and Linda rolled their eyes, waiting for me to order.

"Have the vegetable plate," Linda suggested. I used to do that, forcing the choice. "Have the liver," I would say and my date would usually obey. I liked to say liver because it was a test of my date's devotedness. Most took the liver, even though liver is not a well-liked dish. Some even gagged. The ones who didn't like liver but ordered it I knew I could get into bed that night. The ones who gagged I figured would go down on me. I didn't like vegetables. I refused to eat vegetables when my mother or Frances begged me to. I ordered the vegetable plate. What I should have ordered was lox with a side dish of ammonia.

"So what's new?" I said after dinner was ordered. A brilliant question. It is only when I am with a person from the seventies that the fifties in me glaringly reveals itself. I have sideburns, but my mouth says flat top and I might as well be wearing Glowickie socks. I am a Jewish Eisenhower man and it shines through my faded Levi's.

"Things are fine. I take it day by day. Tomorrow I might get

129

a great idea for a novel or a lousy idea for an article on massage parlors. I might wake up and be Schlesinger or Bogdanovich." She was answering me. She wasn't grunting. She wasn't wearing a bra and she was talking and I was trying.

"You never tried with me," would say Frances.

"You never tried with me," would say Louise.

"You never tried with me," would say Judi Rosenberg and her mother.

Ladies, *please*. I couldn't try with you. My father told me I didn't have to.

"I like Bogdanovich's work," I told Linda, hoping to keep things going.

"All of it?" she said in shock.

"Well . . . just about."

"When I was living in New York, I was going with this guy. We were even thinking of getting married. When *What's Up, Doc?* was released, we went to see it. He laughed out loud at some of the inane humor and I realized I never wanted to see him again. I walked out of the theater."

"You broke up with someone because they laughed in a movie?" I said in shock.

"You're missing the point. I broke up with him because we didn't have the same sense of humor." I tried to look very somber. I wanted her and I wasn't going to blow it by laughing at the wrong things.

"I know what you mean," I said, sounding like a tragic figure.

"I just don't want to go through life with someone who laughs at inane things." She was not easy, this Linda Minsk. Won't sleep with people who like the Queen. Won't marry people because they laugh.

"I once broke up with a girl because her pubic hair was sticking out of her bathing suit," I said, trying to show we thought along the same lines.

"That was very mean of you," said Linda Minsk. I kept quiet for a very long time.

Linda ate with gusto, not like all those girls who pick at their food because they can't eat in front of men. I sat there picking at my food, but not because I couldn't eat in front of women. When you're a single Jewish male, you can eat in front of anybody. I was nervous, afraid that the lovely Linda would walk out on me because I was for or against the wrong things. I was afraid she would find me too square, despite the fact that, of all the guys in the restaurant, I had the most studs on my Levi jacket.

Usually I could handle a beautiful girl without any fear or trepidation. An average-looking guy can handle what is commonly known as a Miss America, just because in the old days a simple formula existed—an average-looking guy equals a Miss America. I could handle superior intelligence, because a lot of girls were uptight about their intelligence. I know for a fact, through the mouth of Judi Rosenberg, that girls sat in the dorms hoping their husbands had higher IQs than they had. Little girls were never told they were regular Einsteins. Little girls were regular Shirley Temples.

I could handle rich girls because I was a boy from a "very comfortable" family. Any girl who went out with David Meyer knew she had a chance of getting a two-and-a-half-carat ring with big baguettes and no flaws. I could handle top drawer. If they were interested in me in the first place, they were rebellious, and I was perfect to be rebellious with—not social register, but clean. I could handle twins. I had the Sontag twins on two successive nights and they found out and both were still willing to see me.

So it seems I could handle just about everyone, including their mothers—everyone except for Linda, the young-Jewish-writer-researcher-hip-whore. She had me ordering carrot cake when I wanted cheese cake. She had me asking questions. She had me begging Paul the expensive hair stylist for appointments and she had me scared of liking royalty. Look, I know this is nothing startling, that a thirty-two-year-old man, for the first time in his life, is scared of making wrong moves and looking square. You read it on the printed page, it looks like nothing; but when you're living through it, you're a Jew in Egypt, or worse, you're a Jew in the New York Athletic Club.

I was pushing myself to be charming. I was listening harder than I had ever listened. I was smiling until it hurt. I know my face wrinkled that night. She left the table for a minute and I sort of half stood—you know, that half-stand where your ass is up in the air. I want to be so right for this girl but I don't know whether to stand or sit, so I end up with my ass in the air. I'll bet that's something even a Rockefeller can't escape. I don't care how much money you have. There are times in every man's life that you end up with your *tochas* up.

Check time. I asked for the check and the race was on. We both produced Master Charge at the same time. If you really want to analyze it, pre-Master Charge, credit cards were male-oriented. You didn't see too many chicks whipping out Diners Club or American Express. Those cards were harder to get. You had to be making at least ten grand or something like that and you had to look like the guys in the shirt ads: tall, dark, good hair, great manicures, patch over one eye. Then along comes Master Charge and any five-year-old with fifty cents allowance can get a card. Listen, women are as entitled to credit cards as men. All I'm saying is Master Charge did a lot to even things out before a lot of us were ready for it.

"I'll take care of it," I said, immediately insecure about my words. I felt I should have said "I'll take it," or "I have it." "I'll take care of it" sounded like I laughed at *What's Up, Doc?*

"There's a flood and the whole town will be wiped out unless something is done about it."

"I'll take care of it," said David Meyer, showing his masculine

strength. All the ladies swooned and were appreciative that such a strong man was in their midst. They all wanted the hardness of his cock within them.

Linda moved her Master Charge card over mine—like in that game you play with your hands when you're little. You put your hand on top, then they put their hand on top of your hand and it goes on until someone really gets slapped. Eventually there are tears and your sister gets blamed because she's older. My Master Charge was on top and then hers and then mine and then hers. She was on top: no good—the man's supposed to be on top.

"Don't be silly, David, I asked you to dinner," said the girl, sounding like Jane Fonda.

"Really, I insist," said the boy, sounding like Ozzie Nelson.

"Come on. I owe it to you. You spent an awful lot on me," said the girl sweetly, kicking the boy in the balls while he was down.

"Please . . ." begged the boy, his eyes trying to conjure up masculine power like they had in the past. Shit. Katharine Hepburn with all her liberalness, with all her cleverness and drive and equality, always let Spencer Tracy pay.

She relented, throwing her Master Charge back into a very cluttered bag. I wanted to get down on my knees and kiss her hands and bury my head in her lap and thank her for letting me be the daddy. Actually, she was so casual about the whole thing I didn't even feel I'd won.

Linda looked at me while I was signing the receipt. Hey, Linda, unfair. Your eyes are supposed to wander about the restaurant, avoiding noticing me deal with the check. Linda, don't you know you're not supposed to look? When you go to the movies, he pays and she looks at the pictures under "Now Showing." You're not allowed to look, Linda, like on Yom Kippur you're not allowed to look at the men who are praying for you. If you had paid, I wouldn't have looked.

133

So you want to talk about embarrassing? I'm telling you, Gloria, for every time I copped a feel I've been repaid double. This one was probably for the time I felt up Louise Lichtner under the bleachers during a basketball game. She had a hot dog in each hand and I took advantage of her.

The waiter and the owner both returned to the table and it seems they are very sorry but they have looked up my Master Charge number in a little book and it seems my number is on the shit list—probably some mistake. (It was some mistake. My secretary, who I entrusted to pay my bills, was walking around with two months' unmailed checks in the bottom of her pocketbook. She cried when I yelled and told me, through her tears, she was going to bring the incident up in group and name names.) The waiter and manager were terribly, terribly sorry. (They will pray for me to be reinstated.) They are so terribly sorry that they are forced to embarrass me in front of my date. Why not shoot me through the heart, gentlemen? Why not announce on the eleven-o'clock news that David Meyer abuses Master Charge?

Linda whipped out her card again, which is not at all fair since throughout history it is the knight in shining armor who saves the damsel in distress by whipping something out. Fuck it. Master Charge is responsible for damsels never being in distress. My receipt was ripped in half. The pain was unbearable. Her card was stamped and sealed and perfectly acceptable and I sat there, my eyes all over the place, while she signed. I wasn't just getting repaid for Louise. This had to count for Judi Rosenberg too, and maybe even for leaving Frances.

"We're glad you were made to look foolish in a public house of worship and eating": the girls.

We got back in the car. I didn't dare suggest we go someplace or do something. A person whose number is in that little book doesn't feel like suggesting things. Linda had trouble getting the car started and she hopped out and looked under the hood and tightened something and hopped back in and the car was working again. I looked under a hood once. Why, I don't know. Jewish boys don't know what's going on under hoods, and Jewish boys don't want to get oil on their hands. Suppose I got oil on my hands. It might get all over my tennis whites and wouldn't that be a terrible mess?

Linda didn't mind oil on her hands. As a matter of fact, she got a smudge on her nose which was irresistible. The fact that she fixed the car without having it carted off by the AAA and having it cost a hundred and fifty-three dollars, which is always what the bill comes to, was almost erased by that smudge, which made her appear vulnerable and soft and helpless. I guess I have looked vulnerable, soft and helpless as I stood there in tennis whites writing out my check for a hundred and fifty-three dollars to Tony the mechanic.

Linda just drove, not revealing our destination. I've done that. There's something very powerful about being behind the wheel and not telling the other person where you're going. She maneuvered that old Porsche, shifting like a car was meant to be shifted. I had an old Mercedes with a shift once, but I had to trade it in in less than a month because I kept stalling on the hills. I'll bet the boys at the AAA talked about me behind my back.

"Tom, you go this time. I went last time. It's that Jewish boy who doesn't know how to drive a shift car, stuck in the hills again."

"I'm not prejudiced, Jack, you know that, but I think Jews should live on flat land. They make great doctors and lawyers, but they sure can't shift."

Linda could shift. She shifted as well as Nureyev dances. If there was a contest for shifting, or a Pulitzer Prize, this little lady would win. She never jerked, never stalled, and could shift and talk at the same time. Funny—before I met Linda, I thought only Gentiles and dykes could shift.

We ended up at her place, a small, very small house (one of

those houses that are smaller than apartments) in Laurel Canyon. (Linda, you could tell from the semi-isolated location of the house, wasn't one of those girls who wouldn't take a shower when no one was around after seeing *Psycho*.) It was pleasant, friendly, needing some repair but overrun with ferns and geraniums and the kind of chaos that can only be perpetuated by careful planning. If you wanted to rent the place, you would describe it as woodsy. It was the kind of house you'd expect Joni Mitchell to have once lived in.

So she had snuck me back to her place. Did she think I was an easy lay? Was she going to lure me inside and take advantage of me? Sure she took me to dinner, but that didn't mean I had to put out.

"Come on in. I got the new Dylan album." Sure, Linda, force me inside with promises of albums. She really wasn't as good as I was at this. I could get a girl inside my house with the promise of a new Dylan single.

I followed Linda in. Sure I was scared. Suppose she had strange sex machines inside? Suppose she wanted to fuck but I couldn't get it up because being able to perform sexually is directly related to whether you're in good standing at Master Charge?

Suppose God has a list of who can't have sexual intercourse each night and my number was on the list? God would be terribly sorry and this time Linda couldn't save me by whipping it out.

Fears grew. What if she used incense and strange oil? What if she wanted to do awful things with pyramids? What if I couldn't get it up and I lay there limp next to someone who was beautiful *and* could shift. I should have taken her back to my place. I would have had more control. I couldn't. She drove. There was no way out. In California you can't yell "Taxi." You end up going into houses and admiring ferns, no matter how scared you are.

The interior of the house was like Linda, natural, pretty, nothing expensive, but pleasing—books that are read, records that are played, plants that are talked to, a cat and a dog living in harmony. For the first time in my life, the smell of cat food didn't bother me. What impressed me the most about the three tiny rooms—just living room, bedroom and kitchen— was that it had permanence. There wasn't a feeling of I'll find something to go in that corner later. I mention this because many homes and apartments of single girls (and men . . . and men) have the feeling of it'll do for now. They somehow live, ready to put everything into Bekins boxes if love comes their way. Linda's place could never be packed up.

In a matter of moments she had everything controlled— animals fed, wine in our hands, fire going. First woman I ever saw build a fire. Gee, I always thought the only women who built fires were married to Abraham Lincoln. We sat on the floor, facing the fireplace, and what happened next is what always happens when two people of the opposite sex sit down and face fires. It was good. I was a little fast, but she didn't say anything like Monica Steinberg would have, and I was grateful. The plants probably knew it wasn't as good for her as it was for me. One large palm seemed to be frowning and maybe it was my imagination, but the ivy seemed a little hostile. In any case, it worked—fairly well considering the circumstances. My plants would have been happy.

We lay there for a while. I don't know what she was thinking. I was thinking that I wanted to stay close to this girl. I was hoping that Linda would let me spend the night. I wanted to kiss her in the morning, even before she brushed her teeth.

"Come on, David. I'll drive you home," she said sweetly.

Happy, girls? Are all you girls thrilled that I got kicked out? She didn't want me there for breakfast. The palm got to stay and I was being driven home.

We kissed good night in the car.

"Linda, I want you to know I'm glad we finally got together." That was good. It came in the right decade. I really do better when there aren't plants around.

"I'm glad too. Really. It was fun. The sex was good." My God, my heart. She liked me.

"Yeah," was all I could think of.

"What do you think of Nixon?" she asked.

"I hate him." That, I figured, was a safe opinion. If she didn't like royalty, she wasn't going to go for Nixon.

"Everything about him?"

"Yeah." Why not?

"I broke up with my fiancé because of Nixon. You know what he said?"

"He liked Nixon?" I asked incredulously.

"Don't be silly. He said, 'We should leave the man alone already. He wasn't all bad. At least he took a trip to China.' " I was expecting more. There was no more. Linda had broken up with her fiancé because Nixon took a trip to China.

"What a disgusting thing to say." Might as well get in there and knock the ex-fiancé and president.

"Yeah . . . one fucking trip to China."

"Linda, are there other things that really make you angry that I should know about?" I figured it was safer to find out in advance rather than make a big mistake of saying something like I didn't care for Fidel Castro.

"Oh, God, David, I wouldn't know where to begin. I'm a very political person."

"I'll bet you hate capital punishment," I said, trying to be helpful.

"Of course. Don't be silly."

"And you're a registered Democrat who leans toward socialism?"

"Oh, David."

"I have to know."

"Why? So you can have the same opinions as me? I don't mind if someone disagrees with me."

"I laughed at parts of *What's Up, Doc?*"

Immediate reaction. She tightened up, pursed her lips and started the ignition within three seconds of my statement. "I suggest you get out of the car, David."

"I was only kidding. I hated it. I just wanted to prove to you that you do mind if someone disagrees with you."

"You're right. I do. I have a cousin I don't talk to because he worked for Rockefeller."

"That capitalist," I said, and didn't know whether I was referring to the cousin or Rockefeller. She liked what I said. The ignition was turned off.

"So when can we get together again?" I said, carefully planning every word, the first cocksman in history to do so.

"I'm going to be the busiest. Let me call you tomorrow."

"I'll call."

"It's silly. I'm not easy to reach."

"Please, just give me your number," I begged.

"It's 714–2324, but . . . let me call you." I ran the numbers in my mind, picturing where the nearest pencil was.

"Thanks for everything." That included dinner and sex.

"It was nice." She made a statement in three words. Look, I was no competition for her. She made statements the way she drove cars and built fires.

Linda sped off. I let myself in and I rushed for a pencil. I got her number down on the inside cover of the *Compleat Works of Shakespeare*, the first available blank space in the house. Before falling asleep, I ran over every word Linda had said, feeling good about things. I dreamt I was being chased by a giant palm. Go figure your subconscious.

11

She didn't call the next day. I know she didn't call when I was out because I didn't go out. I sat there the whole day looking at my beige phone. I watched a whole night of television. Johnny Carson came and went and all hopes that the phone would ring were squelched with the one-o'clock news.

"Hello, operator?"

"Yes, may I help you?"

"Is it possible that my phone is out of order and I don't know it?"

"Has it been reported out of order?"

"No, I was just expecting a call . . . well, I've been here all night and the phone hasn't rung. It would be wonderful if you could call me, just so that I could be sure that my phone is working."

The operator agreed to go with my plan. I hung up and the phone rang and for a split second I prayed it would be Linda and not the operator, a strange lady with whom I'd probably never even have sex.

"Hello." It was the operator. So I guess it was working. Operator, when you were a kid, did you ever hear the rumor that Dinah Shore had twins, one black and one white?

"Your phone is working, sir," she said in her operator voice. She wanted out and I let her go. I never even got to bring up the rumor that James Dean was alive, just tired of making movies.

So. Do I take out the *Compleat Works of Shakespeare* and call Linda? I could make believe I was out all night—a brilliant ruse, one that all the women in my life had used when I didn't call them.

"David? Listen, I was out and my service said someone called and then hung up. I was wondering if it was you." They lied. They were home watching their beige phones all night.

"No, it wasn't me." Could have said it was. Didn't want to.

Do I not call Linda and take a sleeping pill or two, hoping not to dream of palms? Who does this Linda think she is to fuck me and forget me? I'm not going to run after nobody. I have a penis, all she has is a hole. There are plenty of holes in the sea.

I called. There was no answer. One-thirty in the morning and no answer. I imagined Linda was dining and shifting her car with some other chump who she would take advantage of. I hoped, whoever he was, that he said he liked the Queen.

Two-thirty and I couldn't sleep, not even on Doriden and hot milk. I called Barbara Hirsh.

"Hello." She had the voice of a sleeper. I should have hung up with apologies. When your Doriden isn't working, you forge ahead.

"Barbara, it's David." I heard her wake up immediately. It's obvious the girl cared for me. You don't come out of a deep sleep for everyone.

"What's the matter?" She might have been the Head of Daytime Television, but she had the heart of a Jewish mother.

"I just wanted to talk. I can't sleep."

"Sure." The interesting thing about this conversation is that I disturbed her and she's flattered. I am male. Women don't care what time of the night I call them.

"Barbara, tell the truth. Did you ever sit by the phone waiting for some guy to call?"

"Always."

"So what do you do?"

"Why?"

"Because . . . I told a girl I'd call . . . and I didn't." I'm not here for myself, doctor. I have a crazy friend with a problem.

"Don't tell me you're getting a conscience, David." That somehow thrilled her. Had she known the whole truth she would have been ecstatic.

"I guess I am . . . sort of." It was in my nature to qualify things, so it made her a little less happy and me a little more comfortable.

"So why don't you call her?" Good, Barbara.

"Too late. It's twenty to three." Good, David.

"She's probably up waiting." Good, Barbara.

"It seems too concerned to call now. So tell me, what do you do when he doesn't call for days?" Good, David, direct the questions, don't answer them.

"The first night I stay up all night. The second night I take a sleeping pill"—I was a day ahead of her—"and on the third day I go to a psychic . . . not that I believe in psychics. It's just that by the third day I feel like flushing twenty-five bucks down the toilet."

When I lived in New York, I didn't relate to psychics. In California everyone knew a psychic person because we were a generation of people who couldn't wait until tomorrow to find out about tomorrow. Everyone thought they had the leading psychic, the one that had been called into the Boston Strangler case. If this were true, about five hundred psychics were called into the case. Your California psychics were all over the place, and they predicted things like: "Los Angeles will fall into the ocean in May." It gave us something to look forward to each spring.

142

My theory about psychics was a simple one. I didn't believe in them because if they were so smart, how come they weren't rich? You figure anybody who knows what's going to happen to me, a perfect stranger, should know when IBM is going to go up. I had avoided all people of the psychic persuasion and continued to avoid them until the third day that Linda didn't call.

"Barbara, listen, a friend of mine would like to know the name of your psychic." It used to be, in the old days: "A friend of mine would like to know the name of your shrink." And before that there was: "A friend of mine would like to know the name of your abortionist." We've come a long way.

"Marsha Shanks."

"What?" I said that because I couldn't believe that a great psychic was named Marsha Shanks. A dental assistant is named Marsha Shanks. You have a cousin named Marsha Shanks. Psychics should be named Madame Roches or Melinda Moon.

The next morning:

"Hello, is Marsha Shanks there, please?" I asked like I had asked when we practiced telephone in the third grade.

"Speaking." She wasn't supposed to say "Speaking," according to Miss Melano, third-grade teacher extraordinaire. She was supposed to say, "This is she." Marsha Shanks probably had a great head for the future but couldn't remember what she learned in third grade.

"My name is David Meyer. I'm a friend of Barbara Hirsh." She, of course, should have known all of that. "Barbara suggested that I . . . uh . . . come to see you."

"I charge twenty-five dollars for a reading." I wonder if the old soothsayers said things like that.

"Yeah . . . O.K." Linda hadn't called me in three days. I felt like flushing twenty-five dollars down the toilet.

"How about Monday at three?" Monday at three was unacceptable. This was Thursday at nine. I'd die by Monday at three.

"This is an emergency. I must see you right away." I sounded like I had just come from the doctor, found out that it was terminal and wanted a second opinion from Marsha Shanks.

"Well . . . how about six o'clock today?"

"Fine. Six o'clock is fine. Thank you. Thank you very much. Thank you." In my life I never thanked anyone so much, except for Paul the expensive barber when he squeezed me in.

"You fucked me and you never thanked me." Shut up, Judi Rosenberg.

"I'm 1811 La Tijera, right near the airport." I have since heard of other psychics who live near airports. Probably they're expecting a vision and want to be able to leave town fast.

"I'll be there at six."

Instead of saying goodbye, she said, "Watch out for someone named Michael." Obviously Miss Shanks wanted me to think she was some terrific psychic. There isn't a person in this country who doesn't know at least six Michaels. There was Michael who lived right next door, a Michael fixed my Mercedes, and guess who my accountant is—a Mr. Michael Trott. Last but not least, the guy who actually did the blow-drying at Paul the expensive hair stylist's was a Michael. I knew Marsha Shanks was full of shit, but somehow from that day on I never trusted a Michael. Suppose every psychic told every person that called to beware of a Michael. This country would eventually ignore the black situation and get into the Michael problem.

I was at La Tijera by five-thirty. This gave me a chance to sit in the car for half an hour, eating my heart out over Linda. At six I ran to the door.

If I were a film director trying to create the atmosphere of a psychic's house, my camera would come nowhere near Marsha Shanks's place on La Tijera. It was one of those Formica houses, everything plastic—flowers, couches, a plastic black-and-white television. (I never pictured psychics watching television. Don't they know the endings of everything?) In the corner was one of those chairs that recline when you sit in them, all torn apart by a cat and incapable of reclining. On a bookcase with no books stood an award for someone's team coming in first in the bowling league. It was September and a fake Christmas tree still stood, or stood prematurely.

Marsha Shanks looked all wrong. You could tell there was no gypsy in her soul. There were those big curlers in her hair and fake-fur slippers on her feet. I'd have accepted all this if only there had been something about her that told me she could look into the future—like maybe one yellow eye.

"Have a seat." She motioned to a plastic couch.

"Thanks." I sat on the couch, sticking to it immediately.

She lit a cigarette and yawned. My whole future is to be unveiled and she's bored.

"You know someone named Michael?" she said.

"Yeah, but no one who's trying to do me in or anything." I chuckled, trying to dismiss the whole Michael thing. For twenty-five bucks I didn't want to discuss Michaels.

"Watch out for a Michael," she said, cleaning her nails with a matchbook.

"The reason I came was to find out about this girl Linda. . . ."

"Gee, that's a first. Usually the girls come. The guys don't call them and they get all upset."

"Yeah, well, I'd like to know . . ."

A dirty little girl about ten years old entered the room. She went and sat by her mother. (I could tell it was her mother because she looked just like her . . . common.) Marsha didn't seem to care about the intrusion and there was nothing I could do about it. The neophyte psychic just sat there next to her mother, picking her nose.

"I went out with this girl Linda . . ."

"You work in show business?" said Marsha.

Aha! Either this woman is psychic or she combs the trades.

"Yes, I do," I said, my voice registering amazement, the kind of amazement that psychics must thrive on. The little girl didn't stop picking.

"Your father is not in show business." Another safe guess. She knew I wasn't Liza Minnelli.

"Great. Listen, the reason I came to see you is because of this Linda . . ."

"What I like to do first is give you a reading on past lives."

I knew it. They always waste a lot of time on past lives. All the people I knew who had been to psychics had been told what they were before they were California neurotics. Great bit: how do you tell a psychic they're wrong about what happened before you were born, that you weren't the first cousin to the Czar? They can't be refuted, and by the way, just in case you think you're really hot shit, psychics tell everyone that they were a first cousin to the Czar, or Hungarian royalty, or the first person to receive the Ten Commandments from Moses. No psychic has ever got a vision of his or her client spreading out manure or washing the palace floors. Everyone was a prince. There were no pishers in former lives.

According to Miss Shanks, or Mrs. Shanks (her daughter continued to pick; she had a little nose—she had to stop sometime), in former lives I was a philosopher in ancient Greece (I guess I was second only to Plato), I was a general for Napoleon (pretty good for a kid whose father hired the best lawyer in the country to keep him out of the Army), and I was a bigamist in London around 1850 (so no wonder I'm the way I am, having had the pleasure of supporting two wives at once; I probably left them both and had to buy two fun furs).

I sat there nodding. I didn't believe a word she was saying, but what was I going to say? "Excuse me, Miss Shanks, but I got a C minus in philosophy at Boston University Junior College. It seems kind of crazy that I wouldn't have remembered something from the good old days when I hung around Plato." You don't bother to mention things like that because there ain't a living soul who isn't flattered that he was a philosopher rather than a peon.

My past done, Miss Shanks finally looked up toward the ceiling, I thought to put herself in a trance. It was to fix one of her curlers. Finally . . .

"You have a girl named Linda." At first I was startled, thinking she had true genius. Then I remembered that I had mentioned Linda's name about a dozen times since I arrived.

"Yes, we have this sort of relationship." I was choosing my words carefully because of the little nose-picker. "I would just like to know what's going to happen . . . you know."

"To tell you the truth, Mr. . . . uh . . ." (My psychic couldn't even remember my name.)

"David Meyer."

"To tell you the truth, Mr. Meyer, I just can't come up with specific information. I work in a more cosmic sense."

"Oh, well, of course . . . I didn't expect you to tell me exactly." I was defending her inability like crazy. I should have donated the twenty-five dollars to underprivileged children who can't afford to find out what their past lives were.

"I do get this feeling that you have had a permanent relationship with someone."

"I was married once. We weren't right for each other. I rushed into it." I apologized to womanhood, mother and child.

"What's a permanent relationship?" asked the girl. Her

mother didn't answer, so I did.

"That's when you're with another person for a while or permanently." I tried.

"Oh." She was satisfied.

"I think you haven't heard the last of this Linda": Marsha Shanks.

"Are you sure?" I was thrilled, heart skipping around the room. I could have kissed the dirty little girl.

"I can't be positive. It's not that clear." Shit.

"But you do see something?" Something, please. There's going to be a lot of traffic driving back from the airport. I don't want this trip to be total aggravation.

"I don't think you've heard the last of her. . . . She lives on a hill?"

"Yes, yes." You realize if I'd said no, she would have said, "I didn't think so."

"She is blond?": Ms. Shanks.

"No, dark hair": me.

"Yes, that's right." See how they work? "Wait . . . I'm getting something." Ms. Shanks was trying very hard to look like she was in a trance. I knew she was checking curlers. "Wait . . . she is . . . she is . . ."

"I'm thirsty," the dirty little girl said.

Even if Marsha "saw" something, the kid got her off the track. The dirty little girl stood up and her mother followed her into the kitchen. She continued to talk, but I didn't know whether to follow. Suppose she had a brilliant insight while pouring milk. Fuck it. It was my money. I stood up and went to the kitchen door. The kid was grabbing about a dozen Fig Newtons. The mother was pouring her a Coke. The kitchen was dirty, with dishes in the sink and knives with jelly stuck to the counter.

"This Linda will be very undependable in affairs of love." That's not news. Anyone would know that. If I came here in the first place it was because things were not exactly hunky-dory.

"Undependable?" I wrote that down on a note pad I'd brought for Shanks's gems. This wasn't a gem, but I wrote it down anyway to let her know I was with her.

"What's undependable?" asked the brat. This time nobody answered her.

"Do you think I should call her?" I said. Marsha Shanks gave me a look that said, "How the hell should I know?"

We talked on. She seemed to feel that someday Linda would be a part of my life. I didn't have to drive out to the airport to hear that. She was already part of my life. Then Marsha saw our houses joining forces, which made the old heart react again. She knew Linda loved animals. Good. She knew that Linda had, at one time, an unusual job. Very good. (How unusual I never told her. The kid was leaning against her, this time biting her nails.) She didn't know whether Linda loved me, but I would be buying a piano in the near future. Great. She said that I liked to see things grow. Who the fuck doesn't? Do you know one person in this entire world who doesn't like to see things grow? She said I'd have some legal trouble later on in life, probably involving a woman. I worried a little about Kathleen Conway's mother. She felt I should be careful about movement in the next few weeks. Cute. (They usually tell you not to fly next Tuesday, so that you can really go crazy.) She said I was trying very hard to achieve something at work and if I didn't get it soon it would be too late. I assumed she was talking about the relevant series. Marsha Shanks was right. If I didn't get it soon, it would be too late. She said I enjoyed art. As many people enjoy art as like to see things grow. She said Linda would bring me both happiness and disappointment. Our relationship would be erratic. The child wanted to know what erratic meant. I said, "Why should you care? It's my life." And turned my head to avoid further questions.

Marsha Shanks concluded our little session by throwing in a lot during the last five minutes. I had a friend named Barbara. (I told her that on the phone.) Watch out for a dog bite. (I thought of Linda's dog. Would it be inappropriate to buy a dachshund a muzzle?) Be careful of someone named Michael. My father had a strong influence on my life. No kidding. My father will have a long life. Be careful shaving on the twenty-first. I'd be taking a voyage—maybe long, maybe short. Terrific. I'd be having trouble with women. (I know. I know.) Be careful of someone named Michael. I'd have trouble with my stereo. I'm a big fan of Streisand's. See my doctor if I have constipation problems. (The nose-picking child wants to know what's constipation.) One of the women in my life had a homosexual relationship. She didn't know who; possibly my mother. I own something in jade and that'll be twenty-five dollars. I tried to give her a check. She wouldn't accept a check because she had been screwed too many times by bad checks. You'd think a psychic would know.

I said goodbye to the child because it's nice to say goodbye to children. She looked up at me and said, "You're gonna get a ticket." I thought she was psychic for a minute until I realized she could see out the window and there was a cop out there giving me a ticket. Five dollars for the ticket, twenty-five to the psychic. It cost me thirty bucks to find out I had been a great philosopher and my mother might have had a homosexual relationship.

When I got home there were two messages from Myron—call back Operator six. It's always Operator six and when you ask for Operator six, they all say, "This is Operator Six."

"Hello." I think in most homes wives pick up the phone. Myron couldn't stand that. He was always there on the first ring.

"Hi, Pop. How come you called?"

"Do I need a reason?" He called to see how his darling son was doing.

"No, just wondering."

"So, what's happening?"

"Nothing much. I went to a psychic. . . ." As the words formed, I knew I was forming the wrong words.

"You went to one of those nuts?" Psychics fell into the category of charter flights and ghosts. Jews don't believe in them.

"She was good. She said some very interesting things. She said I owned something in jade and I just bought this little jade elephant."

"Well, isn't that terrific?" He said it with so much sarcasm he used up his sarcasm quota for life.

"She said you would lead a long life."

"She did?" Suddenly he was interested. "Ah, I don't believe in those crazies. What else did she say about me?"

"She said you shouldn't have that affair," I joked.

"What affair?" He took me seriously. There's nothing worse when you're joking and they're taking you seriously.

"I was only kidding, Pop."

"She didn't say anything about an affair because I never had any affair."

"No, Pop, I was only kidding."

"What about leading a long life? Were you kidding about that too?" He was worried.

"No, honest to God, Pop, she said you'd lead a long life." He thought for a while. Silence on long distance. Operator Six probably listening in.

"Ah, what does she know. If she's so smart, why ain't she rich?"

"She said in a former life I was a general for Napoleon."

151

"We don't believe in that." In what? In former lives or in being generals for Napoleon?

Some more talk and goodbye. Phone in hand, I dialed Linda. There was no answer. I dialed her all night, twelve, one, two, two-thirty, three, three-fifteen, four, five, no answer, no answer. A Michael was probably holding her hostage somewhere. At five I got in my car and drove past her house. God knows what I would have said if I had run into her.

"Oh, hi, Linda, I forgot this was your street. I often come here at five in the morning to wait for the sun to rise." She wouldn't believe me like I never believed the girls waiting outside my house. One said she was lost, another that she was on her way to her dentist. Hard to believe at ten o'clock at night. I never had to come up with a flimsy excuse, because Linda never showed up. She probably knew I had been a general for Napoleon and she, being a pacifist, never wanted to see me again.

I went home exhausted, called the office to tell them I had this intestinal thing, accepted their sympathy, and fell asleep dialing Linda. Due to an overdose of anxiety, I had my old recurring nightmare. I am in the dorm, frantically trying to get ready for class. It's toward the end of the term and I realize that I haven't attended a single class. (It's either math or science, I think—something that is altogether new to me. It couldn't have been philosophy.) I haven't attended one class and today is the final exam. I spend most of the time, in this anxiety-ridden nightmare, looking for the room where the class is held, with things detaining me along the way—running into people who take my time, entering the wrong building, going for coffee, forgetting I'm on my way to class. All this makes me more and more upset. I imagine I'm tossing and turning and moaning by then. I finally find the class, which is totally unfamiliar to me. I take a seat, just as the tests and blue books are being passed out. I'm dying because I am going to be tested on material I know nothing about. I wake up in a cold sweat and am thrilled that I am in television programming and having to face Alan Milner rather than blue books.

I have found my dream to be a classic, peculiar to those of us who have had the pleasure of an anxiety-ridden college education. This dream parallels the classic actor's dream—the one where you spend all day trying to memorize lines, find things get in your way and have to go out on stage without knowing your part. Or the television developer's dream. A show you developed is going on the air and you haven't had time to really put it together and it's crap. (This dream, by the way, ofttimes comes true.) Could there be the classic plumber's dream? You have to get to a house because a toilet is stopped up, things get in your way and you finally arrive at the toilet without your plunger. The classic president-of-the-country dream: You're president but somehow you have never gone to the White House. You try to find it, but things get in your way, like the secretary of state stops you to tell you a funny joke about a crisis in the Mideast. You finally get to the White House, only to discover that you are totally unprepared to run a country and you forgot your plunger.

I slept until about four-thirty, which is a lousy time to sleep until. After bathing and shaving, I decided to take some positive action. My hand was sore from dialing. (I guess the hand was prone to hurt due to an old war wound, gotten in Napoleon's army, come back to haunt me.) I wasn't going to let a girl make my hand hurt.

"Hello, this is David Meyer of 815–6293. I wonder if you could help me."

"I'll try," said the pleasant lady. There was nothing more I could ask. Here was a lady who was going to try and it was almost quitting time.

"I'd like to order push-button phones." Yes, sir, that Linda wasn't going to make my hand hurt ever again.

I met Barbara Hirsh for dinner that night at Hamburger Hamlet, the only hamburger place in the world with valet parking. I told her all that had gone down between Linda and me, including the visit to Marsha Shanks's plastic house. Up to now, even with all my problems, I had managed to retain my position as prince with Barbara. On this night, after hearing that I dialed a girl for forty hours straight, she dethroned me. The prince had fallen and had been dragged through the muck and mire (Meyer). Barbara was mad that my reign was over. If a cute guy like me could be kicked in the ass, what was going to happen to her, a tall girl?

I may have imagined it, but I thought I heard the "valet" who brought my car whisper "Schmuck" behind my back and I gave him a good tip and he didn't even know my story. For what reason would he call me schmuck? Because I drove a Mercedes? Did my father write to him and tell him to call me a schmuck because I was driving a German car?

At a red light I looked into the next car and thought I saw Marlon Brando—in an old Ford, mind you—turn to his companion, who looked an awful lot like Natalie Wood. They both seemed to be laughing and talking about me.

"He's the one, Natalie, who keeps calling the girl who fucked him," said Marlon Brando.

Of course I knew they weren't talking about me, and likewise I knew it wasn't Marlon and Natalie. It's just that even the birds in the trees seemed to be saying "Schmuck." If only the trees could talk, they would have dumped on me too, especially the palms.

Home again, I threw off my jacket and dialed my answering service.

"This is D-twenty-two. Any messages?"

"No, you're all clear." I thought she said, "You're all clear, schmuck."

It was that night that I realized I'd never be a regular Einstein or rich as Rockefeller. I'd be lucky if I ever got to be a person again.

I awoke to a ringing phone. Christ, let it be Linda. If it is I'll give all my earthly belongings to the church, including all my signed lithographs and my bar mitzvah pictures. I'll give them the stained glass from the front of the house.

"Hello."

"Hello," a strange voice said. "You don't know me"—shit —"but my name is Michael"—oh, my God—"Liftstein. I just got out to California and my mother is a friend of your mother's." The church will get nothing. "She told me to call you because"—I know why she told you to call me; I'm hoping I'm wrong—"I'm interested in getting into show business." I wasn't wrong.

"Well . . . I don't know how much help I can be. What is it you do, Michael?"

"I sing and play the guitar and write my own songs. Your mother thought that maybe . . . well . . . I think I'd really like to do *The Tonight Show.*"

Typical. My mother had told about fifty people to call me when they got to California. I'll bet she handed out my number on leaflets in front of the supermarket. A girl who thinks she's a writer called because my mother told her to, to see if I could get her a job as a writer on *The Carol Burnett Show.* A guy who decided to give up his bakery business called and told me he's a Wayne Newton type and could I help him get booked in Vegas. Somebody's grandmother called. She has a great idea for a story. Could I find someone just to write it up for her? She's willing to split the profits fifty-fifty.

I told my mother, after each stranger called, to please not give out my telephone number to everyone who wants to get into show biz. "I would help if I could, Mom. I'm hardly in myself." My mother promises not to and the following day she's out in front of the supermarket with those leaflets again.

I took Michael Liftstein's number and told him I'd try to help if I possibly could. I hoped he was good so he could make it on his own. Maybe he could get me on *The Tonight Show.* I could tell the whole Linda story and then I'd have every insomniac in the world thinking me a schmuck.

Into the shower and out as fast as possible. I called my answering service in case Linda had called while I was cleansing my body.

"You're all clear, Mr. Meyer." Thanks a lot. I don't pay you to be clear. I pay for messages.

I called my office again. "Gee, this intestinal thing has really gotten to me. I thought it would be over in twenty-four hours but it looks like . . . My doctor told me I better take it easy."

"Fine, we'll get along without you. Don't worry." I worry that you can get along without me and don't send any of those darling get-well cards that every secretary I schtuped signs.

I lay on the bed, nude, tuned in to some early-morning quiz show where housewives were answering questions with precision so their families could win lawn furniture and complete living room suites, the total value thirty-two hundred dollars. Do they want to blow it or go for the car? The audience screams, "Go, go." They have to go. Mrs. Fred Hendricks went for the car and blew the lawn furniture and everybody was very apologetic, but she smiled and said she had a wonderful time playing the game. I'll bet Fred beat the shit out of her when she got home.

I thought about going on one of those quiz shows. It looked easy, lying there on my bed in the nude, spouting forth correct answers. I would have won the Camaro, had they been taping at my house. (Had they been taping at my house, it would have been an X-rated quiz show.)

I did, by the way, go on *The Dating Game*. My embarrassment is so deep, I have never told a living soul. (Several million people saw me and I think I'm keeping it a secret.) When I first came to Hollywood, I met a friend of a friend who knew one of the chaperones from *The Dating Game* and could definitely get me on. I had this vision of me putting on a sports jacket, walking onto the set and since I was so cute and charming, winning a trip to Paris. I put on a sports jacket and went to *The Dating Game* offices. I wasn't whisked into the studio. I was whisked into a room with attached chair-desks—the kind they have in modern junior high schools. There I sat among the other bachelor hopefuls, some looking spiffy, others with so much acne you wondered what had possessed them to put themselves through this. Surely they knew they weren't going to be accepted for color television. We didn't talk among ourselves—natural enemies, vying to be bachelor number one, two or three. My friend of a friend, it became obvious, didn't have such tight connections.

Cuteness counts, especially on *The Dating Game*. Seven of us were asked to stay while the rest were ushered into a down elevator. All the acne was asked to leave. Those of us who remained were put through games. I was a mock bachelor number two, whilst the blond lady with long legs and hair was the bachelorette. She was there to weed out the stutterers, the hesitant, and the ones who would take TV time to push Communism.

It wasn't easy. You could be cute as hell, but they had to make sure that you were capable of delivering those double-entendre answers. You had to do all sorts of things in your voice so that when you said "Hi" you were saying: "Choose me. I'm a great fuck."

I got asked two questions by *The Dating Game* staff lady and answered them both brilliantly. It was one of those "our people will get back to your people" situations. I tried to give her

157

some signal saying that I shouldn't be grouped in with the other six. I was special and to be dealt with one to one because I had connections. I finally said:

"Listen, I was sent up here. They told me that I would definitely . . . you know . . . be on."

She smiled her *Dating Game* smile and said with a little too much pep, "Mr. Meyer, I'll be sure to remember that." Those were the words. What she really said was: "Asshole, get into the elevator with the others."

I got on the show and I like to think I made it on cuteness and brilliant answers alone. I doubt if there was any muscle used. I hope not. Muscle should be used only when cuteness fails.

Let me tell you, Gloria, being on *The Dating Game* is repayment for a lot. If anyone wants to create for me my own private hell, they could arrange it so that I live my life out as bachelor number two on *The Dating Game*.

The show began, and the three of us came revolving around. I felt like a live lobster being shown to the prospective diners in a restaurant. Worse—I felt worse than that. At least the lobsters get a chance to be looked at; we three bachelors had to give our answers behind a wall.

Our bachelorette was Betty. We each said salutations: "Hi, Betty," "Betty, hi," "Hello, Betty ol' kid." I had lost round one. My "hi" stank and I knew it. Suppose Louise Lichtner, Judi Rosenberg and her mother and Frances were all watching and I lost? There go my balls—ah, you might as well take the whole thing. The rest won't work without the balls. I had to win. Christ, my old man: suppose he saw me lose coast to coast? I could lose behind the closed doors of Meyer and Meyer but then only he and his accounting firm would know. Here I was in living color and I had uttered a stinking "hi." What if Lou from the candy store was watching?

Round two began. She asked me if she could be any part of

the body, what part would I like her to be? I smartly told her I couldn't answer that because my answer would be a bust. The audience roared, applauded. The applause was so good it could segue into a commercial. So what if Frances was watching? She was watching me get screams. She was seeing that I was doing fine without her. I could make my own breakfast and create double entendres.

It went O.K. I was saying fuck and cock and let's screw without actually saying it. I got in a few good ones, but so did bachelors number one and three. I was wearing my best sports jacket, but Betty, our bachelorette, couldn't see it. Judi Rosenberg could see it, though. She would know my jacket was really terrific, being the daughter of the junior sportswear king.

Betty, who was introduced as a key-punch operator, was asked for her final decision.

"Gosh, gee, I don't know. They all sound really neat." I was praying to God that she would pick me. I'll bet more people pray to God on quiz shows than in houses of worship.

"We're going to have to have your answer," said the M.C. I'll bet when he was a little boy he wanted to grow up and be a quiz show M.C. It looked like he always took care of his teeth. I bet he brushed, instead of just wetting the toothbrush to make it look like he brushed.

All of a sudden Betty was choosing bachelor number two. She didn't know why, she just thought I sounded cute. I did sound cute, but I was flanked by two *goyisha* blonds. Wait till she got a load of the Jewish boy in the middle. They introduce the other two first, a Sean, sports equipment salesman, and an engineer, Eddie. Then comes David Meyer, who's a television director. They always get those things wrong and you always feel guilty because it looks to your superiors that you told them you were a director because you were ashamed of what you really do.

I come running out, thinking I'm going to run into Catherine Deneuve and hoping that Frances and Judi and Lou and my father were watching. She wasn't Catherine Deneuve. She was a dyed blonde, the kind I hadn't been interested in since I bought *Titter* and *Wink*. She took one look at me, registered disappointment that she didn't bother to conceal. The television cameras couldn't conceal it either. The public saw coast-to-coast disappointment. She looked back on Sean, the sports equipment salesman. A chaperone wasn't going to be needed.

The big reason for going on *The Dating Game* is to win a trip. They send people to Paris and Rome. Betty and I were both thinking at least we were getting to go someplace.

"Now, Betty and David, we've got a wonderful trip planned for you. I hope you're not the kind of people that scare easily" —I'm thinking of scary countries—"because you will be visiting friends from darkest Africa." Africa? A safari? A safari isn't something you would buy for yourself, but it's nice to get as a gift. "You, Betty and David, are going to the San Diego Zoo for two fun-filled days. You'll have dinner at . . ."

I never heard the rest. I was going to the San Diego Zoo for two fun-filled days with this dyed blonde. I didn't want to go. Zoos you went to for an hour with a kid or if you're really in love with a chick and she really digs animals. Who spends two days in a zoo? I had to go. They made you sign a paper swearing you'd go before you went on the show. Maybe I could have got Craig Kelly, the lawyer, to get me out of it.

The worst two days of my life. Betty, the dyed blonde, was whiny. Greta, the chaperone, was good-looking, but made it clear that she had a boyfriend and was above me. The zoo people were doing something for the monkeys, so there wasn't a monkey in the place. The monkeys, in my estimation, are the only things you go to the zoo for. When I came back I smelled. I never did get the smell of zoo out of my good suede jacket.

160

I wasn't thinking of Betty, Greta and the monkeys as I lay there answering *Jeopardy* questions. I was thinking of Miss Linda Minsk. Had I been on *Jeopardy*, I would have won twelve hundred dollars in cash. I would have given it all to Linda if she would fucking call.

At about four the phone rang. It was Barbara Hirsh telling me she'd heard about a job at Paramount. It would be a step down, but then I could work my way up to a higher position than I had at the network. I was still naked on the bed. Any position would be higher.

"Myron, how's your son David doing?"

"Haven't you heard? He got a new job. He's really terrific, my son. He took a step down."

"Why do you care what your father thinks? You've got to break ties with your father. You take that job if you want it," said Barbara Hirsh, who thought I should at least investigate it. Being Jewish, you can never just let a job lie there.

Marsha Shanks, whom I called to see if she could give me a hint about what I should do about Paramount over the phone, said I should look into it but she made it perfectly clear that it was an opinion, not a psychic revelation. From her I didn't need opinions. I needed her to have one yellow eye.

The lady in the cleaners thought I should leave the network for movies. She had run out of television ideas but had a great idea for a film, a thriller that took place in a dry cleaners after hours. The murderer hides in a blue pinstripe that's about to be cleaned but is caught when the owner of the shop staples tags in the garment.

The kid who wanted to get into show business thought I definitely should take the job because movies were more important than television. I thought that was good advice until I realized his name was Michael.

I didn't ask Myron, but Myron I knew would want me to stay

put. Changing jobs to Jewish fathers is as bad as bringing home black babies.

I dialed Linda. I had an excuse to call her. I could pretend to really need her opinion. In the good old days the gals called me, pretending to need my opinion.

"David, I wouldn't have called, but I really needed your opinion about whether to buy a Mercedes. I know you have one and I know nothing about cars." That was Rochelle Freeman, two weeks after I told her we really shouldn't see each other again because I wasn't capable of a relationship. I told her she shouldn't buy the car that Hitler drove.

"David, I wouldn't have called, but I really needed your opinion. I know you live up Harold Way. I was thinking of renting a place up there. Is it a good neighborhood?" Yes, Maxine. It's a good neighborhood and I know you have no intention of moving. You called me, Maxine, because you wanted to hear my voice, not my opinion. That was a month after Maxine and I were—you should pardon my Hollywoodese—in Splitsville.

I could see through these calls because they always began with: "I wouldn't have called, but I needed your opinion." Most of the time, the caller could get better information from the recorded weather report.

"Linda, I wouldn't have called, but I really need your opinion." I said that as quickly as possible after the "Hi"s.

"David, you don't need an excuse to call." Damn it. She wasn't going to let me pretend.

"No, really, I called to ask you about . . ."

"You didn't call just to say hi?"

"Well, it's not that I wouldn't call to say hi"—watch the ass make an ass out of himself—"but really I called to ask you whether you thought I should take this job at Paramount." I knew, as I was saying it, it was sounding dumb. I sounded just

162

like Rochelle Freeman. I shouldn't have picked a major decision. I should have got into the plant area: "Linda, I really
need your opinion. I don't know whether to sing to my ferns
or play them records."

"Do you want the job?" She got right to it. I don't care about
the job, I want you in my bed, Linda. Please don't make me
drag out old *Playboys* tonight.

"I don't know." I didn't know—first truthful sentence uttered by me since the conversation began.

"It seems to me you're the one that's got to decide. . . . Tell
the truth, David, did you call just to ask me whether you should
take that job?"

"Yeah . . . sure." I was back to lies.

"That's too bad. I was hoping you called to ask me over."
You couldn't do numbers with this girl.

"I'd . . . I'd . . . I'd really love you to come over," I stuttered
out. After all those years of lying, it was hard to be truthful.

"I'll be there in ten minutes." And she hung up.

Ten minutes. I never met a person, male or female, who
could be somewhere in ten minutes. I was panicked. Even if
Paul the expensive hair stylist could take me, I couldn't make
it. Then there was the choice of shaving or getting the dirty
underwear away from the front door. I decided to shave. She
wasn't going to fuck the laundry.

There have not been many women in this world whom I
have shaved for. Some of my women have been honored with
two days' growth. I could actually hear my face scratching
against their tender thighs, not to mention what havoc my
beard played on their sweet nipples. For Linda I would shave
my legs.

She arrived, we talked, we screwed, we ate everything in the
refrigerator, we screwed again. We did things that people who
are into each other do, like we watched a very funny movie on
television, completely nude, not worrying that when we

163

laughed parts of us shook. We ate peanut butter off the knife. I let her make the fire because she made better fires, and I admitted she made better fires.

At one-thirty in the morning Linda started to dress. I couldn't believe she was leaving. We were in love. It had to be love. You don't eat peanut butter from somebody's mouth if you don't love them. I didn't just want her for fucking and eating and laughing.

"Thanks," she said at the door. "You really have a great place."

"Thanks." I wanted her again.

"Some really terrific prints."

"Thanks."

"Listen, do you mind if I borrow some books? Not now, but sometime?" It would be the first time my books were read.

"No, of course not." I hated people borrowing books, but just knowing my books would be close to her chest turned me on.

"I knew this guy who bought color-coordinated books. He kept Salinger in the den because it didn't match the living room décor."

"I bet you broke up with him."

"Walked right out." She'd never know I bought my books by the yard just to fill my shelves.

"I don't care what color my books are," I said.

"Do you like Roth?" she said.

"Philip Roth?" I said, trying to avoid having to give an answer. Didn't want Linda to walk right out on me.

"Yes." She gave me no hint.

"Well, I do and yet . . ."

"I love him."

"Me too."

"Everything he does."

"Me too."

"*The Breast* was genius."

"Me too."

"Do you know *When She Was Good?*"

"By Roth, right?"

"Yes."

"Know it and loved it." Tell me you found *Mein Kampf* amusing and I'll say "Me too." Love me.

She left with the assurance that we'd have dinner the next night at her place. I didn't think so. I thought she'd find someone else to share dinner with. Someone named Michael, who had a bigger penis, a great job at Paramount and chunky-style peanut butter.

I got up late the next day, called Paramount, found in an embarrassing conversation that the job I had deliberated over was not really a job. Not that the job was taken; they had decided that there was no need for a "consulting liaison." I had to do one of those "I was calling for a friend" numbers. It was a conversation where your voice trailed off and got softer and softer, until "Goodbye" was almost inaudible.

I was not down because there was no job. I was going to dine with my Linda. I took my laundry in, after having let it pile up for three weeks, and insisted on fluff dry. I went to Paul the expensive hair stylist and had a fluff dry myself. It looked pretty good, but not great. I don't think Michael gave it his all. I had the taillight on the Mercedes fixed and read as much of Roth as I could. Only on an up day could I have accomplished so much. I even had time to answer all the questions on the quiz shows. The only thing I didn't have time to do was go to work.

Yes, they sent a cute get-well card with a guy in bandages and crutches on the front, and yes, one of the receptionists had a messenger deliver chicken soup. Yes, I felt guilty. My father never missed a day of work in his life, God bless him.

165

I called Linda and asked what time she wanted me. She wanted me anytime. At six I started to dress. Six-o'clock news on, me whistling, announcer talking about impending war in the Mideast. Sometimes I'm embarrassed when I think about the times I've whistled.

I dressed slowly but was ready to go to Linda's too early. She had said anytime, but showing up early was not cool and I had a need to be cool. I sat on the edge of the bed, like a little kid who has been given strict orders not to dirty his clothes. At a quarter to seven I got up from the bed and went into the bathroom to pee, because it's not cool to have to pee the minute you get to someone's house. (Actually, it's very cool to have to pee the minute you get to someone's house. To be cool is not to worry about when or where you pee.) I peed a tiny speck of urine. It stung and I think there was a little drop of blood. Not a whole lot, just enough to give me a major trauma.

This stinging business had happened before so I wasn't thinking I had something major. I knew it was goddamn cystitis—cause unknown. In the past my doctor had given me Azogantrisin. It stopped the stinging and I peed orange and I was fine in a matter of days. And here it was again, cystitis, and all dressed up and ready to go to Linda Minsk's, the only girl I could ever love.

Called my doctor's office.

"I'm sorry, the doctor is not in."

"Can he be reached? It's important—an emergency. This is David Meyer." I was saying David Meyer like it was Henry Kissinger. "I had stinging and maybe a speck of blood in my urine." I'm telling the answering service about my urine.

"I'll try. Hold on." And she did something that sounded like you were being disconnected but she said hold and I held and soon I heard the voice of my doctor, who had probably said "Shit" when the call came in and he had to leave his expensive wood-burning set, which relaxed him.

"Hello."

"Hello, doctor. I'm really sorry to bother you. I am coming in for a checkup." I said that because I hadn't been in in almost two years and I didn't want him to think he wasn't going to make any money from me. "I think I have this cystitis thing again. When I urinated it stung and I think there was a speck of blood."

"Is there any pain?"

"I can't tell. Maybe a little. It hurt like heck when I went but I don't feel anything now."

"Have your drugstore call me." They don't say take two aspirins and get into bed anymore. It's "have your drugstore call" now.

Then the big question that could ruin my whole life. "Doctor, I don't remember . . . is it all right to have . . . sex?"

"I wouldn't if I were you." You're not me, doc. You probably have a wife who's forty and goes to sleep with toilet paper around her head. You have a wood-burning set to relax you.

"O.K." Oh, my God.

"Now you know what it's like when a girl has a big date and she knows the guy wants to sleep with her and she gets her period. Why do you think it's called 'the curse'? Because it's pain and blood, and that's what you have now, David Meyer. Now you know how we feel," would have said all the girls of my life, had they known.

"It's different. You expect it once a month," I would reply.

"Sure it's different. You get it once in a while. We can look forward to it once a month."

Once I was really horny and Judi Rosenberg didn't tell me she was having her period. I didn't know until I found the Tampax string. I let her jerk me off, but I was really pissed. She should have told me in advance. I could have contacted Desiree Goldblum.

Once I called Kathleen to ask her out. Kathleen knew our relationship was ninety percent sex. She told me on the phone that it was "that time of the month" and I took a rain check. Sorry, Kathleen.

"Men are lucky they don't get it," said Myron to his son, circa 1954. I got it, Pop. I got the blood and the pain and I couldn't have sex with Linda. I got it good, Pop. Spread it around. DAVID MEYER MENSTRUATES. Great couple, Linda Minsk and David Meyer. She shifts cars and he gets his period.

I had a decision to make. Should I be a Judi Rosenberg and try to keep the secret or should I be Kathleen and call Linda and tell her I got the curse? Suppose Linda does to me what I did to Kathleen? What if she takes a rain check on me? Help me, Lord. I don't want to be rain-checked. . . . Maybe I did. Could this be the first case of psychosomatic cystitis, Gloria?

Got the pills, went over, tried to tell her at the door and couldn't. I was going to be Judi Rosenberg.

All through dinner, pizza ordered in, I agonized over what would happen if Linda was interested in sex that night. Suppose, thought I, that I am to Linda what Kathleen has been to me for the last few years—a convenient lay, no questions asked. She certainly wasn't going out of her way to feed me well. Dinner at the restaurant was just probably to woo me at the beginning. Isn't that exactly what I did with Kathleen—took her out to dinner once and then barely gave her cheese and crackers? I was doing all this supposing and yet really thinking it through, over Sara Lee pound cake that was a little too cold. I figured Linda couldn't possibly want me only for my body. There was much more to our relationship than sex. We had laughed in the nude.

Pound cake finished and I'm getting more and more apprehensive. I was excusing myself to go to the bathroom every five minutes and there was a lot of stinging. I braced myself against the toilet paper holder and I was biting my knuckles so Linda

168

wouldn't hear my whimpering. I would have been great in the Army.

"David, don't sit on those cold steps. You'll get a cold in your wee-wee": Myron Meyer to his son, 1943–1959. I was going to get a cold in my wee-wee almost as much as I was going to lose an eye. I imagine at least once in my life Myron said, "Don't sit on those cold steps. You can lose an eye like that."

Dinner over, Linda lit a fire. Fire in the fireplace, could the fire in her be far behind, or (and this question is for Harold Robbins) if her juices were flowing over and she was seated near the blaze, would her juices eventually boil? Linda lay down on her back in front of the fire. Her arms stretched out for me to join her. She wasn't asking me to play chess. I had to pee again.

I excused myself with an "I'll be right back. I swear." The stinging was unbearable. There was no way I was going to be able to make it with Linda, even if the entire AMA said I could.

While I was stinging, Ms. Minsk had put a record on. I don't remember what, but I can guarantee it was music to make it by. I had planned to sit on the couch and try to get a conversation going. Linda didn't give me a chance, pulled me down to her, a little too close to the fire. She rolled over me. I had to go again. She took off her T-shirt—one that said St. Tropez. That T-shirt told a whole story. She tickled me and took off my shirt, lay down on me, bare chest to bare chest. I had to go more than I ever had to go in my entire life, and believe me, in my youth there were times that I barely made it to the bathroom, whipped it out as fast as I could and still ended up with drips on my corduroy pants.

She wasn't content to lie there, she had to push down on me with her entire pelvic area. Pain unbearable. Picture this: I'm lying under a great-looking girl who is pushing down hard. We are too close to the fire and I'm getting hot on all sides. I have to pee. There is a framed picture of a black guy (probably named Michael) in my direct vision. The black dude is smiling and saying, "I'm ten inches and I never get cystitis." Linda moans a pre-sex moan to let me know she's going to enjoy what's coming. I say:

"Hey, I just thought of something. Why don't we go see the new Mel Brooks film? I hear it's hysterical." It is such an inane comment that Linda laughs, thinking I'm quite a joker, and sticks her hand into my jeans, finding heavy cotton underwear that I had worn to prevent leakage.

"No, really," I go on, fool that I am. "If we leave now, we can make the eight-o'clock."

"O.K., David, if you really want to go," was what I wanted to hear. Not even close. She unzipped my fly and said playfully, "Want to go to the movies, huh? What's the matter, you don't like me anymore?" The black guy on the table said, "I didn't go to college, but it never stings when I pee, man."

What if she got my pants down? I wondered if you could see cystitis by firelight. She took her jeans off; no underwear. I was in pain; the effects of her pressing against me were still there. She stood over me, ready to pounce. I lay there helpless, only a pair of jeans and cotton underwear between me and her. She was ready to land. I looked up and said, "Well, if you don't want to go to the Mel Brooks film, how about *The Graduate*? They're showing it again." Too late. She pounced, I screamed. She rolled aside, confused, and the black guy laughed.

I turned and looked at Linda. "I can't do it. I have cystitis," I said.

She said, "Oh my God, your hair is on fire." I screamed, because I smelled burnt hair. Linda put out the sparks with a throw pillow, beating my head a little too hard, I felt. I ran to the bathroom. One drop of urine but plenty of sting. I looked in the bathroom mirror to check out my hair. So, what the hell,

I was singed on one side. I had the best hair stylist in town. He could even it out—see that I was singed on both sides.

By the time I got back to the living room, Linda was dressed, sitting on the couch very near the picture of the guy on the table. She was quietly smoking a joint.

"The girl is on dope?"

"Pop, everyone smokes marijuana. It's nothing. It hardly does anything."

"If it hardly does anything, why does anyone smoke it?"

"Is it better to get drunk? Statistics show that drinking is far worse for you than pot."

"Who said it's better to get drunk?"

You learn never to discuss grass with your father. No matter how hard you try to convince him, he's going to think you're one step away from heroin.

"You mad?" I said in a tiny voice, much too tiny for my size and stature.

"You should have told me, David. If I knew you were sick . . ." she said wistfully, staring at the fire that could have left me bald, with brain damage.

"I should have told you, but I felt funny and . . ."

She softened. "Listen, don't worry about it. I'll survive." I swear she looked at the picture of the black guy. Sure, I make her all horny and then he comes in and takes over. Easy for him.

I didn't know whether she wanted me to go or stay or die or get out of her life or put my head in the fire for her amusement. Surely I couldn't stand there all evening wishing I were in the bathroom.

"Listen, I think I'll go home. It's getting late and . . ." It was about nine-thirty. The only place it was getting late was London.

"You don't have to go."

"I don't?" I said, crossing my legs

"I didn't invite you over just to have sex." You didn't? I'm not just your dumb blond?

"Great . . . I didn't mean 'great.' I do enjoy sex." I'm telling someone I went to a massage parlor for that I enjoy sex.

"I mean, I'm glad you want me anyway." I walked over and hugged Linda, relieved. There aren't many women I've hugged just for the pleasure of hugging.

"I'm going to fight you," Linda said warmly, while we were still embraced. How many surprises can a person take in one night?

"You're going to fight me?" I squeaked, still clinging.

"That didn't come out exactly right," said Linda, leading me to the couch. Although she didn't ask for it, I leaned my wounded head on her shoulder.

"David, I know this is going to sound crazy," Linda continued. I had burned my head and been burned by my urine in one night. Not much was going to sound crazy now. "It's hard to tell you this. I like you, I really do, but I'm going to fight it. I am not going to allow myself to fall for you in any way."

"You're going to fight it?"

"Yes."

"You're going to . . . Why?"

"Because I don't want to ever love anyone like you. You're eligible and Jewish and chauvinistic and everything I don't need in my life. I go out with a million different guys, but I always feel comfortable with the ones like you. You remind me of someone I went to the prom with. The problem is, I like you already." She ruffled my hair. In modern-day America, hair-ruffling is noted as a sign of affection. I moved my head so the ruffling wouldn't expose my receding hairline.

"*I*'m not fighting liking . . . loving *you.*"

"Why should you?" said Linda Minsk.

The conversation would have continued had I not had to go

172

to the bathroom. Cystitis tends to abort conversations. By the time I got back to the couch, Linda was needlepointing. My mother needlepointed and she wanted someone who was eligible, Jewish and chauvinistic. Some people just aren't trite.

"You O.K.?" she asked.

"I'll be fine," I said, like I had just got my leg shot off in World War II. The only way my buddy could save his own life was to leave me behind to die. "Don't worry, buddy. It'll be O.K." I watch him go off. He turns back. I give him thumbs up to let him know I'm doing fine. He turns and moves off with the rest of the company. A grenade blows me to bits but he never knows it. And it's just the first reel.

"What did you do in the war, Daddy?"

"I died."

I sat and watched Linda most of the evening and that was enough for me.

I left about eleven with promises to call as soon as I was well. Kathleen had called me and I would call Linda.

I listened to the car radio on the way home. Want to hear Hollywood? Vandals had broken into the Hollywood Wax Museum and mutilated all the figures, leaving only Winston Churchill, Dwight Eisenhower and Cher in one piece. Wax stars were decapitated and dismembered. The museum was a total mess, arms and legs everywhere—not that the figures had looked exactly right to begin with. This was not Madame Tussaud of London's work. The Los Angeles radio station was giving it as much space as they had given the story about the Pietà being destroyed. And here's the capper: the manager of the wax museum, being an enterprising man, had put the mutilated wax stars on exhibit, opening it to the public, and attendance had tripled. People loved seeing Barbra Streisand with her head in her lap.

And what does this have to do with my cystitis? Everything. How can a person heal in an environment like this?

12

I played it cool with Linda. I didn't call her the minute I got well; I waited an hour and a half. The waiting did me no good. She just figured I was an hour and a half sicker than I was. Barbara Hirsh felt I was making the wrong move, wanted me to hold out for a few weeks. She had a point, but then again, Barbara Hirsh was a thirty-two-year-old single woman, who was desperate to have a relationship with anyone. There's an old saying that goes: "When you're getting advice from Barbara Hirsh, think twice."

I called Linda, went over. We had the same dinner. She built the same fire. Only this time when she beckoned me I was able to be beckoned. I didn't even see the inside of her bathroom that night.

The sex was good. Maybe it takes a good case of cystitis once in a while to get you really going again. I didn't know how Linda felt, but as far as I was concerned, she could kiss the black guy goodbye. David Meyer was back.

As we lay there afterward, sharing a joint and a Mounds bar, I should have been happy. Good fuck, good grass, good Mounds bar—what more could a guy want? . . . I wanted a commitment.

Yeah, I wanted a commitment. I didn't expect her to propose or give me a ring, but for Christ sake, something. I wanted some sign that I was going to be something in her life. I wanted my picture in the silver frame.

I said, "I love you," and she just smiled. For the first time in my life I could say "I love you" to a woman without stuttering, and I was getting smiles. Why couldn't she just say she loved me too? I know. I know. For the same reasons I could never say it before without gagging. I had the same reaction to saying "I love you" as I did to eating squash.

I said a lot of things to Ms. Minsk that night that just got smiles. One really schmucky moment was when I said, "Linda, I've thought it over. I'm not going to see anyone else." Who was I seeing? The lady at the cleaners? Linda smiled. Enough with the smiling. I wanted her to say she wasn't going to see anybody else. She didn't. She did, however, kiss my toes that night—not exactly a commitment, but you don't kiss the toes of someone you never want to see again.

After seven weeks of this (with one week out for a relapse of cystitis, four weeks to the day when it first hit—I was having a goddamn menstrual cycle), I finally had to know where I stood. Barbara Hirsh, in a 3 A.M. telephone call, warned me not to ask questions. Alan Milner warned me that some people feel suffocated by the idea of a commitment and if I pressured her I might lose the girl in the St. Tropez T-shirt. I couldn't help myself. Over icy Sara Lee cherry Danish, I said, "Linda, it's driving me crazy. I've got to know where I stand with you."

She smiled, but I gave her such a forlorn look, the girl had to answer me. The only way she couldn't answer me was if she had got frostbite from the Danish.

"Why can't you take one day at a time?" Oh, sure, Linda, throw it back at me, the very words I had said to every girl who had asked me for a commitment. Be an existentialist after kissing toes. Sure, Linda.

"I can't. I've tried, but I've got to know." The line usually goes on: "I've got to know if I'm wasting my time," or if they're really disgusting it'll be something along the lines of: "I've got to know if I'm barking up the wrong tree." Thank God, I had the sensitivity not to bring trees into it.

Linda smiled again. It was getting ridiculous. She was beginning to smile more than a Miss America contestant and/or Bert Parks.

"Look, David, I'm not doing numbers. If I knew exactly how I felt about you I would tell you. I really don't know. I do know that I'm very into myself these days. I'm getting some really good writing done. It may seem silly, but I don't know if I could love you and me at the same time." It didn't seem silly. There had been times in my life that self-love had made me incapable of becoming one of two.

"I'd like to read what you're working on," I said.

"I really don't want you to. I'm not ready yet," she said too honestly.

Silence.

"Did you like *2001?*" Linda all of a sudden asked.

"Yes and no," I said. Love me. I'll go either way. I liked about a thousand years of it.

"You see what I mean? I hated it. Thought it was a pretentious piece of shit. It's hard for me to love a man who even liked one frame of that piece of crap."

"I really didn't like it," I said, sticking to my nonconviction.

"But you liked some of it. . . . Oh, David, I don't know how I feel about you." She kissed my hand but gave it right back to me.

"I love you, Linda. Love me back."

"Did you like *Clockwork Orange?*"

"No," I said, hoping I was guessing right. My life at that moment was dependent on what movies I liked.

"Maybe there is some hope for us," said Linda Minsk.

Sure, Linda. Sure. You might as well rip off my fingernails and throw me into boiling oil. Pull out every hair in my head, one at a time, chanting, "He loves me. He loves me not." Drag my naked body over frozen Sara Lee Danish. Sure, Linda. You don't know how you feel. Maybe there is some hope for us. Who told you to say that? Did Kathleen Conway's mother contact you and tell you to say that?

"Well, I don't think I can go on like this," I said, trying to hang on to my balls.

"It's up to you, David. I'm happy with things the way they are, but if it would be easier for you if we didn't see each other . . ."

"No, it's O.K. I mean, I . . . uh . . . understand. Really, if this is the way you want it, I won't bring it up again," I said, dropping the balls I was trying to hang on to. They bounced on the floor and disappeared between the cracks in the floor, never to be seen again.

The prince wanted to live happily ever after and ride into the sunset with the princess. The princess wanted to screw around.

I decided to throw myself into my work. When Einstein and Arrowsmith threw themselves in, they came up with greatness. I got to work at eight and stayed so late I had to leave by the freight elevator every night. I was just giving myself more hours to come up with more mediocrity. It didn't matter how many hours I spent or how many half hours I helped develop. I was still not able to come up with any measure of relevance. It had been almost a year since Alan first gave me the assignment. I had to hope he'd forgotten about the whole thing.

"I'm going to put someone else on the series," said Alan with scorn, while we were both waiting for our Mercedeses, the last two on the lot. "Maybe I'll have it for next year."

"Don't be silly, Alan," I said. "There's an idea on my desk. My secretary is going to type it in the morning." The only thing on my desk at the time were the fingernails I had snipped off just before leaving the office. I don't know why, but sometimes I kept the tips of my nails after cutting them off. I guess I had trouble throwing away any part of myself.

"What's the basic premise?" Alan challenged.

My car miraculously appeared. I hadn't even heard it coming. When Alan Milner talked, you didn't hear sounds.

"You'll see soon enough," I said, slipping into my car. About every ten years, I have great timing.

The phone call came at about eleven o'clock.

"Hello."

"Hello, son."

"Pop, how you doing?" I didn't even think that it was 2 A.M. in New York, and that Myron went to sleep every night of his life at eleven-thirty.

"Your mother . . ." All he had to say was: "Your mother." I knew the rest. My mother was dead. My father was saying something about a stroke and a blessing in disguise. My mother was dead. Ironically the eleven-o'clock news was on and the anchor man was talking about a Mexican earthquake where thousands were believed to have lost their lives. It meant nothing to me. My mother was dead and I'd forgotten to tell her I loved her. I only sent last-minute flowers on Mother's Day. I didn't defend her when she took pictures at the Emmys. She told me big boys don't cry. Big boys cry their guts out when their mothers die.

A blessing in disguise, he said. He said she would have been a vegetable. They have medical miracles. If she were the wife of the president of the United States, would she have died? Why didn't she have a great team of doctors to keep her alive? If I had gone to medical school, I could have got my fellow colleagues to pull her through. If I were Einstein or Rockefeller or hadn't moved three thousand miles away from home, I could have helped. People in television don't get to help in the

178

real world. One day she found fourteen issues of *Playboy* under my bed and she smiled. I shouldn't have been embarrassed by my mother at the Emmys.

My mother hadn't died. You don't understand—it must have been someone else's mother. My mother was too young to die. I have a picture of her in a coat with a fox collar on the boardwalk in Atlantic City. If only Myron hadn't yelled at her so much. Why didn't I tell him to stop yelling? I could have talked to him and asked him to stop. . . . He didn't even know he yelled. And she was used to it. Why did she have to live her life with him yelling?

I took out her letters. I had accidentally or subconsciously saved a handful. God, they were sweet, every one of them asking me to look up cousins. I never did, but I was going to now. I was going to look up all of them, I vowed, as if that would make her happy. Oh, God, let her be in heaven. Let her know that I care, that I'll look up her cousins.

I had a friend whose mother died when he was seven. I remember he played with me the day she died. He would never see his mother again and we were flipping baseball cards. At seven, you can play on the day your mother died; at thirty-three you want to die too. I needed her. She gave me pajamas for Christmas still. Who else was going to give me pajamas I never wore, or keep track of cousins I never saw? Who was going to write to me? My mother died. Grandmothers dying I somehow understood, but mothers could swim and dance. A blessing in disguise, he said. Fuck it, Pop. Blessings don't come in disguises. If it were a true blessing it wouldn't disguise itself. I forgot to tell her she looks really good when she wears green. Oh, God, let her know that I'm going to look up her cousins.

The funeral was to be on March fifth, late in the day so I could get there. My sisters called with tearful details, both talking about a blessing in disguise. I told Linda I was leaving.

179

Without hesitation and without having to ask, she said she'd join me. You see why I loved her? She fucked me up, but she was there for me. She was one of the few Jewish girls in the world who could pack fast. My mother could pack fast too. . . . I wish my mother could have lived Linda's life.

How do you fall asleep on the day your mother died? Twenty milligrams of Valium, wine. I lay down on the couch and tried to keep awake, scared that I was going to dream about her and sure that I had to keep reminding God to let her into heaven. Please, God. If my mother isn't admitted to heaven, then who? I can't remember her doing anything wrong. I fought sleep with prayer. Went from wishing her in heaven to wishing it wasn't true to wishing I really believed in God. God, make my mother not dead. Linda, make my mother not dead. Alan, I lied. I don't have an idea on my desk. My mother's funeral saved me.

It's easy to dwell on death. I'm the type of person who believes that if I sit too close to a color television the radiation will cause me to die before my time. I still worry about fallout from the bombs they tested in the fifties. I think about the radium dial on my clock radio. Is it true that dial will erase three months of my life? Why is it they find that everything I like to eat or use causes cancer in rats?

Once our Hebrew school class visited an old-age home at Passover time. Our youth was supposed to cheer the aged up although I'll never figure out how that works. I was eleven and all I could think of on the way home was that I was going to die. For six weeks I didn't bother doing homework, figuring what's the use of doing homework when I was going to die anyway? At the end of the sixth week, my mother was asked to come to school and see the assistant principal. The three of us sat in his office. The psychologically oriented assistant principal led the discussion.

"Suppose you tell us why you're not doing your homework," said the psychologically oriented assistant principal, his hand on my shoulder, trying to be my chum.

"I dunno." I sure as hell wasn't going to tell him I wasn't going to do my homework because I was eventually going to die and when I did, no one in the whole fucking world would care whether I had done my homework or not. They don't even care if you did your homework if you're in television programming.

"Surely there's some reason why you've chosen to ignore your teacher's assignments?": assistant principal again.

"I dunno." He could keep me there until midnight. That was going to be my only answer.

"David has always done his homework before," said my mother, defending me. I looked at her and thought, She's going to die before I am. And she did.

What a psychologically oriented assistant principal couldn't get out of me in an hour, Myron got out of me in five minutes. *"Whadda you mean you're not doing your homework?":* screaming over his pot roast.

"Why should I do my homework? Someday I'm going to die," I shouted, but my voice was quiet next to Myron's.

"I'll give you die. If you don't do your homework tonight you'll die because I'm the one who's going to kill you." A half hour later, I was writing a five-hundred-word composition on what I thought the ending of "The Lady and the Tiger" was.

Linda and some part of me boarded a plane, went to New York, went to the funeral. I felt as if I was watching television. John Kennedy was in this coffin, not my mother. My sisters cried behind Kleenex, but Daddy and David were brave men. Linda held on tight, or was I holding on to her?

Back to my sister's suburban home, family all over the place. Everybody is very sorry. They're all saying she was a wonderful wife and mother. (In the eulogy the rabbi had called her a good Jew and a valuable member of the community.) All these peo-

181

ple consuming coffee and cake and wanting to talk. Three aunts told me that they liked my hair even though it was long. Two uncles told me I had gone Hollywood. Why were people still talking? My mother was dead. Her consciousness was never raised and she was dead.

These were the same people who attended Larry Meyers' funeral. He was my father's cousin and died when I was in high school. After the burial, the family went back to the widow's house. My cousin Beth and I, both around the same age, ended up in her bedroom. God forgive me. I copped a feel from my own cousin at her own father's funeral.

To the Women's Retaliation Committee, in care of Mrs. Conway:

Sisters, I am going to tell you something I have never told another living soul. My cousin David Meyer felt me up on the day that my father was buried. He made me swear, on my mother's life, that I would never tell anyone. Not wanting to be an orphan, I complied with his wishes.

Cousin Beth

I sat down in a corner. The group nearest me were relatives talking about an upcoming wedding. What a shame that Rose's daughter was marrying a goy. Had they forgotten that my mother was a convert? What a shame a goy was marrying Rose's rotten daughter who had a standing appointment with the dermatologist.

Linda, who had gone for tea, tried to work her way toward me; my Uncle Herman stopped her. You could tell Linda wasn't wearing a bra from where I was sitting. My uncle must have known for sure. My mother wouldn't have minded that Linda wasn't wearing a bra. That was the great thing about my mother. She coexisted with people.

My uncle was flirting with Ms. Minsk. She said something and he laughed. Goddamn ass laughed and my mother died.

Actually, I couldn't blame Herman. If I were an uncle, I'd flirt and laugh with Linda too. Why focus on a dead relative when there's a young, live, braless thing in the room? She eased away from him and tried to get to me. My fat cousin Ron captured her. Shit, I needed her. She was across the room and I needed her touching me.

Out of the corner of my eye I could see my father and Uncle Herman talking. The next thing I knew, my father was making head motions toward me. "Let's talk in private," his head was saying.

"David, I'd like to speak to you for a minute?" My father, sounding old, looking old, an old widower.

"Sure, Pop." I'm young and strong. Lean on me.

In order to avoid the crowd, we stepped outside, ignoring the cold March wind. No coats because we didn't have a mother to tell us to wear one.

"David, that girl—is it true what Uncle Herman told me?" He had to talk about Linda. If he didn't talk about Linda, he'd be thinking about Martha.

"What did Uncle Herman say?" I was scared. Instead of finding me looking at the Playmate of the Month, he found me with the real thing.

"Uncle Herman says that girl you brought worked in a massage parlor." Shit, Linda, you're not a dumb girl. Don't you know you don't tell an Uncle Herman things like that?

"She doesn't work there anymore. It was for research for an article. . . . She's really nice. She has all these plants." As if Myron was going to stop talking about Linda and start talking about plants.

"What did she do in this massage parlor? Did she give massages?"

"Sort of. She demonstrated waterbeds, gave massages, but it was only for research for this article she wrote. She's a writer, Pop. She has these great plants . . ."

183

"You brought a whore to your mother's funeral?"

"She's not a whore." What else can you say when someone's called your whore a whore?

"She takes money and gives sex. What do you call it?"

"She's Jewish." Is that a great answer to my father's question?

"A Jewish whore? Where did you find a Jewish whore?" Myron can't imagine there is such a thing. He has trouble accepting that Jewish people ski.

"I met her through a friend." You don't tell your father that you had to go to a whorehouse.

"Do her parents know what she did? Are her parents living?" You could see him thinking of my mother. The lines in his forehead were so deep. I imagine only those who are grieving have such furrows.

"I guess her parents know. They must have seen the article she wrote." I had never thought of that before. Her parents must know. "They live in Chicago. We're stopping there on the way back." I want him to start thinking of Chicago and to stop thinking of my mother. I can't bear his pain.

"What does her father do?" My mother has left him momentarily.

"He drives a cab."

"He drives a cab?" Again my father finds something about Linda incredible. He can't conceive of a Jewish father who isn't at least middle class. Surely he knows there are Jews in all walks of life, but something stops him from believing there is a Jewish person in Chicago who drives a cab.

"There are Jewish cabdrivers, Pop." I say it and he listens, but he doesn't believe.

"Do me a favor, David. I have nothing against the girl. Next time, just don't bring a whore to your mother's funeral." That is a statement from a very troubled man.

We walked back to the front door of the house silently. Just as we got there, I said, "Pop, listen, why don't you come out to the Coast and spend some time with me? It'd do you some good."

My father nodded. I would live to regret my offer.

13

Linda and I left New York, which looked dirty and fulfilling, as it always looks to Californians when they go back, and headed for Los Angeles via Chicago. Getting out was a tremendous relief. New York and my mother were linked. When I went back home to California, my mother wouldn't be dead. I'd just be missing her letters.

The flight was O.K. I'm not one of those guys who enjoy being thirty-five thousand feet in the air with no control. I sit near emergency exits, drink like hell and watch the stewardesses every time they demonstrate the oxygen masks. Linda curled up and fell asleep. I had to stay up in case the pilot needed my help in an emergency landing, and God forbid we should hit rough weather and I didn't feel it.

There was a mother in front of me with her infant son. My mother had taken me to Ohio to show her mother her infant son. I'm over thirty years older than this baby, I thought. If all goes well in both our lives, I'll be dying thirty years before him. I'm getting old. I'm going to the gym so I won't look middle-aged, but I do look middle-aged. I'm losing my hair. I'm the next generation to die.

My mother had saved my birthday cards from when I was a small boy. Those cards look like they're from a different era and could be sold in an antique shop—little boys in sailor suits with sailboats. My Boy Scout Handbook, which remains in my old bedroom (the bedroom is old because I am), has pictures of Boy Scouts in short pants. It looks like Teddy Roosevelt's Boy Scout handbook, but it was mine. David Meyer is perishing.

Linda woke up for the landing, even looked out the window at the lights of Chicago. Looking at landings made me sick.

"David?"

"Yes?" God, please don't let anything happen to this plane.

"I know I don't have to apologize for my parents, but I think you should know that they're . . . you know, not the easiest people in the world." We all made excuses for our parents when our friends and lovers were about to meet them.

"My father isn't easy," I said. My mother is dead.

"Mine are . . . they're not liberal. They're sweet in a way but . . . they're really hard to be with."

"Oh, come on, Linda, you're exaggerating."

"No, I'm not. My mother even left my father for a few years. We moved in with my Aunt Min and Uncle Frank in Parsippany. We went back to Chicago when my mother turned fifty and she finally realized Prince Charming wasn't going to come. She put on a housedress, never used perfume again and hardly brushes her hair."

And I was wondering why Linda didn't want a commitment.

We arrived in Chicago at about nine. Al and Helen Minsk met us at the gate. My mother always met me at the gate. Myron got hysterical at the idea of parking at airports and met me right outside the baggage pickup, where he managed to wait for half an hour in a three-minute waiting zone. Cadillac Power.

Al and Helen and Linda kissed and I shook hands and got looked over and I looked at the people who had produced the woman I loved. They were short, plain people. He was wearing one of those jackets with the fake fur around the collar. She was wearing—I don't remember: something Joanne Woodward would wear in a movie when she wanted to look unnoticed.

We picked up our luggage and carried it out ourselves. Myron carried his own luggage out too, only he tipped some porter because he didn't want the porter to think he was carrying his own luggage to avoid a tip. He carried his own luggage because he feared that he would never see it again. Everyone in airports was out to get Myron Meyer's suitcases.

Outside we got into a cab and I figured we were taking a cab to the Minsks', a normal assumption. We were taking a cab to the Minsks', only Al Minsk was driving. His picture was in front with his license and the meter wasn't running.

"We were very sorry to hear about your mother, David," said Mrs. Minsk, with careful compassion because we were strangers.

"I guess it was a blessing in disguise": me. My anguish had led me into buying the blessing-in-disguise excuse.

"She never knew what hit her?" Linda's mother again. She lived in Chicago, but Jewish mothers are the same all over the world.

"No," I said. "She went into a coma. Never even knew she had a stroke."

"That's the way I'd like to go," said Mrs. Minsk, and I couldn't fault her. That's the way I want to go. My whole life —no, since I was eleven and saw no need for homework—I hoped that I'd be fine up to about eighty-two and then I wanted to have a heart attack and die in my sleep. Second choice would be to die the way that old lady in *Pinky* died. I saw the film when I was very young, but I remember the woman died with very little pain and just enough energy to spout new-founded good-hearted philosophy.

While I was chatting future-son-in-law-style with Mrs. Minsk, Linda was tuned out, watching her home town pass by. Mr. Minsk had no idea what was going on. There was a shield between him and us so we wouldn't rob him. He was trying desperately to hear through the holes on the side.

"There are some nice little homes around here, about forty-five thousand. That's the neighborhood my husband promised me we'd move into when we first got married. Of course, we never did," said Mrs. Minsk. I smiled. Linda grew up surrounded by a vacant promise.

"On your left is a very nice section. They have beautiful new kitchens. I've been in one. About sixty-five thousand." I looked to my left to please Mrs. Minsk.

"Right there they go up to eighty, eighty-five, but they're not worth it."

"I see what you mean," I said, looking at houses in the dark, squinting to see why they weren't worth it.

"Straight ahead is the worst slum in Chicago. That's where we live." Obviously, Mrs. Minsk wasn't totally thrilled by her neighborhood.

"Yep, the worst slum in Chicago." She was making sure she made her point.

"Oh, Mom, it's not that bad," Linda tuned in.

"You can say that because you don't have to live here." She lowered her voice in fear. "It's all colored. I don't even walk around during the day. When Linda was young we used to sit outside in the summer. You don't dare sit outside now, unless you don't mind a knife in your heart. All around us is a sea of black faces."

"Mom, you sound ridiculously prejudiced." Linda was really irritated. I knew what it felt like to have a parent talk like that. I hated when my father complained about the blacks taking over or the Puerto Ricans running the city. He's full of all sorts of cute phrases like: "Let's have chinks tonight, if the *schwartze* isn't here." These remarks are very embarrassing to us liberal children who would have blacks as best friends if we could only find one we really had something in common with. Linda, of course, had a black lover framed in her living room, laughing at me.

Mrs. Minsk was not concerned with Linda's concern. She went on complaining for blocks about "All you see are coloreds." The topper was: "You can't even get a good chicken in this neighborhood. I heard in black neighborhoods they sell all the chickens that have cancer."

When we got to the Minsks', I realized that the Missis was not exaggerating. They did live in a slum—broken windows, garbage in the hall, "Fuck everyone but Ronda C." written on the steps. The Minsks lived in the kind of building you find on the lower East Side of New York, the ones that used to have charm with low rents and now have low rents and dirty words.

Mr. and Mrs. Minsk had been living in the building for over thirty-five years. They could tell you who used to live in every one of the apartments—the Lotkes, the Finemans, the Goldenmans. The whole thing reeked of Molly Goldberg. Obviously, many years ago, Molly and friends headed for the suburbs. The Minsks intended to but never could. They remind each other every night, I imagine, how they could have bought a place in '48, "practically a mansion for twenty-two thousand. You couldn't get near it now for seventy-five." They seem to forget that they didn't have the twenty-two in '48. I'm assuming that they didn't have the money then, because the Minsks talked about the time when you could steal half of Chicago for next to nothing. They didn't steal half of Chicago and you have to figure the reason is the Minsks didn't have next to nothing.

Al and Helen were the type of people who lived financially in the past. If you sat down to dinner and had roast beef, they talked about what roast beef used to cost in the good old days. They mourned for the five-cent telephone call and how you used to be able to drive out to this farm and buy a hundred eggs for eleven cents, or something like that. The Minsks used to go to the farm for the whole building. Now they wouldn't offer their neighbors a grain of salt. "Salt, by the way, costs four cents more here in the slums than it does in the white neighborhoods," said Mrs. Minsk.

We spent two days in Chicago. Me on the couch, worried that the chicken that was served had cancer, Linda in her old room, all faded pink and exactly as she had left it. In those two days we must have heard over five thousand complaints from Al and Helen. I nodded, Linda nodded. All they needed was nods to keep them going.

"Remember when the Minskys lived downstairs?" she would say.

"Our names were so close, the mail would get all mixed up sometimes. We would get theirs. They would get ours," he would say.

"But they always gave it back," she would say.

"Now we have to get to our mailbox the minute the mail comes," he would say.

"If you don't get it right away, the blacks take everything," she adds.

"They're looking for checks so they can buy heroin." He builds on her words.

"They shoot the stuff into their arms right outside our door." She finishes the routine. They're both triumphant that they get all the information out, from mail to heroin, without missing a line.

They would start with talking about Elizabeth Taylor and end up with murder on the roof. Very cute people. I couldn't figure out how they produced Linda. They were loud. She was soft. They were bitter. She was committed. They were short. Her legs began where their heads ended. Their features were all blended together. Hers were distinct. Both of them seemed

191

unmarriageable. Her I wanted.

When the two days had passed they took us to the airport.

"A dollar fifty to park, they get you coming and going," said Mrs. Minsk, as Mr. Minsk pulled the ticket at the parking lot. I wanted to pay for the parking, the roast beef, the taxi, but how do you arrange for things like that? I wondered if the Minsks took Master Charge.

Linda's father, while unloading us, firmly suggested to his daughter that she take out insurance. "God forbid, I hope and pray nothing happens." He didn't want his daughter dead, but just in case, if the plane happened to go down, they could move in with Jews again.

We got to the checkpoint, had our bags X-rayed, me nervous that they're going to find the joints in Linda's carry-on luggage. I *am* middle-aged. We got insurance, beneficiary Al Minsk, we got to the gate. Linda kissed her parents goodbye, and I got kissed this time too. Just as we were about to board, Mrs. Minsk said, "I don't want to hear that you two got married. I want to be there. Even if we have to take a bus to California."

"Mom, don't worry. We're not getting married," said Linda Minsk with finality. We're not? I thought. Oh, my God, we're not getting married? Does that mean never? You haven't caught me disagreeing with you about movies or queens or presidents. I thought now that my mother died we would be getting married.

14

I arrived home to find about five messages from Kathleen Conway. She had been trying me every day for a week, said my service. Either she had met someone who wanted to get into show business and figured I was a good contact, or the batteries in her vibrator were out, or she couldn't find a fourth for sex.

I called her back.

"Hello."

"Kathleen, it's David Meyer."

"Oh, hi. I saw your ad in the *Free Press.*"

"What ad? I didn't put any ad in the *Free Press.*" The *Free Press* in Los Angeles is famous for (1) thinking Charles Manson is not such a bad guy, and (2) its ads. It's the only paper in the world that advertises things like sadomasochistic house painters.

"There was this ad that said, 'Want to be in television? Straight guy in his thirties interested in video-taping sex acts.' I don't know why, I just figured it was you."

"It wasn't me, Kathleen."

"I guess I shouldn't have told my mother it was you."

"Is your mother still working on that Retaliation Committee thing?"

"Oh, yeah, and they're really getting far. They've got this

lady lawyer working with them and she thinks they'll be bringing guys to trial real soon. They are going to get publicity on it and my mother's picture might be in the paper and everything. My father moved out on her."

"I'm sorry to hear that."

"Don't be sorry. My mother is thrilled. She said for the first time in her life she can have the toilet whenever she wants."

"Well, nice to hear from you, Kathleen."

"Yeah. I was sure you were the one who put that ad in."

"It wasn't me. It was some other guy who likes to beat up women. . . . That was a joke, Kathleen. Don't tell that to your mother."

What if Mrs. Conway got her committee going? What if the lady lawyer got the trial going? What if . . . ? When I was about eleven years old, I would come home from school to find my mother in the kitchen preparing dinner and watching the McCarthy hearings on a small television. People had black-and-white televisions in their kitchens in those days and the little gray men who were investigating and the small gray figures who were being interrogated couldn't touch my life. I measured them once. These enemies of the people weren't as big as my thumb. I was scared of the Commies—they had the atom bomb, which could kill us all—but, perhaps instinctively, maybe because they looked so small on television, I wasn't afraid of the people this McCarthy seemed to be afraid of. If Mrs. Conway and her committee were going to bring men to trial and these trials were televised, one could only hope that children would come home from school and measure the men against their thumbs.

Alan Milner was relatively sympathetic on my return to the office. "Sorry about your mother," he said, his eyes refusing a direct confrontation. I was glad he was looking at the ceiling and not on my desk, where the nails I had cut over a week before were nested.

"It's O.K." I excused Alan from emotion.

"My mother is in Minneapolis," Alan said straightforwardly. This was the first I heard that Alan had a mother. Asexuals' past lives are hard to imagine. In the nursery do they dress them in yellow instead of pink or blue?

"How were the ratings?" I asked to save Alan from talking about mothers.

"We're O.K. on the weekends but we lost every week night but Wednesday," Alan said with more sorrow than he expressed about my mother.

"There's got to be a better system than the Nielsens." When the ratings were high, the Nielsens were considered accurate by everyone at the network. When they were in the toilet, they were a totally invalid system.

"I've promised New York some better programming. You know, something . . . relevant."

"Maybe you should put someone else on it, Alan," I said, failing.

"Look, if you come up with an idea . . ." he said graciously because my mother died.

Alan left my office and with him left my chances for success in network prime-time television. David Meyer was all right for giving notes to writers and dealing with agents on actors, but he wasn't the kind of man Babe Paley would marry. Leave him in his smaller office and let him know that this is his life, there is no promise left of future greatness. He's never going to own even one of Hugh Hefner's mansions, or a Rolls-Royce, or not have to be upset over a large plumber's bill. No mother was ever going to look at her five-year-old son and proudly announce, "He's a regular David Meyer."

Linda and I continued along the same lines that we had

before the trip back east. We got together when she wanted to and if she didn't want to I simply died, picturing her beside some stud, saying, "You're great. The guy I sort of see is all right, but he's got this receding hairline that really annoys me." She still wasn't giving me a commitment, and more and more I was blaming it on Paul the expensive hair stylist.

"Why can't you just take things day to day, why do you need a commitment?" said the lady in the cleaners while stapling tickets into my best silk shirt.

"Because my mother died."

"You're confusing Linda and your mother," said Barbara Hirsh.

"I'm not."

"Forget this girl Linda. There are plenty of fish like her. Your mother, she was something special": Myron.

Linda is special. Why was my mother special to you and not Linda to me?

"I don't want to talk about you anymore," said Alan Milner.

"I'd like, on behalf of the United States of America and the WRC to bring Linda Minsk to the stand," would say the prosecuting attorney.

"No, no, you can't. A wife can't testify against a husband. Please, not Linda!"

"She is not your wife, sir."

"I want her to be my wife. I need someone to go out and get me cigarettes if it's raining and I have a runny nose. I need someone to hold my hand if I'm dying. I want a commitment."

"Do you like the book *How to Be Your Own Best Friend?*": Linda.

"I don't know."

"I hope you don't. I couldn't sleep with anyone who would go for that trumped-up philosophy."

"I don't want to sleep with you. I want a commitment."

"Did your father vote for Nixon?": Linda.

"Probably."

"I once broke up with a guy just because his father voted for Nixon."

"Linda, *please*, I want a commitment."

"We all want commitments," said the lady in the cleaners.

"I love her. I'm scared I'm going to lose her. My mother is dead."

"You're confusing Linda with your mother. She's not your mother": Barbara Hirsh.

"I mean it, David. I don't want to hear about it": Alan Milner.

"I'm not trying to hurt you, David, or drive you crazy. I just don't know how I'm going to feel tomorrow."

"I love you, Linda": David Meyer.

"I'm happy you do": Linda Minsk, and she smiled.

About a month after my mother's death, Myron called. He'd been calling, two, three times a week, but this was a call I wasn't going to forget.

"David, I think I'll take you up on your invitation. I'm coming out."

"Sure, Pop, when? For how long?"

"Day after tomorrow and I don't know how long."

Do you know what it's like getting a call from your father that he's coming out and you don't know how long he's going to stay? I got this feeling that I was being strangled by an umbilical cord, and my father and I had never been attached in that way.

The truth of the matter was Linda had fucked me up so much that there were times when I wasn't easily distinguishing between the sexes. My father had an umbilical cord. I had two periods—cystitis, but regular. Linda had masculine independence and I wanted security. I was not suited for work. She was on the verge of putting together a documentary on the woman's role in film. Linda called me, and we used her Master

Charge. I had a standing appointment at a hair stylist. She could shift. I was upset if I didn't have time to get a manicure and I wanted to be Mr. Linda Minsk. I didn't foresee what was happening. Even the great Marsha Shanks couldn't have predicted it. Who could have known that David Meyer, who didn't have to pick up his underpants because he was a boy, would end up not knowing whether to use Secret or Right Guard? He didn't know whether to smoke Marlboros or Virginia Slims. He didn't know whether to identify with Adam or with Eve.

My fuck-up happened because I was dealing with a new kind of woman, one who can say to her Jewish mother that she's not getting married. Put her together with a man—O.K., not any man—me. What you get is the first of its kind. David Meyer, a straight guy who has taken on the feelings, including the two big ones—the desires for permanence and security—that used to belong to women. There were even moments, I swear to God, Gloria, that I wished she'd marry me so I wouldn't have to work anymore. I'd be so happy to keep her dinner warm. I would take our clothes to the laundry and water the plants. I guess this switch was bound to happen. Whenever new people are created, counterparts must evolve for them. It's just a damn shame I had to be the first. I'll probably end up in some book of firsts. Armstrong—the first man to step on the moon: "one small step for a man, one giant leap for mankind." Meyer —first man to remain straight and yet have a feminine emotional system: "One small step backward for a man, one giant leap for womankind." If I had been second or third, it wouldn't have been so painful. I was first, Gloria. *I was the first straight man in the whole world to have vagina envy.*

I picked up my father at the airport and we drove home almost silently, remembering when there were the three of us driving back from the airport. All Myron managed to say was: "You still have the Nazi car."

198

I gave Myron your typical offspring-to-father talk after the mother has passed away. "Pop, you know the best thing for you to do is to get out and not sit around the house and mope. I loved Mom, you know that, but, Pop, you have to go on living." Nice and trite, this obligatory You-have-to-keep-on-living speech. I expected my father to mope around the house, but I had to deliver the words anyway.

That night when I got back from work, my father was in the living room with a twenty-three-year-old girl named Mary Ricker. They were laughing and drinking sangría. God only knows what they smoked. God only knows where she came from. I never asked him and he never told me. I can only imagine California girls can smell rich widowers. That very night my father took Mary Ricker into the guest room. How could you, Pop? How could you make it with this girl on the same waterbed that you slept on with my sweet mother? I shall never again underestimate the power of my speeches.

After Mary there was a Suzie, then a Laurie and a Marcie and a twenty-year-old Nancy. There was a Betty something who I knew for a fact was in *Playboy*—not a Playmate of the Month, just one of those nude girls of Los Angeles, posing with her ass in full view, the La Brea Tar Pits in the background. (I enjoyed that issue. The issue I hated was the one that featured the Girls of Israel. I don't know about anybody else; I hated seeing naked sabras.) All of Pop's girls were dumb, irrational, had tits and looked like they had hobbies—exactly the type of girl I went for before Linda. I guess it applies to fucking: like father, like son.

My father bringing home the broads made me realize that although I once went for the Miss Januarys of the world, I didn't want them now. Linda had spoiled them for me. Once when Ms. Minsk couldn't see me, I took out my little black book and called up a good old-fashioned lay, even took her to dinner. The evening left me empty. I had no desire to make it with this fucking machine. I took her home after dinner. Just dropped her off, wondering what went wrong. I'll bet the girl changed her deodorant the next day. Once I even tried to conjure up an old fantasy. She came but she was, after all, an old fantasy and old fantasies, like old soldiers, just fade away. Was I going to be the first guy in the world to masturbate to *Ms.* magazine?

A few months after Myron came out, I drove home from an especially difficult day at the office (a writer tried to convince me to do a series about a forty-year-old executive who was never toilet-trained) and my father was waiting at the door.

"Son, I have good news," said a father who happened to be mine, who happened to be desperately trying to grow a mustache, who had buried his wife of thirty-nine years a mere few months before.

"What, Pop?" I was scared to ask. He was full of surprises. I wouldn't swear to it, but one night he had had both Suzie and Marcie over and I'm almost sure Myron Meyer had a three-way.

"I'm getting married," said Myron Meyer, who was now unconcerned about community property laws.

I said, "Great." But I wasn't happy. I was the one who wanted the commitment and he was getting married. My new mommy was going to get all my daddy's money that I was in line for. (That was the first thing my dear sisters thought of. They spent hours on the phone begging Dad to reconsider. One even said it wasn't fair. That can only mean one thing— it wasn't fair that some strange lady was going to get lots and lots of financial benefits that she thought she was going to get.)

The lady, it turned out, was twenty-year-old Nancy. Nancy's parents were delighted that Myron was marrying her. She was the youngest of eight children and it seems Myron had knocked her up.

"Oh, Pop, how could you be so careless?"

"She told me she was on the pill."

"And you believed her?"

"Yeah." The whole situation was impossible. My new mom was twenty. There was no way Myron was going to outlive her, unless she sat close to a lot of clocks with luminous dials. Nancy would get the dough.

"Why doesn't she have an abortion? They're legal now, you know."

"I don't want my child aborted. Suppose when your mother got pregnant with you, I asked her to have an abortion. Where would you be then?" Where am I now? In the toilet.

"But if you don't love the girl . . ."

"Who said I don't love her? I do love her. I want her to be my wife. We're going to get married in a forest and make up our own ceremony."

"No rabbi?" I said, clutching my heart. First the mustache and now this.

"Nancy and I believe in God, but not necessarily in religion." This was the man who was afraid I was going to give up Judaism if I moved to California.

"Pop, how could you do this to me?" I said, being a Jewish father to my Jewish father.

"Don't worry, David. If it's a boy, it'll be bar mitzvahed." I was relieved.

I told Alan Milner that my father was getting married. He thought my father's life would make a good situation comedy. Maybe he was right. I just didn't want to hear that my father's life could be laughed at once a week.

I told Barbara Hirsh my father was getting married. She got all teary-eyed. Big girls cry about weddings.

I told Marsha Shanks my father was getting married. She said that the wedding shouldn't be on an odd day. A man in his sixties was marrying a girl in her twenties that he had knocked up. The wedding was going to be in a forest. It was going to be an odd day.

I told the lady in the cleaners that my father was getting married. She asked me when I was getting married. I cried in the cleaners.

I told Linda my father was getting married. She thought he was a fool. "Why doesn't he just live with her?" she said. "Why don't I just live with you?" I said.

"O.K., why don't we live together? Only it's got to be at my place, and remember, David, no commitment." Qualifications, but I was thrilled. Maybe the girls at the office would throw a shower for me.

My father had a beautiful wedding. Nancy wore a lovely white maternity gown and Myron was glowing. The forest they had chosen was a bit chilly, but guests didn't seem to mind. Myron even let his bride go barefoot. He would never let me go barefoot in a chilly forest. I'll bet he won't even make his new child wear an undershirt when he swims, his first day out in the sun. Bride and groom promised, in their own words, to fill each other with laughter and love and things like that. Before I could get the pine needles out of my suit, my father was married. My sisters refused to come to the wedding and at least one brother-in-law was starting annulment proceedings. Brothers-in-law are good at things like that.

There are no rules, but it seems to me that if the man wants to be king of his castle, it better be his castle that he and his little lady move into. The day I moved into Linda's, I gave up all chances of ever being king of anything. She was the queen and I was the court jester, which simply meant I better laugh at my situation or be out on the street.

I was close to Linda. That was good. The picture of the black guy was still there. That was bad. She couldn't ask me to leave after fucking. That was good. There was very little closet space and I had to live out of a suitcase. That was bad. The lady in the cleaners didn't like it either. Linda was faithful to me. That was good. The house had a one-car garage and my mail never reached me. That was bad. Linda, on the strength of the first draft of her documentary, got it optioned by Wolper. You're probably thinking that was good. That was bad. She liked her work better than I liked mine. Bad. I got home earlier than Linda because she was so wrapped up in her writing she lost all track of time. That was also bad. It gave me an hour and a half to get dinner ready. I didn't mind. I didn't really mind doing the laundry either. It had to be done. I just knew it was bad.

Not only was I nowhere near head of the household, I was becoming an excellent homemaker. I pasted Blue Chip stamps into books because I wanted to and knew which bleach got the clothes whitest because it gave me a high. Not that Linda ever noticed how clean and bright her T-shirts were. I was taken for granted, but there were ways of getting back. It was very easy to develop a headache just around bedtime. That was bad.

Two months after I moved in with Linda I got the flu and ended up in bed. I watched soap operas and really got into them. I was hoping that Ted would get Louise off the murder charge even though she was having an affair with James who was in Miami. It took a long time to recuperate and after three weeks of missing work, it was obvious that I wasn't really interested in getting better. I had started this herb garden, and I had gotten into *The Guiding Light,* and between taking things to the cleaners and getting the vacuum cleaner fixed, et cetera, et cetera, I didn't know where my day went. Before I turned around, it was time to get dinner. If Judi Rosenberg could see me now.

DEWAR'S PROFILES
(Pronounced Do-ers)

NAME: David Meyer

SEX: Unsure

OCCUPATION: Housewife

LAST BOOK READ: "101 Ways to Use Campbell's Cheese Soup"

QUOTE: "I did your bras in cold water, dear, and they came out just as clean."

SCOTCH: You bet, and he always makes sure to use coasters.

Linda had got a pretty good deal on the film and liked having me home and getting the vacuum cleaner fixed, so it seemed very logical, at the time, for me to stop working. I told Alan Milner on a Monday morning.

"Well, Alan, I have decided to stop trying to claw my way up to the middle, ha-ha-ha."

"You're resigning?" Alan said, with too big a smile.

"Yeah, Alan, I'm giving up all the glamour of a job in television to do what I do best. I'm going to be a housewife." Alan didn't laugh. I'll bet asexuals are the first ones to adjust to new roles. They've got the least to lose.

"Well, if that's what you really want. I'm not going to try to stop you." If I had told Alan that I was leaving to commit suicide or to become a eunuch, he wouldn't have tried to stop me.

"Isn't it crazy, about Linda and me?" I continued because I felt a resignation needed length to have significance. "We're your typical fun couple, only I'm in the kitchen and she's in the world. She's bringing home the bacon and I'm cooking it and we're both liking it very much this way."

"That's the show," said Alan, getting up to think on his feet.

"Excuse me?" Two minutes out of television and I didn't know what the word "show" meant.

"You're living the show we've been looking for."

"I am?" We were looking for something relevant and I

204

couldn't believe my life held any relevance.

"Let me think it out," said Alan, pacing past me.

"He's tired of the rat race and not very good at it," thinks Alan. "She is tired of staying home. They're both unhappy. One day he gets sick and has to stay home and he asks her to go to work and cover for him. Maybe it's his own construction business or something like that and he doesn't trust his partner. Something like that. She does such a good job that he never gets well. He takes over for her at her bridge club, wants to be president of the PTA. She negotiates with hard-hats. There's something there. Can you write it up right away?"

"I can't. Today is laundry day," I said.

"Do you mind if we use it?"

"Alan, it's yours. My legacy to the network. My contribution for all the years I sat at my desk and came up with nothing but taco stands in the East."

"Taco stands?"

"It's a long story." And I stood up to go. Instead of shaking hands, we embraced, the only time I ever made physical contact with Alan Milner.

I enjoyed just staying home for a while, even bought new curtains for the kitchen, and then got bored with the whole thing. I was just about to rebel when Linda got offered a job in the story department at Wolper, and thank God we could afford to hire someone to come in and clean twice a week. This gave me a chance to take an adult education course in conversational Spanish at U.C.L.A. Twenty-three ladies and me learning how to tell our Mexican maids to clean the toilets thoroughly.

Gloria, life went on. I can't pinpoint the exact day that I became your typical housewife, but I guess it was around the time that I said something very close to: "You never take me anyplace anymore," and she said, "For Christ sake, David, I'm tired at the end of the day. Why can't you understand that all I want to do is spend a nice quiet evening at home? Is dinner ready?" and Linda plopped down on the couch.

"In five minutes. I didn't want the veal to overcook and I didn't know what time you were coming home. God forbid you should call and let me know you're going to be late."

"Veal? Christ, I don't remember the last time I had veal and I had it for lunch today."

After about six months of this kooky fun life, I wanted to have a baby. Yeah, I did. I used to go to this park on Beverly Glen near U.C.L.A. to study my español. I didn't study. I looked at the mothers with their babies in the park and I wanted one. It's fairly normal for a guy to want a kid. I wasn't fairly normal. I would look at pregnant women and wish it was me. If it had been possible, I would have had the first womb transplant.

In our third year of marriage, Frances wanted to get pregnant. I couldn't have cared less, but if Frances wanted a baby, I figured what the hell, I might as well cooperate. If she wanted a kid and wanted to take care of it, it was all right with me. I could give my father his first grandson—up to now my two sisters had produced three girls—and a picture of a kid would look good on my desk and on Christmas cards. I didn't picture myself changing diapers and made Frances understand that the responsibility would be hers.

"It's O.K. with me, but I'm not going to get up at all hours of the night. You understand that kids are a mother's work."

We started trying in December. I remember because it was the Christmas card idea that really got me going. Frances flushed her pills down the toilet. Every month we fucked when we were supposed to fuck. Nothing happened. By June, Frances visited her friendly gynecologist, who put his friendly finger up her and told her he couldn't find anything wrong. He sent Frances home with temperature charts and thermometer,

206

and she faithfully took her temperature and charted the results. When her temperature was up, she summoned me and I came, ha-ha.

An entire year went by and it seems that God didn't want to bless us with a little baby. God also didn't want Frances to stop taking her fucking temperature (that's what it really was—a *fucking* temperature). The obstetrician finally told Frances that she was getting too nervous and should relax. I knew a couple once who tried to conceive and couldn't. The doctor told them to relax. They got so relaxed they didn't want children.

Frances and I flunked relaxation. Another six months went by. God didn't want us to have a little baby even if we relaxed. Frances wanted to adopt. Myron said, "Adopted kids never turn out right. Look at the Friedlanders—they adopted Jerry and he gave them nothing but trouble." Why it was even discussed with Myron I don't recall. What I do recall is that everything was discussed with Myron and you can add adopting children to the things Jews don't believe in.

One day I got home and there was no Frances, just a note: "Meet me at Dr. Kassendorf. 417 East 39th." A note like that is not easy to ignore, so I met her at Dr. Kassendorf's, all the way there imagining her bleeding to death.

She wasn't bleeding. She was waiting for me in kindly old Dr. Kassendorf's office. Kindly old Dr. Kassendorf was on the phone, but when he got off he let me have it.

"Mr. Meyer, are you really interested in having a child?" He said it like a high school principal would say, "David, are you really interested in graduating?" My high school principal did say, "David are you really interested in graduating?" after I refused to write my autobiography in creative writing. I tried to write it. I couldn't. It turned out to be all about Myron.

"Yes, of course I'm interested in having a child." I didn't add, "Only if I never have to hear crying in the middle of the night."

"You're not just saying that because Frances wants one?"

"No." The true answer was "Yes."

"I'm glad to hear that, because we're going to need your help."

"Well, I certainly hope so," I quipped, balancing my chair on its two back legs. I think I did that in the principal's office too.

"It seems that there is nothing wrong with Frances." I didn't know what he was getting at. "It's possible that she hasn't conceived because she's been uptight." "Uptight" sounded wrong coming out of his mouth. He was trying to be my doctor pal, but he wasn't pulling it off. "It *is* possible there is something wrong with you, Mr. Meyer."

You think so, huh? That's inconceivable, doctor! There is nothing wrong with David Meyer. Maybe he gets a cavity now and then, but there is nothing wrong with him regarding anything to do with his reproductive system. Frances was a sneak getting me to come by leaving a note saying that she was bleeding to death.

"I would like to have a sperm count done on you, David." Count all the sperm you want, doctor. You're not going to find one missing.

Frances was looking at Dr. Kassendorf's many diplomas. He graduated from the Trinity School of Medicine in Ireland. Couldn't get into a school in this country, huh, doc? What the hell do you know about counting sperm? When it comes to my sperm, I bet you can't even count that high.

"A sperm count?" I queried. We're talking about bringing a child into the world and I'm quipping and querying.

"We take a sample of semen to the lab. Just to make sure you are producing enough sperm and of a high enough quality to impregnate Frances."

I, doctor, have enough sperm to impregnate every man, woman and child on Manhattan Island. If you want to count my sperm, it's perfectly fine with me that you count my sperm, but you better be prepared, doc, to do a hell of a lot of counting.

The thing about this sperm-counting business is it is quite humiliating, to say the least. The semen has to be delivered from home to lab immediately or something happens to it. That meant I had to collect the sperm at home, on East Fifty-ninth, and go directly to East Thirty-ninth. Frances offered to help with the collecting, but I preferred to take care of it myself. I told her making sperm was man's work and it is, ladies. Come on. It is.

The first batch I brought in was classified as unsuitable for counting because I hadn't brought it in fast enough. The nice nurse suggested that I use the facilities right there in the office to make my deposit. I said, thank you anyway, I was in a hurry, but I'd try again from East Fifty-ninth.

I got another little container and tried again. You know what I found out? Masturbation is no fun when someone gives you permission to do it. Even as a married man with affairs on the side, occasionally I jerked off. I had a hell of a good time. I thought I would really have a good time if a doctor said I could do it and didn't even mention I would go blind or anything. Nope. I hate to be the first one to tell the world, but masturbation doesn't make it when someone gives you the seal of approval.

The second batch was also unsuitable for counting. The nice nurse suggested again, a little more firmly this time, that I give at the office. Her suggestion led me into a bathroom right there in the lab. A bathroom with a faulty lock. I was given a small glass bottle and left to produce that which was to be counted after I dumped it into the bottle.

There I was in a suit and tie, thinking about the nurse, who knew what I was doing. I took my jacket off, loosened my tie and shirt, dropped the pants, leaned against the door because of the faulty lock and tried to get it up for all the little people who were depending on me. I couldn't turn myself on. It was like when they put you in a room to pee in a plastic cup and you can't. You're embarrassed and mortified and the nurse comforts you, explaining that it happens to the best of pee-ers. She gives you the plastic cup to take home and bring it in at your convenience. You drive it in, hoping it doesn't spill all over the car on those turns. This time the nurse wasn't going to say take it home. I'd already had my chance at home. How the fuck was I going to tell the nurse I can't masturbate? The whole world can masturbate. I thought of turning on the water but realized that was for peeing. I called on every fantasy I ever had. The pages of *Playboy* were floating by and nothing happened.

Sex fantasies gave way to other fantasies. Flashing before me was a copy of *Reader's Digest* with an article entitled "I Am Joe's Penis," with the subtitle "Thank God I'm Not David Meyer's." Then I am on the cover of *Newsweek* and there's a diagonal streamer which reads: THIS MAN CANNOT MASTURBATE. On page fifty-four in the media section is a story about one David Meyer, who can't get it up for himself, and how they're going to make a television special starring Alan King.

It wasn't funny, gang. There was a nurse outside, knowing what I was trying to do in there. My hands were tired. I was rubbing myself raw. A half hour went by. There was a knock on the door.

"You O.K., Mr. Meyer?" said the nurse.

"Fine . . . fine," said the brave war hero, whose pubic hair was caught in his zipper.

"I was worried because it usually takes only five minutes, ten at the most." Sure, rub it in, nurse.

"There's nothing to worry about. I just got a late start." Whatever the hell that meant.

"O.K. Just remember, we've never lost a man yet." She

chuckled at her little joke. Sure, nurse, have a good laugh at the expense of David Meyer's member.

It got to the point that my penis was so sore to the touch that folding it into my Jockey shorts was painful. But I was going to take it like a man. I would march right up to the front desk and tell the nurse that because of the psychological pressure this laboratory had caused, due to faulty locks and other unsavory things, I was unable to come in the bottle. My people would be in touch with her people about this. Then I got a better idea.

This place, where they asked you to do disgusting things to yourself in the bathroom, was also a sperm bank. I had seen the labeled bottles and the refrigerated vault on my way into the bathroom. (I'm surprised women's groups haven't picketed sperm banks. I would have expected them to carry signs reading: "Sperm Banks Unfair. Won't Let Women Donate.") I dressed slowly and quietly, getting into a real James Bond mood. I opened the door slightly, as Sean Connery would, slipped out of the bathroom and worked my way slowly and cautiously down the hall, sticking close to the wall. Sean would have been proud of me. I caught a flash of white coat and ducked into a closet. James Bond would have reached for a gun that would have been in his pants. If he was in my condition, a gun in his pants would have killed him. I listened for a moment, heard nothing and opened the closet door a crack, just enough for one eye to look. The coast was clear, as coasts should be. I worked my way to the door of the vault and ran into a bit of luck that James never would have run into unless he wanted to have a fifteen-minute movie. Sitting on one of those trays with wheels were a dozen bottles like the one I was given when I entered the bathroom, only mine was empty and these were full. I grabbed a bottle containing the sperm of Mr. George Fromer and put it under my coat. A lab technician appeared from around the corner and I gave him a friendly

211

nod, as if we were neighbors on Fifth Avenue, not walking around semen.

I got back to the bathroom safely, transferred Mr. George Fromer's sperm to my bottle, warmed the bottle up a bit in my hands, and gave it to the nurse on my way out. I made my getaway with legs spread, but I made it. I wonder, I thought, if I am the first man in the world to rob a sperm bank. Maybe I'll rob other sperm banks all over the country. I could be the Billy the Kid of the sperm bank set. "O.K., nobody move, just put all the sperm you have in the bottle." How many years can you get for robbing such a bank? I imagine nine months.

"What's the matter, buddy?" the cabdriver said. "You got your balls caught in something?" New York cabdrivers can get very personal sometimes. People ignore it because they'd rather have embarrassing questions asked than risk the subways. I gave the guy an extra-large tip to show him that I didn't care what he said about my balls, and waddled into my apartment.

Frances was there. The lab happened to go looking for the Fromer sperm right after I left and figured I had made the switch. They had called Dr. Kassendorf. Dr. Kassendorf's receptionist had called Frances. That made five of us who knew what happened, not counting the cabdriver, who might have taken a wild guess but I can't be that paranoid and think he knew. My wife cried and asked me how I could do such a thing. I shrugged my shoulders because I knew I didn't have to give Frances answers. Disgusting? Yes. We're talking about a disgusting guy who stole sperm and ignored his wife.

I didn't go to work that day. The drapes were drawn and I lay down to rest until the whole thing blew over. I never did get my sperm counted. Frances never did get pregnant. (Which, by the way, has been classified as another one of your blessings in disguise.)

Unfortunately, this incident has a sad ending. Mr. George

212

Fromer was a seventy-year-old man who had never had children, but he wanted to carry on the Fromer line. I had contaminated his sperm. He would have a hell of a time donating again.

The years before the sperm-counting incident and wanting to have a baby had been spent, spermatologically speaking, in making sure I didn't impregnate anyone. I wore rubbers at first, but once the pill came out I expected all my girls to provide their own protection. I only got caught twice in my life. I had to chip in for Desiree Goldblum's abortion at B.U. and there was a five-hundred-dollar abortion for my secretary at Meyer and Meyer. I didn't mind the money. It was the drive to New Jersey on a Saturday that killed me.

Now that I wanted to have a baby, such things as contraceptives became my enemies. Linda was on the pill, so I really couldn't wait around for an accident. Every time we fucked, I kept thinking of all my wasted sperm not being able to fertilize her pill-protected egg. I thought of the mothers in the park while we were screwing.

For four weeks I told myself the only reason I wanted a child was because I thought I could get Linda to marry me. By the fifth week I accepted that I wanted a baby simply because I wanted a baby. The lady in the cleaners felt I wanted a baby because my father was going to have one. I thought she was wrong. My father had seventeen golf clubs and I didn't want even one of those.

Barbara Hirsh, after hearing how much I wanted a child, volunteered to be the recipient of my sperm. Do you believe that? That's a nine-month favor. What could I do in return—take care of her fish and plants for nine months? That really turned me off Barbara Hirsh. What type of human would allow themselves to be a packaging device?

The lady in the cleaners thought I should talk to Linda about

213

having a baby, but first I should put her in a good mood by bringing her candy. "Here you go, Linda, a whole pound of candy. Will you have a baby for me?"

I tried on numerous occasions to bring up the subject of having a child. I would say, "Isn't it nice that Pop is having a baby?" Linda would say, "Yes." I would say, "I think it would be a great idea if we had one." She would say, "No, I don't want to bring up a child in a world where they dub foreign films."

"You don't want to have children because they dub movies?"

"You don't understand. It's not the dubbing, it's the falseness of the situation. We're living in a society where one person moves their mouth and another person speaks."

Whenever we saw a kid in a car seat, in a store, on the street, I would point it out. "Look at that cute kid," I would say, jealous that it wasn't mine. Linda would drag me away, saying something like: "I couldn't bring a kid into a world where people have hair transplants. Do you realize, David, that there are people who take hair from one part of their head and have it put on another part!" It became evident that she wasn't going to give in. It would have to be an accident. Accidents ain't easy. Let me revise that: Accidents ain't easy, Gloria, when the man wants one.

Just for the fun of it, let us examine this situation in reverse. Linda wants a baby. She merely stops taking the pill (or punches holes in her diaphragm or lets her coil slip). Two months later she complains about the ineffectiveness of those goddamn pills (or diaphragm or coil), but she has her kid. Men have never been able to sneak one through, which I think is entirely unfair. There's been plenty of talk about the male contraceptive, but where is it, doc? Are you going to tell me that in my lifetime conception cannot take place just because

I want it to? I'm always going to need her permission and she's not going to ever need mine? Unfair. Women have complete control over their bodies and men are left holding the bag, so to speak.

15

Before any of us realized, almost a year had passed since my mother's death. My father, very pregnant Nancy, Linda and I went to New York for the unveiling of her tombstone.

The morning of the unveiling, Nancy didn't feel well. While we were having breakfast at one of your less glamorous New York pancake houses, she kept saying she felt like she had to throw up. We all told her it was because of the long trip and maybe she shouldn't have taken such a long trip in her eighth month. (My father reminded me to say sixth month, lest we further embarrass him by letting the family know his girl had conceived out of wedlock.) Nancy insisted she felt funny. We insisted she had eaten her blueberry pancakes too fast.

The four of us arrived at the cemetery, my father and I a bit shaky facing the reality of a woman we had loved in a grave. We were greeted by a hostile family. The uncles hated Linda and me because they couldn't have her. The aunts had a feeling we were living in sin and having wild sex. (To them, wild sex was doing it on the same day that they went to the beauty parlor.) My father and his bride with child they didn't want to deal with at all. The entire family was snickering on all sides of us. If snickers were waves, we would all have drowned, despite the fact that I was a lifeguard one summer.

I was a little nervous. Having been to my father's unorthodox wedding ceremony, I was afraid that those two crazy kids (Dad and Nancy) were going to push the rabbi aside and frug or something. I thought two people who got married in a forest, pledging eternal love to trees, would not go for such a traditional service as an unveiling. They remained respectfully silent, however . . . until Nancy's scream.

The rabbi said, "Friends and relatives of the late Martha Meyer . . ."

The relatives said, "It's disgusting that Myron brought the new wife here today."

I said, "I love you, Linda." Linda smiled.

The rabbi said, "One year ago beloved Martha was laid to rest."

The relatives said, "Look at Myron's mustache."

Nancy said, "Jesus Christ, the baby's coming."

The rabbi said, "We all have missed her."

Nancy said, "Myron, the baby's coming."

Myron said, "What should we do?"

Nancy screamed, "The baby's coming. Get me the fuck to the hospital." Everyone heard.

My father turned to the hostile crowd and yelled, "It's premature. Oh, my God. It's premature."

The rabbi (as rabbis do) went on. The crowd snickered, saying things like: "The body isn't cold yet" and "It's a blessing in disguise that Martha didn't live to see this." And the one I love most: "That girl has no respect. How could she have a baby on the day of Martha's unveiling?" Linda ran for the car that had brought us to the cemetery. My father and I dragged and carried Nancy from my mother's grave. Myron kissed select relatives goodbye on the way out and repeated over and over, "It's premature. It's premature." Nancy panicked, yelling, "Hurry, please hurry. I don't want my baby born in a cemetery. It's bad luck." All you could hear toward the end was Myron: "It's premature! It's premature!" He told the

217

guard at the gate it was premature.

Naturally, we got to the hospital in plenty of time, hours before we had to. This being her first child, Nancy had got hysterical despite the natural childbirth classes she and Myron had attended faithfully. It took us the whole way to the hospital to convince her that her baby wasn't cursed just because the contractions began in a cemetery. At one point she said, "I know it was your wife, from the other side, reaching out and starting those pains." Myron gave her a look that said, "Don't you ever mention Martha again. You're unworthy." He loved my mother.

The hospital would try to help us, the head nurse said, though they were not used to people from the West Coast coming in and having their babies. Their labor rooms are booked way in advance, they told us, and a doctor, well, they don't come easily on Sundays, but they managed to get an obstetrician who, out of the kindness in his heart, would deliver yet another child into the world. The whole ordeal was worse than checking into a Hilton hotel that's all booked up when you don't have a reservation.

Finally, because they were such nice, kind, considerate nurses and doctors, Nancy was put on a table and wheeled to the labor room. Linda didn't see me, but I cried. A baby was going to be born and I wanted a baby so much it was almost painful to go to the park these days.

"You're lucky you're a boy, David. You'll never have to go through the pain of childbirth": Myron Meyer in the 1950s.

"I'm not lucky. I'd go through the pain. I want a child": David Meyer in the 1970s.

Approximately four hours after her arrival at Montclair General Hospital, Nancy produced a son. They would call it Joshua Elias. I was extremely upset. Jealous. A little sibling rivalry there, between a thirty-three-year-old man and a newborn infant.

I was in a state of shock and everyone, including Linda, thought this was just a strong reaction to the birth of this child. I did react strongly, but no one will know how strongly until the autopsy, when they discover that part of my guts are missing due to the birth of my little brother.

It never dawned on me that Myron would have a boy. He was going to have a baby—just a baby. If it had to have a sex, it would be a girl. Myron was always having girls, except for me. *I was Myron's son.* Meyer and Meyer means me, not some infant that had the bad taste to start pushing down in a cemetery.

Myron beamed at Joshua through the nursery glass and I wanted him to be beaming at me. Myron held the little baby during circumcision and I wanted him to be holding me. I would have gone through circumcision again just to be held like that by my father. Don't you see, Pop, I was supposed to be the only son? The boy. The one who got to go into the business. Oh, Pop, out of all the sexes in the world, why did it have to be a boy? Pop, if Joshua and I were in a boat that was sinking and you could just save one of us, which one of us would it be? Save me, Pop. I'll bet you're thinking that this little pisher is better than me just because he didn't lose you one point five million dollars. One son is enough, Pop. You had your boy and you stopped having children, remember? You didn't stop after the girls. After me you didn't have to have any more. I'm your son, Pop. Who is this Joshua?

I don't know if what I did was due to the insecurity, or that I was spending too much time at home feeling sorry for myself, or if there was mischief in the air. While Linda was at work one day, I took her birth control pills, flushed them down the toilet and replaced each pill with a baby aspirin. Two months later Linda came home with an inner glow. "I'm fucking pregnant," she said, sighing and slumping. "And I'm having an abortion on Monday."

"Linda, please," I begged. "Let's keep the baby. I can take care of it."

"It's not fair to the child. Do you want to bring a child into a world where there's pollution and wars and Bob Hope Specials?"

"Bob Hope Specials?" She always had a surprise for me.

"Yes, you heard me."

"Bob Hope is only on once or twice a year."

"But the whole country watches. Think about it, David. We live in a country where everyone watches Bob Hope Specials. Is that what you want for your kid?"

"We could not let him or her see them. We would move to someplace like France."

"France, huh? You picked a good one. I'm not going to live in a country where they think Jerry Lewis is a genius."

"Switzerland?" No one ever gets upset about Switzerland.

"David, I'm having an abortion Monday."

"Linda, you can't do this. I want that baby more than I've ever wanted anything . . . except you." Please, Linda, make an honest man out of me.

"No."

"It's not fair. It's my baby too."

"It's my body." Yeah.

There's something wrong, Gloria. It takes two people to make a baby. It is the union of my sperm and her egg. It takes two, and yet only the mother has the right to decide to get rid of it. On Monday morning she alone would choose the fate of that child. (I guess hearing you're pregnant and breaking your garbage disposal have something in common when it happens on a Friday night. There's nothing you can do about it until Monday morning.)

I had only the weekend to save my child, a short seventy-two hours, and they were weekend hours, which makes them less

valuable. "I'm not keeping it"—[she refused to call it a baby]
—"and I mean it, David."

"I want it. I'm keeping it."

"You can't."

"I'm going to try."

"Why, David?"

"Because I have maternal feelings for what's inside your
body, Linda. You don't, so I do. Someone has to care about
babies. This world has changed. The women don't care about
offspring anymore, so the men will. It's called propagation of
the race, Linda."

"David, please. Don't you see there's nothing you can do?
Sometimes when the baby is born the man can get custody, but
this is different. There is no baby."

"There is no baby because I don't have a womb."

"Why are you so insistent?"

"Because, Linda, I have maternal instincts for that baby and
we're new people."

Linda lit a cigarette in a way that I knew she was going to
talk. "We're not new. We're reversed. All mixed up and reversed. God, we're nowhere near new. You're a housewife
from twenty-five years ago without the housedress and curlers,
but with the same ambitions to have pure white laundry and
babies to fulfill your life—and I'm no better. I think of myself
as an up-to-date, modern, liberated woman. Nah. I'm you. I'm
your father and his father. I'm like a man from centuries ago,
abusing people of the opposite sex. It's funny how far we think
we've come."

Linda Minsk had us figured out.

"You're right, Linda, but knowing you're right doesn't stop
me from wanting this baby."

"Of course not," she said. "And it won't stop me either."

221

"I'm going to win." And I closed the door. Didn't slam it, just closed it hard.

I drove to the nearest pay phone. One right on the Strip. As I was getting my dime out, it rang.

"Hello," I said, because I pick up ringing phones.

"Hi," said a voice trying to be sexy. I was confused. "We're in the apartment across the way." I looked. There were two girls in short little nightgowns, waving.

"Yeah?" was all I could think of.

"Want to come over and have a good time?" they said.

"No, thanks," I said. They were wasting part of my seventy-two hours.

"Fag," they said and hung up.

Instead of call girls, they were calling girls. Phone booths have done wonders for some businesses (theirs and Clark Kent's, for instance).

I dialed Information and got a number for Ashley Fenton in Westwood. (Yes, Virginia, there are Gentile lawyers. They appear in movies and are available on Friday nights.) Ashley Fenton was a cousin of my mother's, the first cousin I looked up after making all those promises to God and Martha the day she died.

Mr. Ashley Fenton was home. He would see me at his home in Westwood on this urgent matter that was too important to discuss over the phone. Thank you, Mr. Fenton, you're a true credit to your race. The minute I put down the phone, it rang again. A reflex action had me pick it up.

"Fag," the voice said.

"I heard you the first time. You could have saved a dime."

"You're not going to stay in the booth all night, are you?"

"Why?"

"Because you're fucking up our business, fag." Losing a dime isn't the worst thing that can happen in a phone booth.

I raced to Mr. Fenton. He was very nice in a soft, Christian way. He had a paneled den with leather books and you had the feeling that nothing had been changed since 1948. We talked about my poor mother and then he lit a pipe, sat on the edge of the desk and said, "So, son, tell me what's wrong." I wished I was there to discuss getting into law school or who was going to win the big game. I hated to bring up the subject of abortion in his forties den.

"Mr. Fenton . . ." I began.

"Why don't you call me Uncle Ashley?" he said. Oh, boy, golly gee, it was going to be very, very hard to tell Uncle Ashley about my unborn child.

"Well, Uncle Ashley . . ." I choked it out in a voice I hadn't heard since my bar mitzvah. "Uncle Ashley, I . . ." I was Mickey Rooney talking to the judge.

"What's the matter, son?" He actually had his hand on my shoulder. "Did you get a girl in trouble?"

"Yes, sir," is what I said. Uncle Ashley made me say it.

"Well, son. The right thing to do is marry her." Time was going, but I knew I had to play out the scene. He's telling me to marry her and my gut is hanging out because she's going to kill my kid.

"She doesn't want to get married, Mr. . . . Uncle." I've got to get out of here. Somebody turned the hourglass over and the sand is pissing away.

"Does she want an abortion?" he inquired, lowering his eyes on "abortion," playing with his pipe.

"Yes, sir, she does." I was developing a Midwestern accent for the purpose of this conversation.

"Well, in the case of wayward girls, sometimes abortion is best. I don't prescribe it, being a religious person, but in the case of wayward girls, sometimes it's best." Oh, God, I've got to get out of here. Let my person go.

"You don't understand. I want to keep the baby." I

shouldn't have said that. I should've said he was right, thanked him and left. He actually laughed when I said I wanted to keep the baby, this Uncle Ashley.

"That's silly, David. You must think practically. Who would care for the child?" I would. I'm the child's mother.

"Look, I really want this baby. I was wondering if there is any way possible—legally, that is—of keeping the girl from having an abortion. I helped to create that child. Don't I have any rights?" Uncle Ashley reached for a leather-bound book and I believed that within the pages of that book he would find the answer. Something like: "Let it be known from this day forward, under the Constitution of the United States of America, it is illegal for a woman to have an abortion without permission from the fetus' father, hereby giving the man certain rights regarding his unborn child."

Uncle Ashley didn't find the answer in that book. He read me something about property rights that was supposed to relate to what I was talking about, but didn't. He invited me to stay for a light supper and told me it was a blessing in disguise that my mother died. (We all sound a bit Jewish sometimes.) I thanked him and he told me that he was pleased that he could help. He actually believed he had helped. As I pulled out of the driveway I thought he shouted jovially, "If it's a boy, call it Ashley," but it couldn't have been that. It makes no sense. He was standing in the doorway, tall, white-haired, cashmere sweater, pipe and golden retriever. Norman Rockwell would have eaten it up.

From the trial of David Meyer, as imagined by D. Meyer.

"We would like at this time to bring Mr. Fenton to the stand." He would get up and move forward.

"Do you swear to tell the truth, the whole truth and nothing but the truth, so help you God?"

"Of course I do, ma'am."

"Mr. Fenton, did one David Meyer, the defendant, come to you for help regarding his unborn child?"

"Yes, he did, and you can call me Uncle Ashley."

"What did you do about his request, Uncle Ashley?"

"I invited him to stay for dinner."

"That's not true," I would scream out. "He invited me to stay for a light supper."

Next stop, the Beverly Hills Hotel. I needed phone booths and they had some of the best phone booths in town. In the lobby, racing to the phone, I was stopped by Phil Waxman, a friend from B.U. whom I hadn't seen since B.U. Thank God he was in a hurry. There was just time for: "How's everything with you, Phil?" "I'm in business with my father." "You look great." And he managed to show me a picture of the lovely Mrs. Phil Waxman and children. They were ugly baby pictures but they were baby pictures and they managed to bring tears to my eyes. I felt like a fool, standing there in the lobby crying over some other guy's kids.

"You O.K.?" Phil was totally confused. He expected me at most to say they were cute. He would have been happy with a nod. There I was, wetting his pictures with tears. We both pulled out handkerchiefs, him to dry his pictures, me my eyes.

"I'll be O.K.," I answered, pushing him on. Phil stared at those pictures all the way to the door, wondering, I'm sure, what was so great about them.

I went to the telephone booth and called Legal Aid. A first, I'm sure. I'm almost positive that nobody has called Legal Aid from the Beverly Hills Hotel before. The phone rang about seven times and I was figuring nobody was there on a Friday night at eight-thirty. I was just about to hang up when a woman answered.

"I desperately need legal aid," I told her, thinking she would put me on with her boss, a radical young man with beard who would fight my cause to his death because he knows I'm right and because he defied his parents who saved to send him to law school and lived to see him decide to become a poor lawyer.

"Well, I was just leaving," said the woman, "but if you're that desperate . . ."

"Is there a lawyer I can speak to?" I said, trying to get as much desperation in my voice as possible.

"I'm a lawyer," said the woman. Jesus Christ, foiled again. Of course there are woman lawyers, David. *Her* parents saved up for law school and lived to see *her* become a poor lawyer.

"My name is David Meyer and I need help," I said.

"You realize that Legal Aid is for the benefit of those who can't afford legal help. Do you earn less than two hundred and eighty-five a month? You can add a hundred dollars for your spouse and fifty for each child."

"Yes, I haven't even been working and there is no wife . . . or child. Can I come over?"

"I'm closing up here. Where are you now?"

"The Beverly Hills Hotel." You know when somebody crunches a beer can with their hand? That's what I felt she had just done to the phone. There are certain things you just can't say to people who devote their lives to helping the poor and "Beverly Hills Hotel" is one of those things. Abercrombie and Fitch, Louis Vuitton and Jackie are a few others.

"I'm not staying at the hotel. I just came in to use the phone booth. Calls cost a dime here like everywhere else. You've got to help me, please." Please, lady lawyer.

"Well, look, why don't you meet me at the corner of Santa Monica and La Brea? I have an hour. We can talk at Nino's, which is right near there."

"Santa Monica and La Brea," I repeated.

"I'll be in a white Volks," she said with pride.

"I'll be in a brown Mercedes," I said with trepidation, knowing that Mercedes was in the same category as Beverly Hills Hotel. A Rockefeller would never have trouble using those words. He also would never get Legal Aid to meet him.

She let the Mercedes reference drop. I guess because I never mentioned the year. We met with pinpoint accuracy, parked and entered Nino's, a small bar that thinks just because it's dark it has atmosphere.

Rachel Rubin was the name of the lady lawyer, a short, overweight girl of about thirty-five with not much going for her physically. I think she agreed to meet me since she knew that I was single. I think she decided on Nino's because she knew it was dark. I decided immediately I would fuck her if that's what I had to do to get her to help me save my baby.

"Daddy, tell me the story about the lady lawyer again."

"Will you eat your liver and spinach if I do?"

"Yes, Daddy."

"Well, O.K. Your mommy wanted to kill you before you were born, but I wanted to have you so I laid this lady lawyer so she would help me."

"That's a funny story, Daddy."

"Yes. Now finish up and I'll tell you how I saved the rest of the world."

We were seated in a booth in back; she was doing a lot of eye fucking, with eyes that were wearing false lashes that popped up at the end.

"So, Mr. Meyer, what do you want from Legal Aid?" A very leading question to ask in a dark bar. The answer Miss Rubin probably wanted was: "You, Rachel."

"I got this girl in trouble . . ." Oh, my God, I hadn't changed gears. I was still into talking to Uncle Ashley. Start again. "Do you believe that a man has any rights to his unborn child?" I asked, begging for a yes.

"What do you mean?" challenged Rachel, like she must have challenged her professors at Harvard Law.

"I've been living with a girl for almost a year now." I lost Rachel. "But that's not the point." I got Rachel back again. "She's pregnant with my child." Lost her. "She wants to have an abortion." Rachel was almost back, but not quite. "I want her to have the child. It means a lot to me. I always wanted a baby . . . not always, but for a long time now. I see the mothers in the park and . . ." Rachel was totally confused. Her eyes were moving so fast she couldn't possibly fuck with them anymore.

"You want to stop a girl from aborting your child?" She got it on the first try.

"Yes. Please, can you help?" I was crying again. "Big boys don't cry, David." Big boys cry, Pop, when their mothers die and their babies are being killed.

"There have been cases where the father has been awarded the child when the mother has wanted to put it up for adoption, but . . ."

"But what?"

"But the baby was born. A woman has a right to abort . . ."

"You don't understand, Miss Rubin. I've got to have that baby. I don't know if in my lifetime I will have another chance to help create life. Even if there is another chance, so what? Just because my baby is temporarily housed in somebody else's body doesn't mean I should stand aside and let my child be slaughtered."

"But what about her?"

"What about the kid . . . and me?"

"A woman should have some rights. After all, it is her body."

Shit. Just plain shit, Miss Rubin. I know, for Christ sake, that it's her body. Don't you think if I could have that baby removed from her body and put into mine that I would do it? I would have that baby put in a jar, its umbilical cord a rubber tube. In nine months I could open the jar and take that baby home, Miss Rubin. At least it wouldn't be flushed down some sewage system.

"So you're against abortion?" Miss Rubin challenged.

"I'm not against abortion," I answered wearily. "Abortion is right. There should be no unwanted babies in this world. The baby I'm talking about is wanted."

I never did get through to Rachel Rubin. She spent an hour and a half trying to talk me into the "but it's her body" theory. She spent a half hour explaining that it would do absolutely no good to start legal proceedings; by the time it got to court, the abortion would be long over. There was no such thing as being able to legally detain an abortion. Miss Rubin also spent half an hour trying to convince me to come home with her. I went to her house, thinking it might help, fucked her, thinking it might help, and afterward she cried. Rachel Rubin cried because she had lied to me.

"What's wrong?" I said. The girl was crying. I had to ask. In the old days I wouldn't have bothered. You see, Mrs. Conway, it was a new David Meyer.

"I lied to you," she said.

"You mean there is a way I can stop the abortion?" I said hopefully.

"I don't know about things like that." A tear was rolling down her pimply face. A lash was also rolling down.

"You don't?" I was confused.

"I'm not a lawyer. I'm only a secretary at Legal Aid. I knew you wouldn't meet me if I was only a secretary."

I picked up the receiver, handed it to Rachel and said three simple words: "Call your boss."

"What?"

"You heard me, Rachel. Call your boss. I want to talk to him immediately."

"It's eleven-thirty."

"I know it's eleven-thirty. Call your boss."

Rachel looked petrified. She was reacting like I had turned

into the Boston Strangler. Her whimpering was excessive, but she called her boss.

"Hello, Mr. Finerall. I'm sorry to bother you so late on a Friday night, but . . . Yes, I'm fine. My voice is funny because I have sort of a cold. . . . Listen, I called you because this very nice man has a question. . . . He can't wait until Monday. . . . Please, Mr. Finerall, talk to him . . . please. I don't know what he'll do to me if you don't." She handed me the phone and went to whimper in the corner.

"Listen, Mr. Finerall." I tried to sound sane and nice. "I am certainly not going to do anything to hurt Ms. Rubin. I had to speak to a lawyer and I asked her to call you. You know how hard it is to get a lawyer on Friday night."

"Yes?" He spoke for the first time.

I calmly explained the Linda Minsk–David Meyer situation. I had it down to a good, heart-warming four minutes by now, getting in all the details and enough emotion to make a half-back on the Rams cry.

"I am sorry, Mr. Meyer. There's really nothing you or I can do about it. There have been cases where the father gets custody when the child is already born. If the girl wants an abortion, there's nothing we can do."

"Thank you for your time, Mr. Finerall."

"You're welcome, Mr. Meyer."

"You do understand why I want this baby."

"Yes. I do. You'll probably be a wonderful father."

"Mother."

"Yes . . . mother." Mr. Finerall was the first person who really understood.

I held Rachel Rubin until her whimpering stopped. In the old days I would have left. These were the new days. I held women for no other reason than that it helped them.

"You didn't hold me, David, when you left."

"I know I didn't hold you, Frances. I've changed. I understand what

holding means. I'm like a woman now, Frances."

I drove around awhile, got home at two. Linda was asleep, but I could tell she was expecting me home. The way she was sleeping—just on one side of the bed.

I got up at seven and placed calls to Melvin Belli, F. Lee Bailey and Louis Nizer. Got two answering services and one answering machine. Linda got up, dressed and went to the studio for a Saturday taping. Neither of us mentioned our baby.

I called Rachel. Maybe she'd know another lawyer's home phone number. She didn't. She wanted to know if I wanted to meet her at Nino's again. No, Rachel Rubin. I never want to see you again; go tell someone else you're a lawyer.

At nine-fifteen, less than forty-eight hours to go, I turned the Los Angeles Yellow Pages to "Attorneys." I started with *A* and went straight through. Mostly I got answering services and machines. I left my name and number, expecting not to hear from any of them over the weekend, even though I begged. About a dozen of the dozens I called answered the phone, but none of them could help. They didn't understand or they didn't do that type of work or would I call them during business hours. One wife answered and I gave her the whole four-minute spiel. I got to her. She swore to God that her husband would call. He did. Unfortunately, he was in theatrical law and although my case was dramatic, it wasn't his line. I pleaded. No, Mr. Meyer, no. He had heard of a case where the father got custody, but that was after the child was born. . . .

There are thirty-two pages of attorneys in the L.A. directory. I stopped at around the *E*'s and switched to the Beverly Hills Yellow Pages. I just needed a change. Same story, except Beverly Hills had more answering services. As a matter of fact, a lot of them had the same answering service. One answering service lady didn't even have to ask me for my name. She'd say,

"I'll give him the message, Mr. Meyer." About the fifteenth time, I gave her the four minutes. She was the most helpful one of the day. She left word for every lawyer client she had that I hadn't dialed yet, saved me from making all those calls.

I fell asleep at about four-thirty and dreamt that Melvin Belli called me back.

"Hello."

"Hello, I'd like to speak to a Mr. David Meyer."

"This is he."

"This is Melvin Belli." We were talking on the phone, but we were in the same room and Mr. Belli looked like James Mason.

"Mr. Belli, I called because I need your help. My girlfriend wants to abort my child, but I don't want her to." By this time we were off the phone entirely. I was lying on one of those rolling tables in a hospital, exactly like the one my father's new wife had been on, surrounded by pregnant women in labor. Mr. Belli-Mason was there beside me.

"Of course I'll help you, Mr. Meyer. We'll take it to the Supreme Court if necessary, and don't worry about the fee. You can give me a hundred dollars."

Just then a doctor, who looked like Winston Churchill, started wheeling me down the hospital hall. I looked down and saw my stomach was huge. There was a three-year-old child sitting on top of it. The child was there but Winston Churchill kept wheeling me to the delivery room.

I kept screaming something like: "I can't have a baby. I'll be late for work." It doesn't take a degree in psychology to figure out the symbolism here.

Winston Churchill said, "Relax, David, you're going to be a mother."

I never found out why Winston Churchill was with me. Linda had returned home, called my name and awakened me instantly. You know that feeling when you're dreaming one minute and awake the next. I knew where I was and everything, but the emotion of my dream was still with me. I wanted to still be sleeping. Imagine never finding out why Winston Churchill was with me.

It was a strange Saturday night. Linda was tired and wanted to stay home. She sat on the couch reading something about lay psychology. I sat watching her because I loved her. When you really love someone, you can sit and watch them read on Saturday night. It should have been a peaceful evening. It wasn't. Lawyers kept calling back. Not a lot, but at least ten. Each time I had to jump up, drag the phone out of the room, speak in hushed tones, pretending not to want to disturb Linda. She would look up as if to ask who it was. I told her my father, Nancy, a wrong number, wrong number again, that guy should check Information, Barbara Hirsh, my father—he forgot to tell me something—that fucking wrong number again, Alan Milner, and isn't it funny that everybody seems to be calling tonight.

Not one of the attorneys who called was any help. They all had the same story: they'd heard of a case where the father got custody, but that was after the child was born. I was out of my mind, they thought. You'd think there would be one out of the ten I could get to, especially since they took the time to call back. If I had been yelling, "Whiplash, and it's the other guy's fault," they would have been able to relate.

Sunday. Linda had to work. She gave me a peck on the cheek as she left, the obligatory kiss. I watched her car pull out, closed the door and went to the Yellow Pages. Started calling every gynecologist-obstetrician in the 213 area code. Their answering services, hearing it was a life-and-death matter, put me through. You can get through to these guys because they're all in partnership and one of the partners is always on call in case one of their pregnant patients delivers. They didn't want to know from me. Their first impression was that I was some religious fanatic trying to preach anti-abortion. They sounded a bit worried, as if I was an obscene caller, or perhaps they felt that I was going to blow up their sailboats or their Lincolns.

"Sorry to disturb you, doctor, but I have a problem and I was wondering if you could help." I was exceedingly polite and had developed this fourteen-year-old voice, so they usually stayed to listen.

"Yes?"

"My girlfriend is pregnant with my child and is planning to have an abortion on Monday. I would like to stop that abortion from taking place, sir, because I would like the child, sir, and I was wondering if . . ."

"I'm afraid there's nothing . . ." You could tell his mind was back on the football game, worried about the point spread.

"Surely, sir, you must see that the father of the unborn child has some rights."

"I can't help. Why don't you call a lawyer?"

"Please don't hang up."

"Please don't call again." And he'd hang up.

One doctor went into a long explanation of how in Russia they had succeeded in transplanting a fetus from one woman to another. Interesting but no help. If they were doing this type of thing in Southern California, perhaps I could get someone to carry my child. I could place an ad in *Variety* for an actress who wants a life experience and won't be busy for nine months. Barbara Hirsh could apply.

One guy, a Dr. Sykes, was very sorry he couldn't help but would love to talk to me since he was writing an article for some medical journal on the male feeling during pregnancy since the liberated woman has become a factor in our society. I tried making a deal—I'd help him if he'd help me—but he wouldn't go for it. It seems he was more important to my life than I was to his article.

234

Linda was due home at seven. At two o'clock I started calling women's groups like NOW and Women For. I figured if they're really into equal rights, there might be hope for me. Those groups are not at work on Sunday at twelve. I got one girl whose organization, entitled Single Women With Children, had headquarters in her home. I heard the children screaming in the background.

"Hello, I'm calling you because I am interested in your organization." That confused her. I was probably the only man ever to call with that line.

"What is it you want to know?" And then she shrieked at a kid: "Melinda, if you don't get that out of your nose, I am going to personally kill you!"

"I would like to stop my girlfriend from having an abortion because I would like to raise the child."

She slapped a kid and said simply, "Why?"

"I love it. I know it's hard to love something before it's born, but I do."

"Take my advice, mister. Be thrilled your girlfriend is having an abortion. . . . Melinda, if you don't put down your dress by the time I count three . . ." I hung up, tried to get a number for Men's Liberation. There is none in the great city of Los Angeles.

By one-fifteen I was feeling defeat. It's the moment when the general realizes he'd better hang out the white flag, the doctor stops pounding the patient's heart and the president resigns for the good of his home in San Clemente.

God, I thought, why aren't you helping me have my child? It was no use trying to obtain God's help. He's not into men yet. I think there is a God, but he's behind the times. I think he's still looking after veterans from World War II, and that he hasn't even gotten into the Vietnam crisis. I think God is still looking after women and children first. That's what I think. God is not dead. He's just living in the past.

I tried. I figured my biographer couldn't say I didn't try. I had the first case of calluses on the finger due to punching a push-button phone. I had dry mouth from all the pleading. Even my ass hurt. I had let the parade pass by. O.K. I dragged my tired body into the bathroom and let the water into the tub. Funny, I had started taking baths when I moved in with Linda. She took showers and there were times when we were both cleansing our bodies at the same time. When we didn't share the shower, in the heyday of our love, I took a bath. My mother took baths and my father took showers. My sisters took baths and I took showers. Here I was at the lowest point of my life, in a bathtub. Gloria, Gloria, what divisions we were taught to follow.

I often thought while in the tub. In showers you sing, in tubs you think. Head back, eyes closed, hot water on, keeping the water steaming, I thought that my baby would end up just where the bath water was going when I pulled the plug. I wished I was rich as Rockefeller. Maybe, I thought, if Linda was offered a million dollars . . . Nah. She had convictions. She didn't marry people because they laughed in movies.

I thought hard. Prayed. Thought. The light bulb came. I got out of the tub, didn't bother to dry off, ripped apart the L.A. *Times*, went through the ads in the real estate section, ran to the phone, called my father and asked him if I could come over and discuss some very important business. He said yes. It was going to be all right. Maybe.

16

I got to the Myron Meyer home to find my father watching a
Rams game, Nancy baking bread and my brother Joshua hanging from some swing contraption in the doorway—your happy
American family, West Coast style, the wife waiting for her
husband's fatal heart attack.

"Pop, I need your help."

"Sure. Oh, my God, look at that, he fumbled. Idiot! You got
anything on the game?"

"No. Listen, Pop. This is important."

"Idiot, just drops the ball. I've got the Rams and six and a
half. I'm throwing a hundred bucks down the toilet. You sure
you don't have anything on the game?"

"I'm sure. . . . Pop, listen . . ."

"Never bet against me, David."

"I swear to God, I won't."

"A son shouldn't bet against a father."

"Pop, I have three buildings in my name, or rather part of
three buildings, right?"

"You know you have part of three buildings. Is that what you
came over for? Asshole." In this case, I wasn't the asshole. It
was a Ram. They were showing an instant replay and Myron
was still pissed at the fumble. You've got to picture this scene.
My father's eyes were glued to the set. I was about to pour my

guts out and he was more involved with anyone on the field than he was with me.

"Pop, I figure that my share of these buildings is about seventy-five thousand, about twenty-five each. Is that right, Pop?"

"What? They got him!"

"My share is worth about seventy-five thousand."

"I figure ninety by now. Ninety easy." Time out. He was looking at me.

"Pop, I want to sell my share of one of those buildings." He was back to the set. Didn't answer me until the next play was completed. Thank God, it was a first down for the Rams. Myron was up. My child's life was now dependent on a football game.

"You can't sell your share."

"Why?"

"You can't just sell your share. There are three other owners of those buildings." He was referring to himself, my uncle and my cousin.

"What about if I sell to you?" The ball was thrown, a beautiful pass, gain of twenty-three yards. Myron was out of his mind with happiness.

"You want to sell to me? Why?"

"Pop, please, I need the money. I really do." I could tell he was receptive. It wasn't me, it was the twenty-three yards.

"You shouldn't sell. I made those investments for you to have security. Not to sell."

"I have to, Pop. My kidney is no good. I have to go on one of those machines." Great lie and I hadn't even thought it up in advance.

"Did you get a second opinion?" Because of the game, it was only half sinking in. A son just told his father his life was in danger and the father was on the thirty-two-yard line.

238

"I got a million opinions, Pop. Really. I need thirty thousand."

"I'll pay for the machine. Don't sell. Bitch! Did you see that asshole?" I couldn't let him pay for the machine. There was no machine.

"I don't want you to pay for the machine. Look, Pop. Why don't you give me the thirty thousand? You can put my share in Joshua's name." I swear the baby smiled. Touchdown! Myron jumped up and cheered. Turned to me.

"You really have a bad kidney?" He had heard. He just couldn't give me the emotion while he was giving it to the Rams.

"I do, Pop." I crossed my fingers in a reflex action.

"I'll pay whatever. You know that."

"Pop, please. Give me thirty thousand. You put my share in the baby's name." They were going for the extra point. Myron's eyes went back to the set. Good.

"O.K., David," said my father, and the crowd cheered.

Linda and I arrived home at the same time. After hellos and how was your day, I laid it on her.

"I want that baby, Linda."

"Come on, David. You're overreacting."

"If it was a three-year-old and I prevented it from getting stabbed to death, would you think I was overreacting?"

"Don't be ridiculous." I loved her.

"I want to make a deal with you."

"Why do you suppose you're reacting this way?"

"We're semi-new people. You need to work and I need to know that the butcher gives us a good piece of meat. I also need to have a baby. I go to department stores and end up in infants wear. Those little clothes are killers, Linda. I pick out quilts and diaper sets and I leave with nothing." I spoke softly and she smiled. Maybe she loved me too.

"David, try and understand. I'm having an abortion. Not to hurt you. It's the way I feel. Do you want a kid of yours to see *Hollywood Squares*? If a star in one of the boxes dies, they keep showing him answering questions for months. Is that an environment in which to raise a child?"

"I want to make a deal."

"I don't."

"Don't you even want to know the deal?"

"What's your deal, David, and the answer is no."

"If you have this baby—and once it's born you don't have to have anything to do with it, it will be completely my responsibility"—I hesitated because here it was, the whole thing—"I will see to it that your parents have a safe, happy life."

"What?" I don't know what she was expecting, but I had caught her off guard.

"I have obtained enough money to get your parents out of Chicago and into a beautiful home in Leisure Village, right here in Southern California, a hundred miles away, mind you, so they won't be dropping in all the time." She didn't say anything, so I went on, sounding like an overzealous salesman for Leisure Village. "There are garden apartments, just like individual homes, with tennis courts and a golf course and a temple and a hospital right on the premises and guards at the gate. No one can get in and out without a pass. It's very safe."

"My mother was mugged," she said sadly.

"She was? Why didn't you tell me?"

"I couldn't talk about it. . . . They pushed her down and took her bag."

"That wouldn't happen in Leisure Village. It's so safe. I swear there are guards with guns. They say people don't even have to lock the doors," I pushed.

"They'd like it . . . I guess."

"You'll have the baby?"

Linda Minsk nodded and that nod saved a life. You can count on a Jewish girl to come through for her parents.

She asked me to move out. She loved me, she said, but having me there during her pregnancy would establish the family unit and she didn't want to commit herself to that. Linda would have the baby and give it to me. She wanted visitation rights and would be delighted to pay child support.

On November fourteenth I moved into a garden apartment on Sweetzer. There was a little lawn, room for a playpen and a small court to ride a tricycle in.

Barbara Hirsh, out of the goodness of her heart, hired me back into daytime television. She understood that my hours would have to be flexible.

In the beginning of December I told my father the truth about why I needed the thirty thousand. He took it well. The Rams were winning.

At the end of January the Minsks took up residence in Leisure Village. They loved it and never failed to mention that you didn't even have to lock your doors.

In February I started natural childbirth classes because I wanted somehow to be close to the birth of my child. I was the only single guy in the class but I arrived late and left early so there were no questions from pregnant classmates.

In March I bought a crib. I knew I wouldn't be needing it for months, but having it there gave me security.

In June I bought everything else I needed. I went down the layette list at Saks. Everything was trimmed in yellow; the saleslady said that was the safest thing to do. I needed to be safe.

On July seventeenth I woke up in the middle of the night with a sharp pain in my back. I called Linda and said, "We're going to have the baby." She answered, "Yes."

I had terrible fears. I was afraid that after going through

labor and holding the infant in her arms, Linda wouldn't be able to let go. Women have changed their minds about giving their babies up for adoption and I feared Linda would do the same. The four days she was in the hospital I didn't sleep.

I didn't have to worry. Linda Minsk walked out the front door of the hospital, kissed me on the cheek and handed me my daughter, Martha. I clutched the baby to my chest and kissed her small forehead, hardly any forehead at all. Did you hear David Meyer is a mother? He started out life as a mother-fucker and ended up a real mother; how do you like that? Before I knew it, I was up to my ass in Enfamil and Pampers and Martha spitting up all over me. I loved it. It was so much better than the world spitting up all over me.

Thank God, she's a girl. She'll never have to go through what I had to go through. It's a woman's world.

"We would like to bring Martha Meyer-Minsk to the stand." The child would be carried to the front of the court.

"Do you, Martha, promise to tell the truth, the whole truth and nothing but the truth, so help you God?"

Silence. Someone would whisper in Martha's ear and the child would say a quiet "Yes."

"Martha, your daddy takes care of you, right?"

"Right, and he loves me."

Yes, Martha. He loves you.

Epilogue

The worst that could happen is that I live my life out, raising my daughter and never finding a husband.

The best that could happen is that Linda comes back to me and that when she comes I'm the person she would like me to be. (I hope someday I'm the person I would like me to be.)

An alternative: What could happen is that Kathleen Conway's mother gets her Women's Retaliation Committee to Washington. One day I could turn the television on just in time to hear Walter Cronkite announce the names of the ten men who have most violated womanhood. On the list among others would be a doctor, an actor, Mr. Conway and me. There would be a full-screen picture of me smiling an old devil-may-care smile. Walter Cronkite would chuckle, amused by the whole thing, as he announced that anybody knowing the whereabouts of these men should please notify the WRC. The men would be found, prosecuted and if found guilty, punished accordingly. Yes, castration was discussed. The baby would cry, sensing something. I would take her to me and we would stand there, we two, father, mother and child.

The phone would ring. I would answer it, not thinking I shouldn't.

"David?" It would be Linda. I wouldn't be surprised; Linda

called occasionally. She took Martha out on Sundays when she wasn't working.

"Linda, oh, my God, Linda. Did you see the news?"

"You can't let them get you, David."

"That was an old picture. It's the old me they're after. I'm sure if I explain that I have a baby and everything . . ."

"I know these women. There are times when they're not fair. If they were so fair, would they have allowed this Retaliation Committee?"

"What am I going to do?" It would hit me.

"David, listen, you've got to get out of there. You'll come back to my place tonight, then we'll move. It's O.K. I want you and the baby. David, I really do want you. I love you both," she would say.

And I loved her. I would take her name for safety: Mr. David Minsk.

There would be nothing to worry about. They'd never find me. They wouldn't look in playgrounds and laundromats.

ABOUT THE AUTHOR

Gail Parent was born in Manhattan, graduated from New York University, and married Lair Parent, one of her professors. She has written for virtually every possible medium: magazines, newspapers, the book for a Broadway musical, *Lorelei* (with her partner Kenny Solms), off-Broadway revue material (Upstairs at the Downstairs), comedy albums, and material for such television shows as *The Carol Burnett Show*, *The Mary Tyler Moore Show*, *Rhoda* and the *Anne Bancroft Special.* She has received an Emmy and four nominations for her outstanding television work; and she and Kenny Solms are now writing a screenplay.

Gail Parent's first novel, *Sheila Levine Is Dead and Living in New York*, was a best seller. She and her husband live in Los Angeles with their two sons.

ACKNOWLEDGMENTS

I am grateful to many people for their help and support: Lair Parent, Dale Burg, Owen Laster, Arnold Stiefel, Lisa Weinstein, Jay Tarsas, Sandy Gallin, Raymond Katz, Dr. Stephen Rosenberg, Ann Harris—and of course Kenny Solms, and especially Rhea Kohan.